THE MOMENT OF TRUTH

"I think it's about time to stop acting."

Too startled by Channing's pronouncement, Maggie dropped her guard just long enough for him to turn her head to just the right angle.

Nothing could have prepared her for the explosion of his sudden kiss. His hand slid around to the small of her back, pulling her tight against the hard, lean contours of his body.

Against all logic, Maggie found herself surrendering to the spontaneous crush of emotion that had drawn them together under the Seattle stars. Even as her heart hovered over the fine line between love and fear, the tantalizing invitation to lose herself in his embrace overrode any desire to escape.

Also by Christina Hamlett

The Magic Touch

Available from
HarperPaperbacks

Harper
Monogram

CHARADE

◆ ◆ ◆

Christina Hamlett

HarperPaperbacks
A Division of HarperCollinsPublishers

This is a work of fiction. The characters, incidents, and dialogues are products of the author's imagination and are not to be construed as real. Any resemblance to actual events or persons, living or dead, is entirely coincidental.

HarperPaperbacks   *A Division of* HarperCollins*Publishers*
10 East 53rd Street, New York, N.Y. 10022

Cover illustration by Jim Griffin

First printing: November 1993

Printed in the United States of America

HarperPaperbacks, HarperMonogram, and colophon are trademarks of HarperCollins*Publishers*

❖ 10 9 8 7 6 5 4 3 2 1

With love and appreciation

to Gayla, John, Clyde, Thatch, Linda, Kari & Kris, who
not only read this book chapter by chapter during its
development but conscientiously pestered me to finish
it ahead of schedule;

to Susan,
who refused to read it until it was all done but kept me
laughing through the rough spots;

to Wendy-Susan Lovejoy,
for her assistance with the research on
historic Seattle;

to Craig,
for dogs in the hallway, the Bickersons next door, and
the absence of waffle shops on the waterfront in the
dead of winter;

and to Janie,
who has more courage than anyone I know.

Courage is the price
that Life exacts
for granting Peace

—AMELIA EARHART
American aviator

Faith isn't faith
'til it's all you're holding on to

—JANE ELLEN
American composer

Prologue

Derek Channing. Even after five years, the very mention of his name by a total stranger had the capacity to stir unbidden memories.

"Miss Price?"

Maggie looked up at the fair-haired man whose arrival in her office half an hour before had shaken her tranquil world to its core. Embarrassed by her lapse of concentration, she turned her attention back to Detective McCormick's cryptic proposal. "I can appreciate your concerns about this," he was saying. "Channing's a dangerous man." His voice was low and smooth, a voice she might have found sensuous under different circumstances. "Unfortunately, the chance to get this close to him might not come again. Without your cooperation . . ."

Maggie apologized for the hesitation that he had mistaken for indifference. "Of course I want to help," she insisted. "It's just that this whole thing is so . . . ." the words fell back into her throat. How could she put her feelings into an answer he could understand when she still had trouble understanding it herself?

He seemed empathetic to the distress that the contents of the slim manila envelope had generated. "I can check back with you after you've had a few days to think it over," he said as he rose to leave. "I'm staying at Parker House on School Street—are you familiar with it?"

Maggie nodded distractedly as she accompanied him to the door. "I'll call you," she said.

Troy McCormick's hand lingered in hers as his eyes of steel gray implored her along with his verbal message. "We really do need you, Miss Price," he said. "A guy like Channing should've been put away a long time ago for the kind of—well, I'll drop it at that. I'm sure you can understand why we can't lose much more time putting someone on the inside."

Long after he left, Maggie's thoughts were still locked on the man whose exploits had dominated their conversation. Successful, handsome, and possessed of an arrogance that would have fit improperly on anyone else, Derek Channing was exactly the sort of match her father would have openly applauded and her mother would have quietly discouraged in favor of someone less "overwhelming." That he might also be a man as capable of murder as he was at amassing wealth sent a chill down her spine.

With a shudder, she reread the letter that McCormick had delivered, disturbed now to discover that she had unwittingly committed every word of it to memory.

Her gaze wandered to the silver-framed picture on the corner of her desk. "What the hell did you get yourself into?" she murmured. But the photograph gave no reply.

1

Channing's house on Lynx Bay in the San
Juan Islands was the closest thing to a contemporary
fortress that Maggie had ever encountered. Surrounded
by the natural moat of Washington's Puget Sound and
monitored by a stock of surveillance equipment that
would rival that of Fort Knox, the wooded island retreat
was a clear reflection of its owner's wish for privacy.
"No one gets in there unless Channing says so," Troy
had told her. Maggie couldn't help but wonder whether
the reclusive millionaire also controlled one's exit privi-
leges.

Without warning, her prior uneasiness returned,
spiced with the irritation that she would be little more
than a servant on Channing's sequestered turf. For a
woman whose reputation at the Boston Heritage Commission was predicated on independence and initiative,
it would take every inch of her willpower to pretend the
opposite and assume a passive role.

That Derek Channing would be a powerful opponent was an understatement, stretching ever tighter the tension she already felt. No turning back now, she reminded herself. For five years come September, she had pacified her soul with a reluctant acceptance of the Seattle coroner's report. Five restless years of denying there existed a direct connection between her father's death and the enigmatic man with whom she was now seeking employment. "By summer's end," Troy had promised, "at least you'll know the truth."

Somewhere beyond the foyer through which Maggie had passed upon her arrival, the resonant tones of a grandfather clock were chiming the hour, nudging her out of her musings. In annoyance, she pursed her lips, conscious of the fact that she had not only been abruptly deposited behind the closed doors of the drawing room by Channing's bodyguard but had then been forgotten about as well.

The blunt reception was consistent, of course, with what Troy had already forecast in preparing her for the interview. Whether Channing's noticeably overdue appearance was by design or accident, the underlying message was clear: neither Maggie nor her time was particularly important to him.

Perhaps that was all the better, she thought. Channing's indifference to her presence might make it that much easier to nose about undetected. "Channing's a workaholic," the detective had told her. "If you don't move, he'll think you're a piece of furniture and walk right past you."

In the next breath, Troy McCormick had been quick to criticize his quarry's obsession with work, particularly to the exclusion of an attractive assistant. "If it were me," he candidly confessed, "I'd have to be *dead* not to

notice someone like you." Maggie returned his compliment with a smile, by no means blind to his unabashed
interest in her or to the shrug of spontaneity that suggested it wasn't just a line he tossed off to every woman
he met.

"Keep a low profile," Troy had advised her when
they parted. "If that's even possible . . ."

She had opted for a minimum of makeup this morning and donned the ecru linen suit she had purchased
at Filene's on her last day in Boston, along with a silky
scarf of muted peach to complement the blush of color
on her high cheekbones. A whisper of shadow was all
that she had applied to the lids of her jade green eyes,
her mouth lined with just enough lipstick to show its
perfection.

The brisk journey by ferry from Anacortes to Lopez
Island, then by private craft to Lynx Bay, had only mod-
erately mussed her cropped, honey blond hair, so there
was no need for extensive repairs before her meeting.
Channing, she was certain, would have little tolerance
for an associate constantly attending to cosmetic first
aid.

Maggie examined the surroundings in which she had
been left to await her interview, purposefully studying
every detail so that she might glean a better understanding of the man who was now half an hour late for
their appointment.

In spite of the sunny weather that beckoned beyond
the French doors, the interior's dark paneling and
heavy oak furniture suggested a perpetual state of winter. It was a predominantly masculine room, the show-
place of a man who purchased only the best. Maggie
could picture her father enjoying himself in a setting
such as this, retreating to its depths with a brandy to

ward off the Northwest evening chill and a selection of classical music to erase the quiet. Had he ever been invited to join Channing in this room? she wondered. She scanned the tables and bookcases for signs of an ashtray, half expecting to see one of her father's pipes where he had left it in midthought, the scent of chocolate tobacco lingering behind.

The south wall was dominated by a river rock fireplace that rose to meet the cedar-beamed cathedral ceiling, but the room did not invite lounging before the fire. Concessions to comfort were clearly at odds with Channing's penchant for ordered elegance. He probably never sat still long enough to watch a fire burn from whole logs down to ash. From what she knew of him, Maggie surmised that Channing was a man of action, not leisure.

Maggie's gaze wandered across the room to the portraits of stony-faced patriarchs, casting expressions of stern disapproval at her intrusion in their descendant's life. Channing men, every one of them, she decided, their handsome visages linked by the common denominators of jet black hair, piercing eyes, and cleft chins. Most assuredly, whatever physical traits their mothers might have contributed to their appearance had been all but extinguished by the Channing genes' tendency to dominate. She was hardly surprised that, in six generations, only sons and no daughters had been born to carry on the empire.

Her glance at last settled on the room's largest and most impressive piece of furniture—a vintage partners desk not unlike those found in East Coast law firms. That a man who had never been known to work with a partner should have a desk designed for two users struck Maggie as unusual. A Channing inheritance? A purchase at auction? There was no telling where the man's treasures had originated, much less whether he valued them for their beauty or for the message they projected to others.

No photographs or personal memorabilia graced the desk's wide surface, but only the most expensive-looking leather and marble accessories. No untidy scraps of paper. No yellow pencils missing their erasers. Not even a paper clip absently bent into free-form design.

But what piqued her curiosity was the set of drawers with brass pulls polished to perfection. For an instant Maggie wondered whether those facing her had been left unlocked, inviting investigation of their contents. Then she decided against snooping. There were probably no less than a dozen video cameras planted in the room, trained on her every move.

Instead she rose from her seat and strolled toward the bookcases. It would be no crime to check out Channing's library, she rationalized. And there was no sense letting time go to waste.

The sound of the double doors opening behind her caused her to turn sharply, her face conveying a look of startlement.

"Relax," Channing said, sounding amused. "You look as if I'm going to bite."

In what seemed like only two strides—owing to his height—he had reached her and extended his hand in a firm grip that had sealed many a merger and destiny. His eyes of electric blue swiftly swept over her in practiced assessment, missing nothing.

"So you're here about the position," he said, crossing to the desk and pulling a manila folder out of the center drawer. "Tell me about yourself."

2

It was the type of opening that men like Channing were accustomed to making. Direct. To the point. No frivolous banter.

Anyone else might have inquired first about her flight from the East Coast or apologized for keeping her waiting. Anyone else might have even volunteered something about himself or his work before putting her on the stand as a hostile suspect.

"I'm not sure you're exactly what I'm looking for," he remarked, casually flipping the file folder closed with one hand.

In the cool silence that followed, Maggie wasn't certain whether he had just dismissed her as a candidate or was waiting for her to prove his assumption wrong. "And what exactly is that, Mr. Channing?" she pleasantly countered, refusing to buckle under to his intimidation tactics.

Surprise registered in his left brow and the corner of his mouth. "Why don't you keep talking, and I'll let you know when you've met the parameters. If, of course, you do."

Does he disarm everyone that easily with a smile? Maggie wondered, conscious of his arresting good looks and steeling herself against their potent distraction. The newspaper photographs she had seen had fallen far short of capturing just how handsome a man he was in person . . . or how dangerous.

Undoubtedly like those Channings who had come before him, Derek Channing was an authoritative presence at six feet four inches, comforting himself with the confidence of a courtroom lawyer on the verge of extracting a confession. There was a strength in his face that she could not help but find attractive. His bronzed skin was pulled taut over his high cheekbones, squared jaw, and patrician nose. Only the feathered lines at the corners of his eyes and mouth betrayed his forty years, yet even those Maggie attributed to the pressures of his profession rather than the aging process.

He wore a classic navy blazer that hugged his broad shoulders perfectly, and gray slacks that gave only the most subtle hint of pinstripe. Had he chosen to doff the jacket, Maggie could easily picture knife-sharp creases in the sleeves of his tapered white shirt. He probably owns dozens of them, she thought, each one elegantly monogrammed with his initials in English script on the left cuff.

His voice—as rich as the flow of expensive bourbon—was still edged with the aristocratic drawl of his native West Virginia, in spite of almost two decades on the opposite coast. "I see you've been to the Far East," he remarked. "Why was that?"

Not "when." Not "where." Why. Maggie felt her muscles tighten.

"Why not?" she replied, buying herself a few extra seconds to catch a breath and proceed. Then she went into the story that she and Troy had practiced—a forged chronology of travel and work experience designed to convince Channing that his current project would be doomed without her. "The Far East has a wealth to teach us about civilization," she concluded. "I wouldn't have missed it for the world."

"I should think that Europe would be more your style," Channing said. "You strike me as a castles-and-cathedrals type."

Maggie arched a brow. "And what type is that?"

Amusement lurked in his eyes as he replied, "The type who likes to sidestep simple questions. All of which makes me more curious. Something about the Far East you're trying to hide, Ms. Johnson?"

It was the first time he had addressed her by the surname that Troy had made up for her, the same name that graced her résumé and was now on all of the documents she carried in her purse. Johnson. Margaret Johnson. For the first time, it truly hit her just how dangerous a role she was playing.

Maggie shrugged to mask her discomfiture and dismiss his question. "I've always had a fascination with the Far East," she said. "An opportunity came up to go there with other students and I took it. I'm not sure why you're reading so much mystery into my answer."

"Maybe because the Far East isn't the cheapest place for a young woman on a modest salary to run off to. Was it supplemented by a scholarship of some sort? A government grant?"

"An inheritance," Maggie murmured, lowering her gaze so that he might interpret the money's source as the result of some tragic loss in her family.

To her relief, he chose not to pursue this avenue. "So what exactly did you do while you were there?"

"Mostly categorizing artifacts. I was also responsible for transcribing Dr. Rynearson's notes for his research on the Tang period and—"

Channing chuckled. "Rynearson's still alive, hmm? What a fossil."

"Actually—"

"Shame, wasn't it? Did they ever determine if it was cholera or something more colorful?"

"I really wouldn't know," Maggie replied. "I heard about his death secondhand from one of the students."

Channing regarded her with a wry smile. "After all that glamour working for Rhino," he said, "I suppose it's only obvious to ask why you've been collecting dust lately in an archives office." His blue eyes sparkled with challenge. "Boston, no less."

It was, ironically, the only portion of her résumé that *was* the truth. Against Troy's protests, she had insisted on leaving it in, maintaining that she could trust her boss, Clive Bowman, with any secret under the sun. It made sense, Maggie had pointed out to Troy, that a man like Channing would want to follow up with her current employer for a reference. Considering that every supervisor on the fabricated résumé was either dead, completely fictional, or off on exotic missions, Bowman's endorsement would lend her at least some authenticity.

"My time overseas," Maggie replied, "rekindled an interest I've always had in American history." With a passion that was genuine, she proceeded to defend the Commission's work in preserving Back Bay's stately brownstones and the Bulfinch townhouses clustered on Beacon Hill.

Channing regarded her with a long, silent scrutiny. "So what do you know about Seattle?" he finally asked. "Anything?"

"Enough to know that I'd like to work here."

"That's the *right* answer," Channing remarked with a wink. "What I want to know is why you *really* want to be here."

Maggie wavered, trying to comprehend what she was hearing. Was it possible that he had already seen through her deception and was baiting her to admit to the truth? Or did he just relish the power of being in control?

He was waiting for her answer.

"Injustice of any kind," Maggie said at last, "is a black mark against all of us." Channing cocked his head in interest as she continued. "What happened to the Chinese community here over a century ago shouldn't have happened to anyone. If the work you're doing can at least restore some of their history, their heritage, I'd like to be a part of it. Isn't that reason enough?"

It was Maggie's turn to wait for a reply. Only then did she catch a flicker of movement at the double doors and realize that Channing's manservant, Brecht, had been openly listening to their conversation. "Channing's shadow," Troy had called him. Based on the detective's description, it had been easy enough for Maggie to pick him out at the ferry terminal on Lopez. A stocky Germanic-looking man of indeterminate age, Brecht's most distinguishing feature besides a perpetual scowl was the magnificent crest of silver hair against black that emphasized his widow's peak. He was clean-shaven and only a few inches shorter than Channing. Dressed in a three-piece suit, he might have been a banker or attorney, were it not for the shoulder holster that Maggie had caught a glimpse of under his jacket. Had she been relaxed enough to feel amused, Maggie might have wondered what dire threat she posed to Channing that necessitated Brecht's watchful eye.

Unnerved by the bodyguard's hawklike fixation on her at that moment, she nearly missed Channing's next remark.

"I've put aside some reading to get you started," he announced, rising from his chair to indicate that their meeting was over. "Brecht will show you to the library."

"You're offering me the job?"

"That's what you came out here for, wasn't it?" Channing inquired, arching a dark brow.

In spite of the knowledge that she had just cleared the first hurdle, Maggie felt her skin bristle with apprehension. "I was hoping you'd give me a few more details before I made a commitment."

"We can discuss it tonight at dinner," Channing informed her. "If you decide you still want to sleep on it, the choice is yours."

Not waiting for her reply, he was practically out the door when Maggie found the voice to ask him when he wanted her to come back. With the balance of the morning and a few hours of afternoon, she'd have plenty of time to touch base with Troy in Anacortes and let him know how the interview had gone.

Her tension crept up another percentage point with his reply. "Your leaving the island won't be necessary, Ms. Johnson," he said. "Brecht has already arranged for your bags to be picked up at the hotel and brought here."

Only then did the realization grip her that she had never mentioned to him where she was staying.

3

The view of Lopez Island across the strait was unobstructed, owing to clear skies and a bay-window vantage point from the second-floor library. For the isolation Maggie was feeling, however, the neighbor island might as well have been on the other side of the planet. Likewise, the irony of an accessible telephone just three feet away only increased her misgivings about the charade's chances for success. Even after only one meeting, it was clear that Derek Channing intended to keep her on a short leash until she had won his confidence—if she ever did.

Not that she would even have considered calling Troy from anywhere close to Lynx Bay. The Seattle detective had provided her with a special number to reach him with the explicit instructions that she not use it on any line that her host or his shadow had the capability to track. "Besides," Troy had added, "with no living relatives and no acquaintances on the West Coast, who could you possibly say you were calling if you got caught by either one of them with a receiver in your hand?"

Did Troy wonder why she hadn't checked in with him yet? The original plan had been for Maggie to phone him when the ferry returned to Anacortes. Maybe he had already gone there himself, hoping to catch her in person when she got off the boat. Was he still waiting? There was no way for her to know. Consoling herself with the knowledge that at least he knew where she had gone and could implement a course of rescue if necessary, she settled back and mentally replayed what had happened downstairs in the study.

Channing already suspected something, that much was certain in Maggie's mind. Why else, she wondered, would he have pressed so many questions about the Far East and alluded to secrets and motives? Even his query about Dr. Rynearson had seemed suspicious.

And yet he had still offered her the job, still made her a guest under his roof. Furthermore, he had left her some of the logbooks and notes of the waterfront excavations to study before they met again at dinner that night. While there was probably nothing scandalous in those particular papers, his outward display of trust in letting her read them contradicted the reservations he had projected during the interview.

Either that, Maggie mused, or he was planning to throw her a pop quiz on the material as a basis for the evening's entertainment.

Nothing that the man did should really surprise her, she thought. Even her own father had suggested as much when he'd summed up his experience as Channing's chief engineer with the remark, "Never a dull moment."

Dull, of course, would have been the last adjective she would use to describe the man she had just met. Self-driven, shrewd, and ruthless, he had garnered an equal match of allies and enemies in the continuation of his ancestors' accomplishments in commerce and industry. No fewer than six corporations bore his name. Over three dozen international firms claimed him on their letterhead as a board member. All of which made it seem odd to her that he had invested so many years thus far in a relatively obscure venture to dig out the tunnels along Seattle's vintage waterfront.

"Even if he finds the treasure he's looking for," she had pointed out to Troy, "it can't be worth as much as he's spending in salaries and equipment."

Troy's reply had been enigmatic. "The treasure's just a ruse to look good to the public," he said. "If he's after what we think he is, Miss Price, that poking around in the dirt he's doing could cost the U.S. more than it can afford to pay." He had left it at that, leaving her imagination to take flight and consider the worst.

On the surface, at least, Channing was covering all of the bases. She recalled her conversations with her father about the crew's excitement in discovering various artifacts buried deep beneath the city's streets, an excitement that had been recorded by others in the books that now lay open on her lap. Each of these discoveries had reinforced Clayton Price's estimation of his employer as larger than life. "He really knows what he's doing," he had often boasted to Maggie in the letters he sent to Boston.

As she sat in Derek Channing's library now, her father's words came back to her. *Channing knows what he's doing, all right,* she thought. He just wasn't bothering to let anyone else in on it, especially not a newcomer who had been sent to spy on his operations.

Determined to play through at least the first twenty-four hours of her new identity, Maggie turned her attention back to the books and papers Channing had left for her. No sense in letting him show her up at dinner with questions on historical trivia for which she wasn't prepared.

California and Oregon had already been admitted to the Union when the first stirrings of expansion north of the Columbia River in 1851 set off a migration to rival the Gold Rush. From every corner of the globe, adventurers came forth to test their mettle in the lumber camps of the Cascades, on the plentiful waterways of Puget Sound, and in a new and bustling city named for a Duwamish Indian chief: Seattle. Unlike the eastern tribe that had traded Manhattan for a paltry $24, Chief Sealth had held out for the sum of $16,000 before finally selling his name to the waterfront township.

Its mild weather proved a pleasant respite from harsh, Midwest winters; the abundance of Douglas fir and cedar colorized the territory with a fresh vitality long missing in communities on the Atlantic. Like a magnet, its untainted wilderness drew the most hardy—and foolhardy—settlers northwest.

In less than half a century, Seattle also earned the distinction of being born twice—first from the muddy banks of Elliott Bay and then, like a phoenix, rising from its own ashes after the devastating fire of 1889. It was that summer inferno, in fact, that literally gave Seattle a better foundation than it had before. The major reconstruction prompted by the fire soon laid the groundwork for replacing the flimsy structures with solid masonry. What had originally been thrown together in haste was redesigned with precision. By the 1890 census, Seattle not only boasted a modest skyline but an increase of six thousand in its number of inhabitants.

While the city streets teemed with energy to rebuild for the future, the subterranean world below them clung to the past. Distressed by the gradually sinking shoreline and treacherous tideflats, the town council embarked on an emergency plan to utilize a network of stilts and boardwalks, creating a landscape not unlike an oversized waffle. Second-story exterior walls were modified to accommodate the new, elevated entrances to shops and hotels, and the original ground floors were gradually boarded up and sealed over.

Save for the present-day waterfront's underground tours and an occasional publicity piece, few hints remained in modern Seattle of the nearly eight acres of dank catacombs that wended their way beneath the city in the darkness—a darkness that not only concealed treasure but buried lies as well.

Accidents were not uncommon on a project of this type or magnitude. Clayton Price had known that at the outset and yet had zealously attacked each Dig Day with his shirt sleeves rolled up to his elbows and his enthusiasm high. Maggie caught herself shuddering at some of the logbook entries of his co-workers, graphically citing the near-misses of falling debris and poorly braced supports.

How Channing had ever secured permission from

the city to go in with a crew of five dozen was a minor miracle in itself. "Money talks," Clayton had said when Maggie had first inquired about her father's new job. By assuming the entire insurance liability himself and enticing the museum board with promises of priceless artifacts, Channing had managed to cut through the bureaucratic red tape in less time than it took most people to shower. With the carte blanche he needed to pursue his latest obsession, the millionaire laid temporary claim to a cavernous territory that had not been seen for eighty years, entrusting the bulk of the planning to a veteran engineer named Price who had a minor degree in geology.

Out of loyalty to his boss, Clayton's few remarks about the project particulars were couched in secrecy and melodrama. "The place would be crawling with amateurs if word got out," he had said to Maggie when he went to Boston, the last time she had seen him alive.

Channing's assignment released Clayton from a boring desk job and added the thrill of adventure that had been too long absent from his life. The physical risks clearly had not deterred him from signing the papers that bound him to Channing's side. For almost eighteen months, he had happily kept to himself the secrets of the dark maze that lay beneath Seattle's modern streets. Eighteen months, until the fatal day when he had chosen to put one of those secrets in writing.

4

"Excuse me, madam," said a voice in a precise German accent. Thoroughly absorbed in what she was reading, Maggie hadn't heard Brecht advance halfway into the library until he spoke up.

"Your bags will be arriving within the hour," he said.

"Thank you," she murmured, knowing better than to ask how he had discerned where to find her luggage in the first place.

"I've been asked to show you to your room," he said. "If you'll come this way, please."

As if I had a choice, Maggie thought as she set aside the logbook and stood up.

"There's some really interesting material in these journals," she remarked, hoping to engage Channing's bodyguard in conversation. "Have you read any of them?"

Brecht's face was impassive as he held the door for her. "My other duties preclude reading for pleasure, madam."

"That's strange. I'd think that working as closely with Mr. Channing as you do that you'd know everything he knows."

"We have our respective areas of expertise."

Maggie thought of the weapon she had glimpsed earlier beneath his jacket. "Well, I can see why your boss has put so much work into the project. Something like that must be absolutely obsessive."

Brecht nodded but said nothing.

Maggie quickened her pace to keep up as they approached the broad staircase to the third floor—not that a man like Brecht would have allowed her to stray too far from his sight. She wondered what he had done before going to work at Lynx Bay.

"So how many people live here?" she asked.

"As many as Mr. Channing feels are necessary," was the reply as they ascended the stairs.

From Troy she had learned that the Lynx Bay house had been built from the ground up in the early 1930s, yet it seemed that it could easily have been transported lock, stock, and widow's walk straight from Marblehead or Cape Cod. No expense had been spared in recreating every detail of an age in which men spent days at a time whaling and women contented themselves with sitting at home, watching the sea for their husbands' return.

It was definitely a man's house, Maggie decided. It was so stiff and formal—not the kind of house where children would noisily slide down the banisters. As she noted the stark absence of feminine influence she remembered asking Troy whether Channing had ever been married. "Who could live up to *his* kind of perfection?" Troy had retorted. This reply was interesting to Maggie, given her father's outspoken hope that his only daughter and his favorite employer might one day meet and hit it off.

Brecht withdrew a key from his vest pocket. "Is that supposed to keep people out or keep them in?" Maggie asked as he paused beside one of the doors before inserting it in the lock. Her attempt at levity went unnoticed.

"Perhaps you should ask Mr. Channing," Brecht answered, pushing the door inward to reveal a bedroom awash with natural light and comparable in size to Maggie's entire apartment. Intrigued by the sight that awaited her and anxious to escape the man's diligent scrutiny, Maggie stepped inside.

It was impossible not to be impressed by the room's beauty or puzzled by its dissimilarity from the rest of the house. Softened by the color scheme of rose and ivory in the comforter and draperies, it invited romantic thoughts and purposeful laziness. The brilliantly polished hardwood floor was partially covered by two beige and mauve rugs of Chinese design, their placement gracefully directing the way to a four-poster bed on which one might have expected to find a wooden breakfast tray of croissants or a box of fancy chocolates. Twin armoires of rosewood graced either side of the bed, one of them open to display an orderly row of padded satin hangers. A Victorian chaise, upholstered in the same fabric as the draperies, was the temporary resting place for the latest issues of *Architectural Digest* and *Elle*.

It was the seascape view, though, that Maggie's gaze kept returning to, the same view of Lopez Island that she had seen just one floor below.

"Is something wrong, madam?" Brecht asked.

"Nice view of the island," she replied. "It looks

pretty close from here, doesn't it? A couple of miles maybe?"

"Distances," Brecht curtly informed her, "can be deceptive."

"Then I guess I'll rule out the option of a midnight swim."

Brecht's only response was to measure her with a cool look.

"So am I free to wander around?" Maggie asked as she strolled the room's length. "Or do I need a hall pass?"

Whatever answer he might have given was pre-empted by the arrival just then of a dark-haired, matronly woman bearing an armload of fresh linens and towels. Brecht's words to her in a language Maggie didn't recognize set the housekeeper straight to her task of readying the room for occupancy, her eyes never once meeting Maggie's.

"SkySet will attend to your needs," Brecht said.

"SkySet?" Maggie repeated. "Interesting name. What kind of—"

"She doesn't speak English, a condition for which she admirably compensates with American charades."

Which translated to zero conversation, Maggie thought. If it was Channing's intent to cut her off from all human contact except himself, she had to give him credit for succeeding.

"What was that language you were just speaking to her? It didn't sound familiar to me."

"Dinner will be at six sharp," he said, ignoring her question. "Mr. Channing will expect you to dress for it, of course." With that, he left.

"I'll be there with bells on," Maggie replied, wondering whether Channing's definition of dressing could adequately be met by the wardrobe she had packed for the summer.

"Well, I guess it's just you and me, SkySet," she said as the woman busied herself across the room with unfolding the sheets she had brought. "What do you say we let our hair down and you give me the scoop on this place?" Save for a faint smile at the recognition of her first name, the housekeeper gave no indication of understanding a single word.

Maggie had to credit her host for providing her with costly and elegant quarters befitting a queen. For a lowly summer assistant to land so cushy a space to retire to at day's end only increased the man's mystique. What was he up to, besides keeping her off balance? Dwarfed by a ceiling as high as a museum gallery's, Maggie couldn't help but wonder how many guests had stared up at it and pondered their fate beneath the millionaire's omnipotent spell.

Guests. The word didn't fit a man like Channing. Prisoners? *You're overreacting,* she chided herself, nonetheless wishing that Troy McCormick were not quite so far away.

She unzipped the interior pocket of her purse and ran her fingers over the letter it concealed, tracing the paper surface as if it were a talisman to protect her. Against Troy's advice, she had brought it to the island with her. "At least hide it somewhere safe if you insist on taking it," he had warned her.

While the obvious choice would have been to carry it on her body at all times, it also seemed to Maggie that it would be an equally obvious place for Channing to focus his attention, thus inhibiting her attempt to act casual in his presence. Her eyes scanned the room in search of a suitable place to hide it.

To the left of the bay window, café doors opened into a sparkling bathroom of blue and white tile. Lights reminiscent of a Hollywood dressing room bordered three sides of the mirror, a mirror that now reflected the fear she could not afford to reveal to the man who had just hired her. *Toughen up,* she commanded herself, affirming that her ability to expose a secret would ultimately surpass Channing's talent to hide one.

Beside the marble sink was an orderly basket of Caswell-Massey soaps and shampoos set out by the housekeeper, as well as a tortoiseshell brush and comb. She reached for the lower edge of the nearest drawer to see what other treasures she might find, and winced in pain as the nail of her index finger broke off to the quick. Pressing the injured finger to her lips Maggie now gave the partially opened drawer a decisive tug to determine why it had jammed.

What rolled into sight was the last thing she would have expected to find: a tube of lipstick.

5

"*Brecht tells me* you have an interest in swimming," said Channing as he filled her wine glass with white zinfandel at dinner that evening, shedding his domineering manner for that of a gracious host.

It took Maggie a moment to make sense of his peculiar comment. "I usually restrict my water exercising to a pool," she replied. "I don't recall seeing one on the grounds."

Channing's smile was dazzling white against his tanned skin. "*I* don't recall letting you see the grounds at *all*." He raised his glass. "Perhaps we should get to that after dinner if you're up for it."

"And when," Maggie asked, "are we going to get to the purpose of my being here?"

"You're referring to the job, of course?"

"Of course." She focused on squeezing the lemon on her grilled fish so he would not catch the flash of apprehension in her eyes. "What exactly am I going to be doing on the project? The 'assistant' title is pretty generic."

As she might have expected, Channing ignored her question as he conducted his dinner agenda as masterfully as his interview. "I hope you enjoy Pacific salmon," he said. "It seemed a good choice for someone who's grown up on all the Boston fare. SkySet has a way of preparing it that makes it melt in your mouth."

Maggie opted to follow the change of subject rather than try to push as immovable a force as the man who sat opposite her. "She seems very nice," she said. "Did she come with the house?"

"SkySet's ancestors came with the territory," Channing replied. "Back before the Dennys and Doc Maynard ever settled on Elliott Bay, the whole Sound was full of Duwamish, Nisqualli, Snohomish. SkySet's a Snohomish, seventh generation."

"I'd think that she'd miss being with her own people." Maggie thought of how isolated she felt there after only a few hours.

"Not when she has all the comforts she needs on Lynx Bay. And not," Channing added, "when you consider the plight of her peers back on the mainland. She's done better than most."

Maggie nodded, remembering what her father had said about the Northwest Indians' deficiencies in modern health, education, and housing, and the high incidence of alcoholism, drug abuse, and suicide among them.

"I assume you're familiar with their conditions, then?" Channing said.

"I've read a lot about it," Maggie lied. "There's a parallel to the Hawaiian Islands, I think."

"And every other culture to whom we've introduced civilization," Channing added. "All in the name of doing a favor."

"So how long has SkySet been with you?"

"Almost ten years," he replied. "How's your salmon?"

Ten years. Certainly long enough for someone to learn a passable command of English. "Delicious," Maggie answered. "And how did you happen to meet her?"

Channing's blue eyes met hers over the top of his wine glass. "Do you always ask this many questions on a first date, Ms. Johnson?"

Maggie refused to respond to the romantic connotation. "I find it's usually the best way to learn things."

"Then maybe there's something I should ask about *you*."

Maggie hoped her smile was convincing. "And what's that?"

His white teeth gleamed in the lights of the chandelier. "Why do you go by something as stuffy as 'Margaret'? You strike me more as a 'Maggie.'"

It was a coincidence, she tried to reassure herself as Channing gave her a tour of the grounds, a respite she might have enjoyed after spending the entire meal as his object of scrutiny. Yet the earlier utterance of her real name, the name her father had called her since childhood, had set the alarm bells in her head ringing.

She tried to be rational and attribute it to the annoying habit most people have of shortening formal names, even without asking. But as they made their way down the steps to the pier, she was unable to dislodge the mounting suspicion that he knew more than he pretended.

"This is where you came in," Channing said, pointing to the snug harbor where her new life as a spy had begun less than twelve hours before. "Recognize it?"

"Looks like someone stole your boat," she said, anxious to learn who monitored the craft's comings and goings. Without an introduction to the man who had accompanied Brecht to Lopez Island to meet her and then chartered them both to Lynx Bay, she had no idea whether the silver-haired skipper was a permanent fixture in Channing's retinue or a special hire for the day.

"Brecht had a little errand to attend to in the city," Channing replied. "I don't expect him back with us until tomorrow morning."

"He doesn't smile very much, does he?"

Channing's voice, uncompromising and yet deeply sensual, sent a ripple of awareness through her.

"I don't pay him to smile, Maggie. I pay him to protect me from my enemies."

"And is that a full-time job?"

Even in the moonlight, the expression of humor around his mouth and eyes were evident. "What do *you* think?"

Before she could respond, his hand caught her elbow and gently steered her toward the right. "Let's get started on the tour, shall we?" he said. "There's a lot of the island to see."

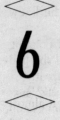

6

As if hurled from the hand of a primeval giant, a cascade of jagged black rocks lay in tumbled disarray from the west side of the house down to the shoreline, a drop of over one hundred feet.

"There are limits to what you can do with the landscaping," Channing said. "I decided to go with the 'natural' look."

"It's breathtaking," Maggie said.

"Not to mention dangerous," he added. "I wouldn't come out here at night by myself if I were you, unless you carry a strong flashlight."

"So roaming around on my own is permissible?"

"I expect to keep you busy enough that roaming won't be part of your itinerary."

He extended his hand to steady her descent down the craggy path. Tapered and strong, his fingers telegraphed a warmth and protectiveness that made her forget for an instant that he might harm her if he knew her true purpose.

"How big exactly *is* this place?" she asked, for in the darkness, it seemed to go on forever.

Channing scowled. "Exactly? About sixty acres, give or take a few barnacles. Large enough for privacy and small enough not to run me into debt."

"I wouldn't think the latter would be a worry to someone like you," Maggie said, regretting it almost immediately.

"You have a lot of preconceptions about me, don't you? Care to explain where they come from?"

Thankful for the shadows that hid her face, Maggie feigned puzzlement. "First impressions," she murmured. "I can't be the first person who's ever said that about you or made a couple of generalizations."

"You're not," he said. "As a matter of fact, there's someone you remind me of. . . ."

Maggie held her breath, but he didn't finish the thought aloud.

"Why don't I tell you something about the project?" he said as they stepped on to the sandy strip of beach that led away from the house. "You've been begging for details all evening, as I recall."

"I don't recall begging for *any*thing."

He chuckled. "No, I suspect a woman who looks like you is accustomed to getting most everything she wants with very little effort. Including the truth. . . ."

Again he paused, and then continued without really completing what he had begun to say. "You've probably gathered that I'm not just digging for chopsticks and yen."

"Not for what you must be spending to do it," Maggie replied, cautious not to reveal that she had a fair handle on the extent of his underground investment.

"Was that a hint of censure I just heard in your voice?"

"More like confusion," she said, trying to sound innocent. "I came out from Boston to meet new people and work on a project where I could apply what I know about the Asian culture. If what you and your crew are doing is something entirely different—" Maggie shook her head. "I was really looking forward to what I was going to learn."

"Oh, you'll learn plenty," Channing assured her. "I just need to know that I can trust you." He gazed at her speculatively. "Everything about your background seems to be in order."

Maggie said nothing, stunned by the realization that her fictitious résumé had actually passed his approval. Concurrently came the awareness that the very hours he had consigned her to the library had been put to use checking her references. Without question, Troy McCormick had done a thorough job in creating a credible identity for her, convincing enough to fool the man who now walked by her side.

"To be blunt," Channing went on, "I only have one problem with this arrangement of ours, and I think you may know what it is."

Maggie was instantly on guard. "And what's that?" she asked.

"Three months may not be long enough for all the work that needs to be done."

They had come upon a seawall at the far end of the cove, and its wide stones offered comfortable seating for a panoramic night view of the Sound. A romantic spot, Maggie thought, disconcerted by the dangerous company with whom she was currently sharing it.

"Care to sit down awhile?" he asked.

She hesitated. In response to Brecht's dictum

regarding formality at dinner, she had donned a rayon challis dress and heels. Channing's proposal to go walking after their meal had not afforded her the chance to change into something more practical—yet another testament to his desire for control.

"I'm really not dressed for it," she finally said.

"Neither am I, but that's an advantage of having your own island."

Maggie arched a brow. "What advantage?"

"You can make your own rules. And one of mine is to enjoy the scenery whether you're dressed for it or not."

"I think I'd be more amenable to the idea in jeans and sneakers."

"You can send the dry cleaning bill to me if that's what you're worried about." His palm skimmed the surface of the stones and came away clean. "Doesn't seem to be a problem, though," he remarked. "It looks like SkySet's already been down here dusting."

In spite of her nervousness, Maggie giggled at the image.

"You should laugh more often," Channing said.

"Another one of your island rules?"

"No, it just seems to suit you."

Maggie felt heat creep into her face and sought a change of subject to dispel it. "So what's holding your interest down in the tunnels? I was convinced it was all for the artifacts."

"It's an answer that reads well for the public. Artifacts always bridge that distance between a troubled present and a peaceful past."

"Peaceful for whom?"

"Primarily the bankers," Channing replied. "Certainly not the common man, the immigrant—they were the ones who suffered just trying to survive."

"And that's where the Chinese come in?"

"Come in or go out, depending on how you look at it." A frown crossed his face as he settled against the ledge of seawall. "There was a movement to get rid of all of them in 1886—you read about it in the books I gave you, didn't you?"

Fortunately, it was one of the stories that had stuck in Maggie's mind, though Channing had no way of knowing that she had learned it years earlier from her father, and not from her studies that morning. "The Sinophobes wanted to round them up in the middle of the night and deport them on a steamer leaving for San Francisco."

"And do you know why?"

"Exploitation run amok." As she proceeded with her explanation, the sight of Channing's smile encouraged her with the knowledge that he recognized an intellectual equal.

"You've done your homework," Channing said. "Now let me add a little to your education." He proceeded to tell her about the discrimination against Chinese immigrants to the area in the nineteenth century and the organized looting of Chinatown in 1882 by a self-appointed "Order Committee" whose goal was to rid the waterfront of its Chinese occupants. "Within two hours, however," Channing said, "the committee not only absconded with everything of value in Chinatown but terrorized a couple hundred Chinese by herding them to the waterfront for a one-way trip on the *Queen of the Pacific*."

"Thank goodness they didn't get away with the full plan," Maggie said as Channing concluded the story with President Cleveland's intervention and the subsequent reparations to the victims.

"Unfortunately, they *did* get away with everything they stole that night." A chill hung on the edge of his words. "Somewhere under the city streets, that treasure is still unclaimed."

"You'd think with so many people knowing about it, someone would have found it by now."

"Not likely," he replied. "In the first place, the public's primary focus during the period of martial law that followed wasn't on recovering the goods but on seeing justice served. As for the Chinese themselves, I think it's a pretty safe bet that they just wanted to get out of the whole mess with their lives. At any rate, the delay and confusion easily gave the committee enough time to bury the evidence where it wouldn't be found."

"And you have an idea where that is?"

"Roughly, yes. The hard part is getting to it." Seattle's reconstruction after the fire, he explained, had covered over all of the original ground floors. "They would have been smart enough to hide it down in a cellar, which means it's two layers down from what we know now as the existing street level." With roughly eight acres to search, he pointed out that the project was impeded not only by city regulations but by the hazards of excavating beneath structures that were not as sturdy as others.

Maggie's heart squeezed in anguish at his mention of the latter as she thought of her father's senseless death.

"Of course you'll have an opportunity to see what I mean tomorrow," Channing said.

"Tomorrow?"

"Explaining the layout is one thing," he replied. "I think you need to see it firsthand to appreciate what we're up against."

Maggie's optimism surged. A trip to the mainland would offer her the chance to contact Troy.

"You mentioned having enemies," she reminded him as they began to walk back to the house. "What exactly did you mean?"

Channing smiled. "I think it goes without saying that there are descendants of the Sinophobes who'd just as soon not let the past come to the surface. Whatever cellar we eventually find the treasure in will reveal a lot more than anyone would like to have known."

"And do they know what you're up to? Your enemies, I mean?"

"Oh, I'm sure of it," he said, seeming amused by her question. "I'm sure they never let me out of their sight."

7

Derek Channing clearly was an early riser. Without preamble, he had voiced his desire to be in Seattle by nine o'clock sharp, leaving Maggie with no choice but to nod in compliance.

"Pleasant dreams, then," he'd said, leaving her at the second-floor landing, his footsteps echoing on the hardwood floors as he made his exit into the library.

Sleep, however—much less dreaming—had not come easily to Maggie. So puzzled was she by new thoughts and haunted by old ones that her first night at Lynx Bay was a restless one. She speculated that the ever-vigilant Brecht was probably standing guard outside her door and wondered if he would fall into the room if she opened the door quickly.

As the morning alarm nastily jarred her from what her father always called "the gray state," she realized that she had caught no more than a few hours of snoozing. She'd have to do better than that, she reminded herself, if she was going to stay alert to Channing's maneuvers.

"I should have thought to feed you first," Channing remarked when they had reached their destination. "Or was that *my* stomach growling?"

"You said you wanted an early start."

"Yes, but man can't live on coffee alone. Or woman, either, for that matter. Would you like to get something at Pike's?"

To anyone observing them at that moment, Maggie thought to herself, they could have been just another couple on vacation in the Pacific Northwest. Maybe even a couple of locals, given their casual outfits of jeans and camp shirts. Brecht, to her surprise, had taken leave of them a few minutes before and been swallowed up by the crowd that was already infiltrating Seattle's open-air waterfront market. If intuition was any measure, however, she suspected he had not strayed so far as to miss his master's voice if summoned.

"I *am* a little hungry, yes," she confessed.

"Breakfast is on me, then," he said, withdrawing a twenty-dollar bill from his breast pocket and handing it over to her. "There's a little place down on the lower level called The Anchor. Not much atmosphere, but I'll vouch for the food." Channing glanced at his watch. "Think you can meet me back here in half an hour?"

"You're not joining me?" Maggie asked, startled that he was about to leave her to her own devices for an entire thirty minutes—easily enough time to find a phone and touch base with Troy.

"You were still asleep when SkySet put mine on the table," he replied. "You looked like you needed the extra rest after your long trip."

Had he looked in on her? Suddenly self-conscious, Maggie lowered her eyes from his face and found herself gazing directly at the wisps of dark hair curling against the open V of his shirt.

"Find your way around here okay?" he asked. "It's confusing sometimes for a newcomer."

"If I can handle Boston, this place should be a piece of cake."

"Half an hour, then," he repeated. "Have a nice breakfast."

Rooted to the spot as if in a dream, Maggie watched his broad back as he moved through the throng of shoppers, a man in command of whatever environment in which he was placed. That other women were also noticing him and appreciating what they saw was a fact that she noticed as well. If they knew just what kind of person he was, she thought, they'd be running in the opposite direction instead of craning their necks for a better view of him.

While her first impulse after he had disappeared from her sight was to seek out a pay phone, Maggie reminded herself to be cautious. After all, who was to say that Brecht's pointed absence wasn't a trick to get her guard down? He was probably watching her even as she stood there debating what to do next.

For lack of a better plan, she turned her attention to the stalls that lined either side of her, their wooden crates and metal tubs overflowing with crab, salmon, and more produce than she had ever seen in the vegetable section of grocery stores back East.

The Pike Place Market had been a favorite haunt of her father's on his days off from the project, Maggie recalled as she shouldered her way through the crowd of housewives with bulging canvas bags and teenage girls admiring T-shirts and earrings sold by street vendors. Though its original purpose was to serve the workaday merchants' needs rather than cater to tourists, Pike's had come to rival Seattle's most famous landmark—the Space Needle—in popularity.

A cacophony of foreign accents assailed her ears as vendors hawked everything from eggplants to psychedelic posters reminiscent of the 1960s. Burly men in oilskin aprons pitched silver-bellied mackerels and rainbow trout to each other, providing impromptu entertainment to prospective buyers. Even children were part of the circus atmosphere, helping their parents lay out displays or getting their faces painted by wizened Indians attired in tribal costume. "Pike's is the soul of the city," her father had told her. Now she understood what he meant.

As Maggie wended her way from stall to stall, engaging the merchants in small talk about their food, her glance periodically swept the crowd in search of Brecht. That she never caught sight of him did not dismiss the prevalent feeling that he was close by, however. When her meandering brought her at last to a flight of stone steps to the lower level, Maggie took them, willing herself not to look over her shoulder. *Act casual,* she kept reminding herself.

As if she had performed such a routine all her life, Maggie slipped around the first downstairs corner and waited, hidden from sight. To her relief the passage of a few minutes suggested that she had either successfully lost Brecht or else had never been followed by him to begin with. Throwing caution to the wind, she emerged from her hiding spot and proceeded down the ramp toward a phone booth in front of a shop.

The answering machine came on, just as Troy had

told her. "You've reached Ballard Dental Center," a woman's voice cheerfully announced on the line, followed by instructions for leaving a message.

Maggie's initial words were barely out of her mouth when Troy came on the phone.

"Maggie!" he blurted out. "Are you okay? What the hell's going on?"

"Well, for openers, I got the job."

"And you're going to get yourself killed if you— Look, I don't mean to snap, Maggie, but it drove me nuts last night when you didn't check in like you were supposed to."

"A change of plans," she said. "Channing's." With an eye on the corridor, Maggie hastily explained what had happened since her arrival at Lynx Bay.

"So where are you now?"

"Pike's Market."

"That's close. I can be there in—"

"I'm not alone. As a matter of fact"—Maggie checked her watch and discovered that she had less than fifteen minutes—"I have to get back to meet him. He's taking me to the tunnels this morning."

"Then what?"

"I don't know. I *do* know, though, that he wants me to plan on three days a week here in town. The rest of the time I'll play it by ear, I guess."

There was a pause at the other end of the line.

"Something wrong?" she asked.

"I just want you to be careful," Troy replied. "Very careful."

The care evident in his voice warmed her. "I will," she promised. "Oh, by the way—"

"What?"

"He let me in on what he's looking for down there."

"And you buy that?" Troy asked after she had told him about the buried treasure.

"Doesn't quite ring true," Maggie said. "I mean, what difference would it possibly make to anyone after a whole century?"

"Like I said before," Troy reminded her, "the man's got more tricks up his sleeve than a magician."

"Listen, I'd better go."

"Check in tomorrow?"

"If I get a chance."

"Please *make* the chance, or I'm going to have to rent a white seahorse and come charging out there after you."

With only a few minutes remaining and hunger gnawing at her, Maggie debated whether to grab a snack or hope that Channing was planning on an early lunch. As she rounded the corner, she saw that the café he had recommended was straight ahead. She decided to make a quick stop there, just in case Channing quizzed her on the wallpaper color or the omelet of the day.

"Could I get a cup of decaf and a croissant to go?" she asked the woman at the counter. "I'm in kind of a hurry."

"Be right with you, hon," the woman replied.

Maggie mentally prepared her explanation to Channing that she hadn't finished all of her breakfast and brought the rest along with her.

The sound of his voice directly behind her startled her. "Still waiting for a table? The service here is usually much faster. . . ."

8

In *the momentary* surge of panic, Maggie seized on the first excuse she could find. "You just can't take me past a store without my wanting to go browse in it. A place like Pike's—well, I guess I lost track of the time. Blame it on heredity."

Channing's right brow rose a fraction. "A shopaholic, hmm? That's a critical weakness you seem to have left off of your résumé."

Thankful for the unexpected respite of humor, Maggie played along. "I didn't think it was pertinent to the job specs."

"Intentional omission?"

"Does this mean I'm fired already?"

"So what did you buy?" he asked instead of answering the question. "Anything interesting?"

Conscious that he had just scanned her person for evidence of vigorous bargain-hunting, Maggie gave what she hoped was a casual shrug.

"Nothing really grabbed me today. Maybe I'll have better luck later in the week."

There was an uncomfortable pause, and then the woman at the counter resumed talking to Maggie. "That was one cup of decaf and a croissant you wanted to take, hon?"

"We'll take a table with that as well," Channing spoke up before Maggie could reply. "Do you have something by the window?"

"I really don't want to slow things up," Maggie protested as they followed the woman across the room to booths that looked out on the harbor. "I can just as easily carry it with me if we're going to be running late. . . ."

Channing chuckled. "It's not as if we have to catch the next train out of Dodge. Besides, I'm interested in this shopping thing of yours. Where did you say you inherited it?"

"My mother," Maggie replied, knowing full well that he was baiting her again. "She and my aunt held records, I think, for the longest hours spent shopping without benefit of food, drink, or trips to the restroom."

"I hope your father and your uncle made secure enough livings to support that kind of habit," Channing remarked. "It sounds like it could get expensive."

Maggie avoided answering by pointing to a fishing boat that was just coming in. "The harbor sure sees a lot of action."

"True, but not as much as it used to. About a mile and a half of piers along this stretch used to be a working waterfront for freighters and passenger lines." Clearly enjoying his role as historian, Channing told her about the major ships that used to depart for Alaska, the Orient, and Mexico. "You can still find plaques out on the concrete," he said, "that commemorate events like the first arrival of gold from the Klondike."

"So what happened to change things?" Maggie asked after the waitress brought her order.

"Progress. Most of the commercial trade has long since moved over to Harbor Island. What you've got left around here are restaurants and teasers to attract the tourists. Too many of them, if you ask me."

"You seem to know a lot about it," Maggie complimented him.

"That and a lot of other things," he replied. "At the moment, though, I don't know that much about *you*, do I?" With elbows on the table and fingers steepled, he studied her as one might study an abstract painting. "Maybe we should do something about that."

"What's there to know?" she countered, trying to project an ease that was far from her inner anxiety. "You read it all on my résumé."

"Except for your compulsion to shop," he said with a wink. "Who knows what other dark secrets you're keeping from me. Chocolate binges, maybe? A closet cardplayer? A neat freak who alphabetizes all of her clothes by color?"

"Nothing nearly that dangerous," Maggie replied, amazed by the man's capacity to keep her nervous and entertained simultaneously. "Just a working woman from Boston with a summer to spare."

"Someone so well adjusted must have come from good stock," he remarked. "Are your parents still alive?"

His ability to bring the conversation full circle back to her personal history was something she would have to get used to. Maggie shook her head, hoping it would be enough to dissuade him from deeper inquiry. Even discussing the deaths of two fictitious people could not help but strike a familiar chord of pain in her.

"And yours?" she finally countered.

Channing hesitated a moment. "No living relatives to speak of," he said. "So have you lived in Boston all your life?"

"Not yet."

"Touché. Seattle's a long way from the East Coast," he continued. "That must make it hard on a relationship."

She could see where the conversation was headed and chose to preempt its course. "It manages just fine," she said, hoping to discourage any romantic advance from Channing as well as establish that she'd be missed if anything happened to her. "He supports everything I do. My number one fan."

"Lucky guy," Channing murmured without missing a beat.

Maggie braced herself for the next question, certain that he would pursue details about her long-distance swain. His name is Richard, she'd say, affecting a brief, wistful look before explaining that he was the manager of a beer distributorship and was designing and building a house in the country for the two of them in his spare time. Next September, she'd reply, if he inquired how serious their plans were. September twenty-fourth at a chapel they had already picked out in Cape Sevier. She wished she were wearing a ring for emphasis.

To her surprise, however, Channing asked none of the probing questions for which she was mentally rehearsing. "As long as we're sitting here," he said, withdrawing some papers from his pocket, "I may as well show you what you're going to be seeing this morning."

It was like nothing Maggie had ever experienced before, standing beneath the city streets for the first time in a subterranean world that smelled of earth, moisture, and—most predominantly—sewage.

Channing read her mind as well as the wrinkle of her nose as they descended into the dank netherland. "There was definitely a plumbing problem in Seattle's early days," he said. "Remember what I told you about the city being built on mud flats?"

Maggie nodded as she took in the stone retaining walls and amber floodlights illuminating cobwebbed corners, an eerie scene reminiscent of a haunted house thriller.

"The tides of Puget Sound," Channing went on, "used to back up the sewer system on a regular basis."

"Sounds like a sanitation engineer's worst nightmare."

"Worse than that. Between exploding pipes and toilets that geysered at high tide, it wasn't the most charming city to call home." Channing chuckled. "If you think Mount Saint Helens was a force to be reckoned with, try to imagine a scaled-down version erupting in your bathroom twice a day for half an hour."

"No thanks."

"Watch your step there," he cautioned, extending his hand to assist her over a piece of rotted wood. "And don't step on any rats."

If he was anticipating a squeamish reaction, he didn't get one.

"You don't frighten very easily, do you?" he remarked.

"Did you think that I would?"

"I was hoping not," he said. "There's a lot you'd miss out on if you were afraid to set foot down here."

More than you know, Maggie thought, ever mindful of the danger she was in just by being alone with him in the rubble-strewn caverns.

"Over on First Avenue at Doc Maynard's restaurant," Channing continued, "there's a group that brings tourists down here a couple times a day."

"Doesn't that interfere with your work?"

"The section we've been concentrating on isn't public access. Watch your head."

Maggie ducked as she followed him beneath a brick archway.

"The whole thing was once condemned as a firetrap. That and a breeding ground for plague."

"I'd believe it."

"Pretty seamy territory, even minus the physical hazards. Criminals used to run a speakeasy and gambling operations out near the west end during Prohibition. After *they* moved on, the winos, rodents, and cockroaches moved in."

"And now they bring tourists," Maggie commented. "What does that say for natural evolution?"

Channing laughed.

"So where are we now?" She was disoriented by the turns their route had taken since they had first descended twenty minutes ago.

As he opened his mouth to answer, Channing's attention was diverted by a sound from behind them.

"Yes, Brecht?" he said.

Maggie was disturbed that she hadn't even known he was behind them. His footfall was as quiet as a ghost's.

"If I may speak with you a moment, sir," Brecht said. And in the lethal calmness of his eyes, Maggie saw a man who trusted her as little as she trusted him.

9

"*Something's come up* that I have to take care of," Channing said when he returned from a hushed exchange with his bodyguard. "Looks like I'll need to turn you over to Cleveland for a couple of hours."

"Cleveland as in Ohio?"

Maggie was wary that Brecht's intrusion might have some connection to her charade. Had he seen her make the phone call at the Pike Place Market? Or worse, had Channing himself witnessed it?

"Cleveland as in Ken," Channing replied. "One of my employees. He'll get you started on what you'll be doing for me." With a tilt of his head, he motioned toward a portion of rock staircase carved into the wall and twisting upward to street level. "We'll take this way," he said. "It's a little quicker than the tunnels."

Without protest, Maggie followed him up the stairs, now and again glancing back to see if Brecht was behind them. He wasn't.

"Let me give you a hand," Channing offered after sliding back a trapdoor and hoisting himself onto the planks in the upper level. A shower of dirt and dust filtered down through the floorboards, stinging Maggie's eyes. "I've got you," he said as, temporarily blinded, she fumbled to regain her balance. With solid, strong arms he pulled her up through the opening and, in doing so, drew her tight against his chest.

"I'm okay," she hastily assured him, conscious of the contours of his body and the electricity of his touch on the small of her back.

"Well, that's good," he replied as he released her, seemingly indifferent to the effect he had just had on her. "Ready to go on?"

Determined that he not have the satisfaction of seeing her flustered by their proximity, Maggie asked what kind of building they were in. What minimal light shone through crooked slats in the walls revealed a ten-by-ten-foot cubicle and a pile of wood scraps in the corner that at one time might have been furniture. Beneath their feet, however, were crushed cigarette butts and crumpled candy wrappers—evidence of modern visitors.

"This used to be part of a brothel," Channing explained as he led the way out through a musty corridor and across a reinforced catwalk. "Madam Gianecchini's, if memory serves. Another colorful chapter of Seattle's racy history. For the census, the women used to list their occupation as 'seamstress,' probably as a play on words for helping the customers sow their wild oats."

"I'm never sure when you're serious," Maggie said, stifling a smile at the poor pun.

"About the world's oldest profession? Of *course* I'm

serious," he insisted. "Who could make up a story like that? At any rate, even after the houses were closed up, the waterfront continued to draw that kind of trade. It just wasn't formally organized like in the old days."

They had reached a low door at the corridor's end. "Down we go again," he announced, sliding back an iron bar and opening the door to reveal a flight of spindly stairs that couldn't have been much wider than eighteen inches.

"Looks like the spiders have been putting in overtime," Maggie remarked of the webs that formed a gray lace canopy above the entry.

"Didn't I promise you a glamorous tour?"

"I'm glad *you* know what you're doing," she replied, thankful that, by going first, he was the one to test each step's dependability. "So how far are we from where we started?" she asked. Given the circuitous route they had traveled thus far, they could just as easily have gone twenty feet as two hundred.

"Only about a block and a half," he replied. "Disappointed?"

"Just confused. Somehow I had a picture in my mind of everything connecting like an ant farm."

"Unfortunately that's not the case. The state of decay down here is so bad in a couple places that we've had to keep them blocked off. One bump against the wrong wall and a person could literally bring the whole house down."

Maggie's stomach instantly knotted, his words bringing back the hurt and anguish that five years had yet to dispel. Somehow, she found the voice to ask what she knew she had to. "Has that ever happened?"

"You mean have there been any accidents on the project?"

"From what you just said, it sounds like the people on your crew are taking their lives in their hands every time they come down here."

"Not if they know what they're doing."

Was it her imagination, or was there an edge to his voice that hadn't been there before?

"It's still a risk, though," she said.

"Things worth having usually are."

"But has anyone on the crew—"

"Better close your eyes a second," Channing advised a moment before opening the door they had just come to. "Civilization is dead ahead."

Frustrated by his evasiveness, but knowing better than to press the issue any harder and arouse suspicion, Maggie let the subject drop.

After over half an hour down in the darkness, his suggestion to close her eyes was not without purpose, as the bright lights of the adjoining storeroom were almost dizzying in comparison.

"I'd like you gentlemen to meet someone," Channing said. "My new assistant, Ms. Maggie Johnson."

As her eyes adjusted to the light, Maggie saw four men huddled over a table that would have comfortably seated only two. Spread before them were diagrams and maps the color of parchment and the width of wallpaper rolls. Pieces of equipment—none of which she could identify—rounded out a haphazard decor of packing crates, hard hats, industrial flashlights, and a cluster of black metal lunch boxes.

It was the room itself, though, that puzzled her the most. Almost new in appearance, it contrasted sharply to what she had already seen of Seattle's original level of architecture. Almost, she thought, as if it had been built from scratch to accommodate Channing's needs.

Only the rough brick archway in the far corner suggested any connection to the past.

"Welcome to the basement boardroom," Channing said, drawing chuckles from the other men.

"Am I missing something?" Maggie asked.

"You're standing on the foundation of one of the few buildings to survive both the mud floods and the fire," Channing replied.

"And the sewers!" one of the men said.

"Sewers, too," Channing added. "At any rate, it served our own purposes. If you ever want to find the boss, this is the most likely spot."

The largest of the men, a burly redhead, stepped forward to shake Maggie's hand vigorously. "Ken Cleveland," he said, displaying a huge grin. His callused palms and broad shoulders gave him the appearance of one who had always held physically demanding jobs. And though he towered over his peers by several inches, it struck Maggie that his presence still paled by comparison to that of the man who had brought her here.

"Ken's my foreman on the project," Channing said. "Best engineer in the Pacific Northwest."

"Yep," the tall man unabashedly nodded. "Been on it now for four—no, make that five years." Cleveland grinned again. "Greatest damn thing that ever happened to me."

Maggie only half-listened as Channing told her the names of the others, suddenly disturbed by the realization that the large man standing before her must have succeeded her father upon his death. And perhaps, she speculated, had been instrumental in bringing it about.

"Since you've still got the money from breakfast," Channing said, "I'm putting you in charge of picking up tonight's dinner."

Maggie forced herself to reply, though her mind was elsewhere. "It's hard to even think about it after eating so recently."

Channing winked. "I guarantee that Ken here will work up your appetite by the end of the day."

She decided to indulge the millionaire's penchant for calling the shots, even those not work-related. "Anything in particular you'd like?"

"A couple of king crabs and some sourdough bread should do," he replied. "I hate to cook on SkySet's night off, and I imagine that you feel about the same."

He was gone before she could ask if Brecht had the night off, too.

10

"*Sure I can't* twist your arm for some coffee, Maggie?" the foreman asked for the third time that morning as he filled his own plastic cup from a seemingly bottomless thermos. "It's real good."

"Thanks, no."

She wished that there was something disagreeable about the man to support her predisposition of his guilt. In truth, however, he was practically bending over backward to make her feel at home, patiently explaining how to log the finds that they made as well as plot them on the transparent overlays accompanying the labyrinth's detailed maps. Cleveland's tutoring had consumed most of the morning, an investment of time that Maggie thought odd for someone whose expertise should have warranted his presence elsewhere.

"You're picking this up real fast," he said.

"It helps to have a good teacher."

Cleveland shrugged off her praise with the insistence that it was her own talent that made his job easier. "You must've done a bunch of this stuff before," he said.

Maggie nodded. "Similar, but on the other side of the world."

"How's that?"

Cleveland could have been coached to play confidant and test her, so she'd remain steadfast to the original story. "I spent some time in the Far East," she began, skillfully dropping enough details to mesh with what she'd already told their employer.

"Never been over the Columbia myself," Cleveland remarked. "Not much of one for living in a suitcase. So how come you're in Seattle?"

"Well, when I heard about the position, it seemed like a perfect match to my background. The weather you get out here also sounded like a nice change from another New England summer."

Cleveland chuckled. "So you like plenty of rain, huh?"

"At least it keeps everything green."

"Maybe that's why they call it The Emerald City."

Maggie laughed.

"Well, it's a real high honor for Mr. Channing to pick you," he continued. "He doesn't just pick anybody, y'know. Not with what's at stake down here."

"Yes, everyone certainly seems professional at what they do."

"That's the way he likes 'em. Get in, do the job, do it right. That's what he pays us for."

Would he fall for the bait if she phrased it cleverly enough? "Isn't it great," she said, "to get paid for something you enjoy? When you have a job like that, it doesn't feel like work."

The foreman laughed. "Oh, it's work all right. Damn hard work, too. But yeah, I know what you mean. Sorta makes you feel strange taking the money for something you'd do for free."

"So what did you do before you did this?"

Cleveland scrunched his face into a frown. "Hard to remember. Goes way back, y'know."

Maggie feigned confusion. "I must've misunderstood you then," she said. "I thought you said that you'd only been here for four years."

"Five years as foreman," he corrected her. "Before that, I just sorta worked my way up to assistant."

"Oh, really?" Maggie forced a smile of glowing admiration. "And now you're foreman of the whole thing?"

"That's right."

"That's quite an accomplishment."

The look on the man's face mingled pride with embarrassment. "Well, yeah," he said. "One of those things you never think is gonna happen to you and one day it does."

Maggie pretended to go back to the notes she had been writing, willing herself to stay as calm as possible in the face of learning a truth that would be painful.

"Your boss must have thought pretty good things about you," she said. "Was he like a mentor to you?"

"You mean Mr. Channing?"

"I meant the last foreman. Isn't he the one whose job you moved into?"

"Yeah, we got along okay, I guess. Taught me some stuff you don't learn in books."

"So did he retire or move on to something else?"

Cleveland suddenly shifted gears. "Listen, we've got plenty of time for yakking, but not near as much to teach you all the particulars like Mr. Channing wants. Where'd we leave off?"

By noon several men had come into the room to eat their lunch and engage in friendly conversation with the newcomer.

"Boston?" said one man. "I got a speeding ticket once in Boston."

"Ever see the Sox play?" another asked.

"Got any more like you at home?" a third wanted to know as his eyes made a sweep down to her ankles and back up again. A sharp glance from Cleveland set the man in his place.

"You're welcome to half my sandwich," the foreman offered. "We usually eat in every day. I guess Mr. Channing didn't tell you."

"And I usually go out at lunch," Maggie said, anxious to get her bearings straight on the world up above and, with any luck, find another phone booth. "Mind if I go up for a walk and some fresh air?"

"Give me a couple minutes to wolf this down," Cleveland volunteered, "and I'll go with you."

"Oh, I've monopolized you all morning," she said. "I'm sure you could use a breather from my company."

The disappointment on his face looked genuine enough to be real. Maybe it was.

"The truth of the matter is," Maggie went on, "I'm feeling a little claustrophobic."

"This place'll do it to you, that's for sure. That and the dark. But it can get real confusing finding your way back, and there'd be hell to pay with Mr. Channing if you got yourself lost."

"Then maybe I should take you up on that sandwich

offer after all. I could use the bread crumbs to leave a trail."

Cleveland's full-throated laughter filled up the small room. When at last he regained his composure, it was with the realization that she was determined to leave alone. "I guess it'd be okay," he said reluctantly, "just don't go to far 'til you get used to it."

He escorted her through the brick archway and up a flight of steps, until they reached a narrow corridor. "End of that, and on the left's a door that comes out in a storeroom. A door to the alley's across from that, and around the corner's South Washington Street." The foreman fished into his pocket and produced a key. "You'll need this to get back in."

Maggie thanked him. "Back in a flash," she promised.

Savoring her temporary freedom, a smile spread across her face as she reached the end of the corridor. A smile that would not have been there had she been aware of the man who silently fell into step behind her not thirty seconds later.

11

The welcome respite of cool, fresh air at street level renewed Maggie's senses. She was tempted to seize the opportunity to escape. Critical as her participation might be to the Seattle police in obtaining information on Channing's endeavors, Troy McCormick would be the last person to fault her for changing her mind. She could tell from their conversation that morning that she was treading on uncommonly dangerous ground, and he knew it.

As she rounded the corner and came upon the midday bustle of Pioneer Square, she realized how easy it would be at that moment to simply slip away into the crowd and leave the Derek Channings of the world for higher powers to deal with. *You're in over your head,* she warned herself.

Certainly none of the pep talks or hours of coaching on Troy's part had prepared her for the mental drain of keeping up such a facade of innocence in the millionaire's company and that of his workers. Nor, her conscience added, had she been prepared for the effect of Channing's touch when she had lost her balance. To be sensually ignited by the enemy—even briefly—seemed anathema to the whole quest for justice. Yet, try as she might to deny the knot that had since formed in her stomach, its very presence was testimony of the man's power to overwhelm her.

She chided herself at the notion of his interest in her. Channing had probably touched hundreds, maybe even thousands of women, as casually as he had touched her, and had never felt a thing in response. No sense in letting *that* little episode influence her decision of staying or going. It was the element of danger, not the proximity or the attraction, that was responsible for such a heady rush.

And as for the charade—Maggie silently complimented herself on how well she had done so far. No screwups, no discrepancies, no bumbling hesitations. Even the incident at the café with Channing's sudden appearance had been countered with a believable explanation. Troy's assessment of her ability to think fast on her feet had been put to the test and passed.

Why then, she wondered, did she now feel so intimidated by the challenge of keeping it up for an entire summer . . . or until she learned the truth?

The exchange with Cleveland about her father's death had ended on the same disconcerting note as her earlier conversation with Channing. Both times she had felt close enough to the answer to reach out and grab it with her hands. And both times it had been snatched away from her, escalating her frustration.

What had *really* happened in the catacombs beneath Pioneer Square five years ago? What secret alluded to in her father's letter had cost him his own life? The thought that she had come this close and yet might never know the answer tore at her, fueling her hatred.

In Channing's case, of course, the motivation to evade her questions was painfully obvious. Unless he derived some heinous pleasure in recounting his deeds to others, it would only make sense for him to change the subject whenever it came up, slyly averting any suspicion of his involvement. Even on the chance that he hadn't orchestrated the accident, his very treatment of another human being's death as inconsequential was a mockery she could never forgive.

It was Ken Cleveland's reaction, though, that was even more perplexing. For someone who had supposedly come up through the project's ranks on the basis of hard work, dedication, and respect for authority, his sudden discomfiture with her curiosity wasn't consistent with his otherwise friendly demeanor. Something—or someone—held sufficient sway over the foreman to dictate what topics were verboten.

Were the others who worked for Channing as susceptible to his pervasive influence? Clearly, there was only one way to find out. As amenable as they had been to accepting her as a peer, it was just a matter of time and patience to find the weak link among them and determine which one could be tricked into talking about the past. Whether she herself could maintain the momentum and courage to pursue it remained to be seen.

The chime of bells marking the hour stirred Maggie back to her purpose in coming up from the tunnels, and she began to take stock of her surroundings for future reference. Delighted by the initial discovery of at least two phone booths within half a block of the place she had exited, her confidence increased slightly, allowing her to enjoy the colorful antiquity of the city's historic district.

Not that many years before, the sandstone and brick buildings, meandering cobblestone streets, and weathered totem poles had seemed destined for extinction. Pioneer Square had become mostly a tenement neighborhood, an eyesore populated by vagrants and vermin. Then it was renovated and reborn as a Victorian mecca of activity, filled with dozens of restaurants, boutiques, galleries, taverns, and theaters.

It was incredible to Maggie that its ghostly, abandoned counterpart still existed below the surface. Oblivious to the subterranean level that held its secrets of treasure and death, the people milling in the streets today seemed more concerned with finding a bargain or a good cappuccino than resolving any twisted puzzles of their past. She envied them.

As she continued her mission of exploring, the temptation to call Troy again was strong. So, too, was the desire to hear his voice, to affirm that she had a protective ally outside of Channing's world. For a moment, his face floated back into her memory, his fair and boyish good looks contrasting sharply to the roguishly chiseled features of her handsome adversary. A white knight and a black one, she thought, struck by the irony that, had it not been for her father, neither one would now be in her life.

Not more than eight or ten years could have separated the men in age, she guessed, and yet from her limited perspective it might have been twice that difference, due to Channing's worldly bearing and satisfaction with himself. Born into an arena of wealth, he was as accustomed to manipulating personal relationships as he was to expanding his empire. As Troy himself had suggested, Channing's quest for an equal probably stopped just short of his own mirror.

The same could never be said about the Seattle civil servant. Content with a sensible car, a comfortable apartment, and a job that gave him challenge, it was obvious to Maggie even from their first meeting that Troy's orientation was to make other people his priority. Even though they had begun as relative strangers, his compassion for her loss was genuine. "I know what it's like to lose someone by violence," he had said. The almost imperceptible note of anguish at the corners of his mouth kept her from asking—but not from wondering—what he had meant.

Buoyed by Troy's concern for her that morning, she realized just how much she was beginning to miss him. Their single date—if their evening out together could be labeled as such—had hinted at potential for more. So, too, had his gray eyes hinted that his interest in her safety at Lynx Bay might extend beyond the professional.

Why, then, did the warm image of him in her head keep getting pushed aside by the more dominant presence of Derek Channing? Troy McCormick was the kind of date that any mother would like to see her daughter bring home to dinner, whereas Derek Channing was the wicked kind that hapless daughters always pursued into dark alleys in the hope of reforming.

Not *this* daughter, she reminded herself. Men like Derek Channing spelled nothing but trouble. She vowed not to forget that.

Even without anything substantial to report about operations down in the tunnels, a call to the detective seemed like the best thing to assuage her confusion. Just steps from a pay phone, though, Maggie hesitated.

Instead of stepping inside the booth, Maggie turned around.

She might not have noticed the youth at all, she realized, had their eyes not locked at that exact moment. Certainly there were enough other people around her to have caught her attention and diverted her from looking his way. With no one between them at that very second, however, his riveting stare startled her. As if paralyzed, he stared a moment longer before turning and running in the opposite direction, his long black hair flying loose from the baseball cap that had concealed it.

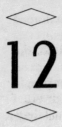

12

"*Something bugging you,* Maggie?" the foreman inquired after her third erasure of one of the easier entries. "Ever since you came back from lunch,
you've been—"

"Guess my brain's just awfully taxed," she interrupted
him, running both hands through her hair in a gesture of
exhaustion. "Listen, would you mind if we picked this
up again tomorrow?"

The room had suddenly become constricting to her,
just as Channing's tactics had finally gotten her goat.
Was there no end to his planting spies on every corner
to watch her? Try as she might for the last hour to dismiss the latest incident, her irritation with the man
behind it had reached a flash point, making it impossible
to concentrate.

"Well, sure, I guess that's okay with me," Cleveland
said reluctantly, "but I don't think that Mr. Channing
will—"

"Tell him I'll meet him over at Pike's Market instead of here," Maggie said as she grabbed her purse. "I'm supposed to pick up dinner there anyway, so it'll just save me a trip back."

Cleveland scratched his head. "Big place, Pike's. Is he gonna know where?"

"No problem. We already talked about which stall had the best seafood when we were there this morning." Let Channing figure out for himself where she'd be, since he was so fond of playing cloak and dagger.

"In *my* book, it's Captain Haskell's," Cleveland said. "Best cod in the Pacific. Their salmon's not a bad buy, either."

"To each his own," she replied.

"So which one's Mr. Channing's favorite?"

"Oh I'm terrible with names," she said, "but I'll recognize it as soon as I see it again."

The foreman scraped back his chair to stand and say good-bye. "Hope you're feeling okay." The beginnings of an apology started to form on his lips.

"Thanks for understanding, Ken," she murmured, availing herself of his sympathy. "I'm sure I'll feel a lot better when I adjust to the West Coast time zone."

She was almost out the brick archway when he suddenly said, "I'm gonna be late tomorrow. Have to pay a traffic ticket."

"Bummer."

"I'll leave you some stuff to do, though," he promised. "Shouldn't take too long for a smart girl like you to figure it out."

Maggie reflected when she had reached the street level again that she had offered a lame excuse, but being fired for insubordination would at least give her back her freedom, something that Channing had an unnatural compulsion to limit. And if by chance her headstrong attitude had the opposite effect and won his respect . . . Maggie dismissed the idea as quickly as it had come. Termination was a much more likely scenario at the hands of a man as ruthless as Channing when he found out she had cut out early without his permission.

At First Avenue, Maggie took a turn and was reminded by the aroma of fresh bread how little she had eaten all day. The open doors of a patisserie beckoned, drawing her off the street and into its cozy ambience. The combination of bakery and country café was quaint, with English ivy cascading forth from brass planters hanging above the dining area and soothing classical music playing in the background.

"Are the restrooms in the back?" she asked the waitress after placing an order. The girl nodded and directed her past the cash register and the glass counter.

That she should find a telephone in the privacy of the ladies' room was pure luck and an opportunity that could not be passed up.

"Stay exactly where you are," Troy instructed. "I'm on my way."

"Don't you think the management will get suspicious if I don't come out?" Maggie countered, trying to maintain some levity.

She could picture Troy smiling at the other end of the line. "I meant don't leave the café," he said. "You might also want to sit back in a corner, away from the front entrance."

"I already thought of that."

"That's my girl."

*   *   *

"You're a sight for sore eyes," he remarked about fifteen minutes later as he eased into the empty chair next to her.

"But I don't remember those eyes of yours wearing glasses," she said. Her first impression of the round, dark lenses was of the late John Lennon's trademark wire frames—an image contradictory to that of the conservative professional she had met back in what now seemed like light-years ago. "New look?"

Troy smiled. "Just my slumming disguise—does it work?"

"Better without," she replied, smiling.

The detective obligingly slid them off of his nose and laid them on the table. "Your wish is my command."

"Then hang up the corny clichés and tell me what you think I should do next."

For a moment Troy was silent. "What do you *want* to do?" Then he chuckled. "I hope you know I didn't mean for that to come off like a shrink or something."

"Which it did."

"You just sounded pretty frustrated on the phone."

"Who *wouldn't* be?" Though she had already told him the story once, it felt good to Maggie to repeat it, replaying the dialogues with Channing and Cleveland out loud in the hope of catching something she had missed before. "It's as if a red flag goes up when I get too close. Down slam the doors, and I'm left with as little as when I started."

"All of which means that you're closer than Channing would like."

"So?"

Unexpectedly, Troy's hand came down over hers on

the table, his fingers cool and smooth. "*I* can't tell you what I think you should do, Maggie."

"Because I'm the best thing the department's got going right now and you're biased about my decision?"

Troy's smile was almost apologetic. "You caught me on the biased part," he confessed, "but probably not in the way you expect." The detective hesitated a moment. "If he didn't trust you," he said at last, "I guarantee he would never have let you set foot on his little rich boy's playground out there. Channing's far too smart for that."

Maggie nodded. "He does seem to have bought the background story. Thanks to you."

Troy ignored the compliment. "Tell me again about the guy you thought was watching you. You said he was Indian?"

"That's my best guess."

"How about age?"

"Teens, I think. He didn't look that old to me."

Troy winked. "Maybe he just likes watching pretty ladies and you got the luck of the draw."

"Not by *my* intuition."

The detective scowled. "Well, the description sure doesn't fit anybody on Channing's crew. I can check into it, but it sounds to me like an isolated incident. A fluke."

"As opposed to his resident watchdog?"

"Brecht?"

"The man gives me the creeps. I bet he'd stare me down for twenty-four hours a day if his boss told him to."

"Maybe you're reading Channing's reasons all wrong. Maybe he's just protecting his investment."

"Run that by me again?"

"The man's not without enemies, Maggie. We already talked about that back in Boston."

"Meaning?"

"Meaning someone working as closely with him as you are might be privy to secrets that others would like to get their hands on. Considering the kind of people that Channing's been known to deal with—"

The implication infuriated her. "Meaning, that you got me into something deeper than I bargained for. Is that what you're saying?"

Troy's grip on her hand tightened in spite of her attempt to pull it away. "Maggie, believe me, the Seattle Police Department—"

"—isn't on Lynx Bay." Her green eyes met his. "It isn't."

13

For every ten reasons that it would have made sense to get up and walk away, there remained in Maggie's mind the one obsessive reason that underscored her willingness to be in Seattle at all. That Troy diplomatically chose not to remind her of it in the heat of argument, Maggie thought, was of small consolation.

"There are things I *can't* tell you about Channing," Troy said, "and all I can do is apologize for that."

Maggie's reply abandoned any pretense of blind understanding that he might have expected. "His island out there is every inch the fortress you told me it was. Apologies won't keep me safe."

"Then you'll just have to trust that yours truly *will*." Troy met her accusing eyes without flinching, resolute with the sense of conviction that he was doing the right thing. "Believe me, the less you know, the less chance of Channing finding out and using it against you."

"That's not what we agreed to."

"What *I* agreed to," Troy replied, "is to make sure nothing happens to you. That's why I've taken precautions that—"

"Easier said than done."

"I wouldn't say it if I didn't mean it, Maggie." His hand came up as if to touch her chin, then withdrew, closing instead around his half-finished glass of iced tea. "Would it make a difference if I told you that what I think you're doing is very brave?"

"A difference in what? In whether I go back to Lynx Bay . . . or back to Boston?"

Troy shook his head. "Neither one. We both know you'll make whatever choice you feel comfortable with."

"Then what did you mean?"

There was a shyness in his smile that made him look years younger, a smile that might have melted her down to her Reeboks if she hadn't been so frustrated with his tactics. "Nothing I can put into words right now." Troy shrugged. "It's probably not appropriate to try to, anyway. Just trust me."

Trust. As she made her way back to the Pike Place Market after taking leave of him, it occurred to Maggie that she now had two men instead of one whose respective agendas were not all what they seemed on the surface. A game of cat and mouse, with an extra cat thrown in to give the mouse twice the stress.

"Give it a week," Troy had advised her when she announced her decision to stay with their original plan. "Give it a whole week, and if you decide after that you really want out, I'll personally come and get you. In the meantime—well, just be careful, okay?"

Secure as his promise and the tenderness in his eyes should have made her feel at that moment, Maggie could no longer deny to herself that, for the most part, she was alone. Derek Channing had not only the resources to do whatever he wanted but the influence to buy others' silence. If he chose for her to fall through a crack in the planet and never be heard from again, the deed was probably as good as done.

It was going to be a long week.

She saw him coming before he saw her and, for an instant, Maggie glimpsed an uncharacteristic flash of anxiety on Derek Channing's face as he scanned the marketplace. A worried look, she thought, as if he had misplaced something of value.

Too soon, his visage hardened, revealing a mouth thinned with displeasure. She wondered if he would make a scene, or instead she would feel the blunt poke of cool steel at the base of her spine, accompanied by the sound of Brecht's voice ordering her not to make any sudden moves. But certainly real life wouldn't take on such bizarre dimensions. He'd probably just fire her on the spot and calmly walk off.

Prepared for the worst, Maggie pretended not to see him striding toward her. "How much did you say those were per pound?" she asked of the clerk who was weighing her order.

"Banker's hours, Ms. Johnson?"

Maggie feigned surprise at his arrival by her side. "I guess maybe I should have mentioned the claustrophobia," she said. "Ken says it takes some getting used to down there."

"There seem to be a *lot* of things you left off of your résumé," he remarked, his blue eyes sharp and assessing. "Would you like to get them all out of the way now, or would you rather start looking for a job that will accommodate them?"

"That'll be fourteen fifty total, ma'am," the clerk interjected.

Maggie withdrew the money from her purse. "What I'd like," she replied at last, lifting her chin so she could look Channing in the eye, "is to be respected for the job I can do instead of being watchdogged like a three-year-old."

"I wasn't aware that you were being watched."

It was, she realized in retrospect, exactly the kind of answer she should have expected him to give.

"Weren't you?" she challenged him.

To her surprise, his next remark was a compliment. "Cleveland says I've made a good choice in hiring you."

"He's a good teacher," she replied, disconcerted by the conversation's shift.

"People with a short memory usually annoy him."

"Who has a short memory?"

Channing indicated the clear plastic package in her hand. "I thought you were picking up crab for dinner."

"I thought the sea scallops looked better."

He cocked his head slightly. "I don't have much use for cooking," he informed her, daring her to put forth a rebuttal.

"Then you're going to miss a very good meal."

Maggie found herself puzzled by what seemed a definitive change in Channing's treatment of her over the next few days. Maybe confronting him was all it had taken.

"You've lost me," Troy confessed as she tried to explain it to him on the phone. "You say he's not following you anymore?"

"Either that, or he's gotten a whole lot better at it."

"Maggie, I don't—"

"I'm being careful," she reassured him. "I don't doubt for a minute that he'd love to catch me doing something I'm not supposed to."

"So what's this change you're talking about?"

"I'm not sure," Maggie said. "A little more openness, a little more respect—"

"—a little more of that infamous Channing charm to keep you off balance," Troy interrupted. "I'm not sure I like the sound of any of this."

"Then how do you like the sound of *this:* He needs me to go back and fax some papers to New York for him this afternoon."

"I hope there's more to the story than that. What *kind* of papers?"

"The papers aren't the point, Troy. The point is that he and Brecht are staying on the mainland until this evening. I'll have the place to myself."

She could feel the significance striking its intended chord with her listener.

"What about the housekeeper? SunSet, was it?"

"SkySet."

"Whatever."

"I don't think that she's a problem."

"And *I* think you could be underestimating her. The woman's got eyes in the back of her head. But go on— what's your idea?"

"I don't know that I have one other than to just look around."

There was a pause at the other end. "Something just tells me there could be a trap behind it. It's almost too convenient, if you stop and think about it."

She *had* thought about it, Maggie wanted to tell him.

She had thought it through from one side to the other and yet kept returning to the same conclusion: it was a chance too good to pass up.

"I'll call you first thing in the morning," she promised.

"Maggie?"

"I know, you want me to be careful."

"That and something else."

"What's the something else?"

Troy hesitated a moment. "I miss you."

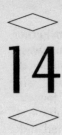

14

Maggie mapped out a rough "snooping plan" in her head for when she returned to Lynx Bay, but there was at least one problem that still had to be factored in: SkySet. Channing's casual mention that morning that the housekeeper was only working half a day gave no indication of how she was going to spend the balance of it.

While Maggie normally would have assumed that a domestic would opt for a respite away from her workaday surroundings at the drop of a hat, it was clear even from minimal observation that SkySet considered the island her permanent home. On her night off earlier in the week, she had not set foot from her room. Fortunate as it would be to find the woman on the dock with an overnight bag packed and awaiting transport back to the mainland, Maggie knew it was unlikely.

She found SkySet instead in the mansion's foyer, meticulously measuring out liquid plant food for the indoor ficus. Maggie greeted her with an explanation of why she had come home early without Channing. Sky-Set merely looked up and smiled at her, then continued about her duties.

For an instant, the sight of the woman jogged something in Maggie's memory, something obscure that she had thought strange when it happened and yet had let slip by without questioning. Just as quickly, the sensation was gone.

"I'll be in the study if you want me," Maggie said. Given the complete lack of reaction on the Indian woman's part, she could just as easily have proclaimed "Your hair's on fire," or "I'm going to steal all the petty cash in the safe." Totally impassive to Maggie's agenda, SkySet concentrated on the plant.

The papers were exactly where Channing had said they'd be, and the leather-bound directory was to the right of the fax machine. As instructed, Maggie found the New York number and proceeded to program it in, pausing for a moment to finish scanning the first sheet before she entered the final digit to start it feeding through.

Replete with legalese and party-of-the-first-parts, the document seemed little more than a rough draft of his intentions to purchase more property in King County. There was probably nothing critical or confidential in that particular transmittal, she told herself, or else why would Channing have sent her back to take care of it for him? Anything really important would have been entrusted to Brecht instead.

On the heels of Troy's claims that Channing had world-class enemies, though, it was entirely possible that the recipient might have a significance to the Seattle Police Department, though to her it was just another name. Maybe it wasn't even a law firm at all but a pseudonym for one of Channing's cohorts in crime.

Maggie crossed to the partners desk in search of a pen and paper so she could write down the number.

As she approached the desk, she realized that she had just provided herself with a convenient excuse to do exactly what she had been wanting to do since the day of her interview: to see if the drawers were locked.

Did Channing trust her that much, she wondered, as the middle one smoothly slid open at her touch. Undoubtedly he was smart enough to keep any incriminating evidence in a vault to which only he had the secret combination.

Like the top of the desk, the interior was flawlessly neat. Onyx trays neatly separated the paper clips from the Post-It notes, the felt-tip pens from the metal drafting templates. A sheet of current commemorative stamps lay beneath a short stack of parchment envelopes whose upper left corners displayed his initials—but no address—in black English script.

Maggie pulled the drawer out a little farther and skimmed her fingers over the space behind the dividers. Nothing.

Disappointed not to have found any bloodstained handkerchiefs or at least a treasure map marked with a charcoal X, Maggie started to close the center drawer and move down to the next. It was then that the crystal caught her eye, its point poking out from under one of the envelopes.

At first glance, her impression of the icicle-shaped glass was that it must have come from one of the chandeliers. That Channing would keep such a bauble in his desk tray instead of putting it back where it belonged, though, seemed to contradict his penchant for perfection. Maggie lifted it out for a closer inspection.

It was definitely a crystal, and not from a hanging fixture. The short strand of clear fishing line knotted through the tiny hole pierced at its top typified the sort sold in New Age shops that burned incense and offered sitar lessons. Maggie frowned. The prism's very association with the occult and magical was definitely at odds with the man who had hired her, a man whose black-and-white logic no doubt dismissed anything occult. How he had come by such an odd trinket in the first place, much less tucked it away in a drawer for safekeeping, only fueled her curiosity about who Derek Channing really was.

"As if I'll ever find out," she muttered under her breath as she slipped her discovery back under the envelopes. If she lived with him for a hundred years—Maggie laughed off the speculation before it was even completed. It would be hard enough just living with the man for the space of one summer.

Neither the lower drawers nor the opposite side offered any tangible clues. Her faxing done, Maggie's pulse quickened at the thought of where she really wanted to go next—the one room that knew her host more intimately than did the rest of the house. His bedroom.

The stamp of Derek Channing was so overwhelming that Maggie felt her breath catch in her throat as she closed the door behind her and took in the powerfully masculine setting of the private suite.

Rich, dark walnut furniture dominated the room. Massive and thick, its Early American style echoed the theme of pioneers and seafarers, men who measured their wealth by the quality of goods that would last through the ages and be passed down through the generations. Maggie found her imagination toying with just how many ancestral brides had been deflowered in the king-size four-poster bed, or how many hats had been tossed on the antique coat tree with its hooks carved in the shape of animal heads.

Heavy drapes of emerald green and gold brocade were pulled back from the windows and secured to the wainscoting by antique chains. Did he sleep with the curtains and windows open at night, she wondered, trying to picture how the room might look with the ocean view cut off and the walls swathed in fabric. The appreciation of a spectacular view and a brisk breeze off the sound probably were important to Derek Channing.

Like the hardwood floors in her own room, his had been left bare, except for a single Oriental rug in greens, browns, and golds—a color scheme repeated in a trio of wilderness paintings above the dresser and the writing desk. Even at a distance, and with her limited background in contemporary art, Maggie recognized the artist. Linteau's work, widely praised by international critics, had been on tour in the Boston Museum only months before she had met Troy. That the three she was looking at now were originals and not prints was surely a safe bet.

Intrigued by the double doors to the right of Channing's bed, Maggie approached them and opened one to reveal a walk-in closet. The kind of closet to kill for, she thought, remembering her apartment on the East Coast and its limited storage space.

Row upon row of expensive suits, jackets, and shirts on wooden hangers lined the closet's generous interior.

Deep built-in shelves were the nesting place for sweaters and wool scarves. The mingled scent of cedar and Channing's after-shave tickled her nose.

Her attention was drawn upward to neat stacks of shoeboxes on the entire upper shelf above the hanging clothes. Maggie wondered whether his orderliness had been inherited or acquired and refined over all of his years of bachelorhood.

It was too much to hope, of course, that he stored anything besides shoes up in those boxes. That, after all, was the practice of ordinary people, people who also kept rainy day money in coffee cans, loose buttons in ashtrays, and candle stubs in a bottom kitchen drawer. Unlike her father, who had been known on occasion to stack his canceled checks in an empty cereal dish, a man like Derek Channing would never utilize something as common as a shoebox for the storage of receipts, souvenirs—or other damning evidence. Still, it was worth a look, as long as she had the opportunity.

As she reached up to slide out the first one, the sound of footsteps just outside the bedroom door brought her to an abrupt stop.

15

There was no time to pull the closet door closed, only time to shrink behind it and press herself as far against the wall as she could. Thank goodness she hadn't turned the interior light on, Maggie thought, as the door to Channing's bedroom opened and someone stepped inside.

Not daring to move or breathe for fear of discovery, she could only listen as the quiet tread of soft-soled shoes crossed the hardwood floor toward the far corner, then stopped. Something was set down. A newspaper perhaps? A book? The steps resumed, coming back toward her, but at a slower pace. Once again, they stopped, as a drawer was gently pulled open.

All color drained from Maggie's face in the tense silence that followed. Unable to see who it was and not daring to inch forward for a better look, she could only hope that the visitor's stay would be short.

At last the drawer was pushed shut and the steps continued. Too soon, though, Maggie's relief was superseded by sheer panic. Whoever it was must have noticed the opened closet door just then and was crossing back to it to investigate. Maggie's entire body tightened, her nerves at full stretch.

A split second later, she was shocked to hear the switch clicked on from the outside wall and see the wardrobe around her suddenly bathed in bright light. Should she bolt? Should she freeze? Should she even try to improvise some excuse for being there?

The merciful intervention of a ringing phone saved her from having to make a decision.

"Channing residence," a woman's voice replied upon lifting the receiver next to the bed. "Yes, just a moment. I'll go find her for you."

Almost lyrical in its sweetness, the unexpected voice in the room with her was startling to Maggie's ears. Sky-Set? The smoothly enunciated words seemed surprising, considering that Maggie thought the woman barely spoke English.

The receiver was set down, and the steps grew faint as they reached the hallway. A hundred questions hammered in Maggie's head, not the least of which was where she should turn up if the telephone call was intended for her. Grateful for the reprieve from being discovered, Maggie quickly slipped out of the closet, pausing only a moment at the bedroom door to make sure that she wouldn't be seen exiting it.

If SkySet really *did* understand the language, she would probably look for Maggie down in the study. Since there was no way to beat her down the stairs and pretend she had been there all along, Maggie opted for the next best choice and ran to her bedroom.

"Yes?" she murmured drowsily from her bed a few minutes later when a sharp knock came at the door. Amidst the propped up pillows and with her hair lightly mussed out of its usual stylishness, it would be a convincing suggestion, Maggie thought, that she had lain down with a headache. Certainly SkySet would buy it.

It wasn't the housekeeper, though, who opened the door at Maggie's invitation.

"Mr. Channing is on the phone for you," Brecht coolly informed her.

Maggie followed him down the hall to the nearest extension.

"I must have misunderstood you," she said to Channing after assuring him that the faxes had gone through to New York. "I thought you and Brecht were coming back together."

The pause at the other end was just long enough to make her uncomfortable. "Is that a problem?" he asked.

"Just a little surprised to see him, that's all."

"Probably mutual."

Probably planned, Maggie thought, annoyed with his ongoing duplicity.

"I had some things for him to take care of out there," Channing continued. "Must have gotten our wires crossed. Oh, by the way, I'm going to need you on the mainland for the next three days—can you pack a bag and be ready to go in the morning?"

"Above ground or below?"

"Pardon?"

"If I'm packing a bag, it would help to know what should be in it."

"It'll be a change of pace," Channing said. "Didn't I tell you the job had variety?"

"So?"

"Definitely above ground. You'll be interviewing some ladies on Queen Anne's for me. Descendants of Seattle's elite." He explained that it was a good opportunity to tap into a new resource of private records.

"Wouldn't they be more charmed by a man instead?" Maggie asked.

"I'm sure they would, but I doubt Brecht would have the patience for it. At any rate, pack something pretty but conservative. We can go over the questions in the morning."

Maggie's pause prompted him to ask if there was something on her mind.

"It just seems strange," she said, "that for all the time I spend on the mainland, you've got me living out here at Lynx Bay."

"Meaning?"

"Meaning that no one else on the crew—" Maggie hesitated, wishing that she had rehearsed a smoother probe on the perplexing arrangement. "I guess I was just wondering," she said, "how I happen to rate room and board in addition to salary."

Channing pondered her question a moment before replying. "Maybe," he answered at last, "I just think you're intriguing to have around."

"Intriguing?"

"I'll leave you to think about it," he said, and then hung up.

It was impossible not to be swept up in the romance of the era, Maggie decided as she spent her second consecutive afternoon sipping coffee and listening to the family anecdotes of the Marquart sisters.

Octogenarian twins in confusingly similar floral dresses, each one kept interrupting the other by insisting that hers was the more interesting story.

"Now, it was Great-Grandpa Eugene," Cora Marquart explained, "who said that old Doc Maynard used to get up every morning and he'd—"

"No, it wasn't," Nora cut in. "Grandpa Eugene hadn't come out yet. It was Great-Uncle George who knew Doc Maynard." Nora shook her head apologetically at Maggie. "The older she gets, the more she forgets."

"You're five minutes older," Cora was quick to remind her.

"What about that old dry goods store you were telling me about?" Maggie asked. "The one you said is where Barron's is now?"

"Nice store, Barron's," Nora said. "They always have just the right thing, you know. Never too pricey like some of the rest, either. Have you been there?"

"No, not yet. I'm still learning my way around the city."

Cora sighed. "You already asked her that yesterday."

"I just thought she'd like it. Stop being such a goose. Would you like more coffee, dear?"

Maggie smiled. "I think I'm coffeed out."

"Isn't that a cute expression, Cora? Coffeed out. You could say that about a lot of things, couldn't you? Souped out . . . Monopolied out . . ."

"Booted out," Cora murmured.

"Do they say things like that back in—where was it—Philadelphia?" Nora asked.

"Boston, Nora. She told us she was from Boston."

Nora nodded. "Boston's such a nice place. So where are you staying now, dear?"

It was a pure slip of the tongue, Maggie realized the

moment she answered "Lynx Bay." Content with her supposed role as a writer doing historical research, she had successfully followed Channing's instructions to the letter and masked any connection to him or the underground project. Until then.

"Lynx Bay?" Cora repeated. "Wasn't that where—"

"Oh, you're thinking of that other one," Nora broke in. "Fog Fox Cove."

Cora was insistent. "No, no, I'm sure it was Lynx Bay. I remember it because it was some kind of animal and a body of water."

Nora leaned forward and tapped Maggie's wrist with her bony index finger. "It was probably Elephant Lake," she said with a giggle.

Cora saw no humor in her sister's teasing. "It was a small animal," she said. "And I think it was a lynx."

"Excuse me," Maggie said, "but what exactly are you talking about?"

"Oh, it was the most terrible scandal!" Cora exclaimed. "Of course they never proved anything one way or the other, but it was terrible all the same."

"*What* was terrible?"

Cora sighed. "I don't really remember anything about it, dear, except that—well, for the times, it just wasn't the kind of thing you liked to read about." Her face crinkled into a smile. "Would you like some more coffee?"

"She's coffeed out," Nora said. "Don't you ever listen?"

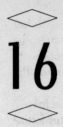

16

"*They sound pretty dotty* to me," Troy remarked when Maggie called him from her hotel room later in the afternoon. "Must be the altitude on Queen Anne's."

"I'm not so sure," Maggie said. "They were lucid enough about the layout of Pioneer Square. And this one old map that they had—"

"Where was Channing all this time?"

"Down in the tunnels, I presume. Why?"

"Just curious. As you were saying?"

"I go back again to see them tomorrow," Maggie continued. "They told me they have some old photographs from their mother's side that'll help pin down what exactly was where. Should cement some missing pieces on the project, I think."

"So he's still sold you on the story about the Chinese treasure?"

Maggie settled back in the pillows, the receiver tucked under her chin. "Whatever other motives he's hiding, he hasn't dropped a single hint."

"Did you really think he would?"

"Speaking of hiding things—"

"Hmm?"

"What do you think the Marquart sisters were referring to about a scandal out at Lynx Bay?"

Troy pondered her question for a moment. "I think it means that they may have helped themselves to the cooking sherry a tad too often. You said yourself that they couldn't even agree on where it happened, much less *what* it was to begin with."

"It would be in the newspapers, though," Maggie pointed out. "All you'd have to do is go to the library and look at—"

"Look at what?" Troy interrupted. "Every city issue between World War One and last week? For all you know, they might have been talking about something that happened two hundred years ago."

"Lynx Bay," Maggie reminded him, "has only been there for sixty."

"It also has nothing to do with what Channing is up to now."

"Maybe it does."

"I can hear the wheels turning in your head."

"And?"

"And I'm not sure I like the sound of them. You're losing your focus, Maggie. There's enough for you to keep an eye on without chasing after false leads."

"But what if it *isn't* a false lead? What if it's somehow connected to what my father had written down?"

The detective sighed. "You're not going to give me a moment's peace on this, are you?"

"I thought my tenacity was one of the things you admired."

"Yes, but some of the *other* things I admire are

going to be in hot water if you don't learn to follow directions."

"Can't you at least check it out? I mean, if there was some sort of crime involved—"

"Like I said, you'd have to get a lot more specific on the dates, or you're looking at a major waste of time. Which it probably is anyway."

"I'll be back at Queen Anne's tomorrow," Maggie said. "I could bring it up again in a conversation with them—casually, of course—and see if anything jogged loose during the night."

"I've got a better idea."

"Such as?"

"A guy I know who works on the docks. Been around forever. If anything of major juice happened anywhere on Puget Sound in the last couple of decades, Ernie would be the man to know about it. It'll probably cost me a couple bucks and a beer, but since you're so insistent about ferreting out crazy rumors . . ."

"Thanks, Troy."

"So what are your plans for dinner?"

"Well, Derek and I—"

"It's 'Derek' now?"

"Are you jealous?"

"Insanely," he said in a low voice.

"He said 'Mr. Channing' was too formal for someone I was living with."

"Oh. So you're saying you have a dinner date?"

"A dinner *meeting*," Maggie corrected him.

"Where?"

"The Space Needle."

Troy whistled. "Expensive meeting."

"I think he can probably afford it."

"Maybe I could meet you afterwards for some coffee and dessert."

"Wouldn't that be dangerous?"

"No more dangerous," Troy said, "than having dinner with your father's killer."

"You look nice in black," Channing said with a wink over the top of his menu. "In a dress like that, I could almost forget that you're an employee."

"Don't worry," Maggie replied. "I wouldn't let you."

The mischievous glint that came into his eyes warned her that her reply may have challenged rather than dissuaded him.

"Spectacular view, isn't it?" he said. "You know they built the whole Seattle Center and the Needle for the World's Fair over thirty years ago." He indicated the compass notations directly beneath the window. "As the restaurant revolves, you can always get your bearings on what you're looking out on by these marks. That's Lake Union over there, for instance. Northeast."

"And by the time we finish our salads?"

"Depends on how fast we eat, but my guess is we'll be facing the Kingdome."

"Oh, really?"

"But personally, I'm not in a hurry."

"What do you recommend?" Maggie asked, conscious that the price of the panorama had been incorporated in the already substantial cost of each entrée. "I assume you've been here before?"

"Never for dinner," he replied.

"That surprises me."

"Maybe that's part of the plan."

Maggie looked up from her menu in puzzlement,

only to discover that his attention was now on the list of featured specials.

"So what do you think of the Marquart sisters?" he inquired after they had made their selections and he had ordered wine.

"Definitely characters. They remind me a little bit of the aunts in *Arsenic and Old Lace*."

"Good comparison." Channing shook his head. "Now *that* brings back some funny memories."

"Memories of what?"

"Junior high back in Virginia. I got recruited to play the role of Jonathan."

"You're kidding."

"Seriously. I wasn't any good, but the drama class was short on males."

"No, I meant your playing Jonathan. It doesn't strike me as your kind of part."

"Isn't that what acting is all about, though? Playing someone that you're really not?"

Maggie stiffened, disconcerted by how closely his remark had hit home.

"So did you act in anything else?" she asked after he had finished his account of the production's success.

"Not enough time." Channing sipped his wine. "It did give me an appreciation, though, of how draining it can be to memorize lines and keep up a convincing facade night after night."

"I'll take your word for it," Maggie said, eager to get off the subject. "Did I tell you I'm getting a look at some more pictures of Old Seattle tomorrow?"

"Good. Every little bit helps. I couldn't do this without you."

"So what am I missing down in the tunnels?"

"Well, for one thing, Cleveland found a way to open

up one of the connectors into Seneca. Probably be a couple of weeks to even make a crawl space, but today was a good start. The guy knows what he's doing. He'll also be damned glad to get you back when you're finished at Queen Anne's."

"Sounds like it was your lucky day," Maggie said.

"I don't think luck has anything to do with it. Empires were never built on it."

He had offered her an opening she couldn't resist. "But I bet a rabbit's foot or a horseshoe never hurt," she said. "It all depends on what you believe in."

"Oh?"

"I used to carry a four-leaf clover for years," she said, improvising as she went along. "Brought me some of the best luck I ever had." Maggie thought she detected laughter in his eyes, but she wasn't sure. "How about you?" she asked, forcing a demure smile of innocence. "Ever carry anything silly like that?"

Channing studied the contents of his glass a moment before setting it down and replying. "You found the crystal, didn't you?"

17

Maggie hoped her initial silence was interpreted as confusion and not as the stab of guilt it really was. "Your train of thought just jumped a couple of tracks," she finally replied.

"Did it?"

"What are we talking about?"

"Omens, talismans, lucky charms." His thumb grazed the cleft in his chin. "Isn't that where you were leading? To get me to bring up the crystal?"

There seemed to be no point in dodging the question. Whatever his methods, Channing must have known that she had opened his desk and looked inside. Maybe he really *did* use closed-circuit surveillance to watch her.

"It just struck me as a strange thing for someone like you to have," she said with a shrug. "You don't seem the type."

"The type? I didn't realize there were enough others like me that we'd now have our own category."

"You know what I mean."

"Yes, but I'm enjoying hearing you explain it."

"It just surprised me, okay?"

"In what way?"

That he hadn't yet asked her what she'd been searching for was as curious as his knowledge that she'd been searching at all.

"You just said it yourself," she said, annoyed that he found such perverse pleasure in turning the tables on her. "Luck doesn't have anything to do with success, remember?"

"A bad paraphrasing, dear, but close enough to make your point." Channing grinned as their Caesar salads arrived. "We'd both like ground pepper," he told the waiter.

"None for me, thank you," Maggie said, vexed that his influence now extended to whether she took seasoning on her food.

Channing teased her after the man had departed. "Did you say that just to be contrary?"

"I said it because I didn't care for any."

"I see."

They passed the next few minutes in silence, Maggie purposefully concentrating on her lettuce.

"We seem to be in a verbal cul-de-sac," Channing said at last. "Would you like me to do something about that?"

"You're the boss."

Channing's reply surprised her. "No, not tonight," he said. "Tonight we're just two associates out for a nice dinner and a view of the city. A view," he added, "that's almost as beautiful as you are."

Unnerved by his sudden attentiveness, Maggie reverted to the subject of the crystal. "So what's the story on the crystal? Or is it a dark secret that no one's supposed to know?"

Her assertiveness brought a smile to his lips. "Oh, I wouldn't say there's that much of a story behind it, Maggie. And certainly if it were a dark secret," he went on, "I wouldn't leave it out where some inquisitive young female from Boston would be apt to find it and contrive her own version of how it got there."

"Well?" Maggie said as he procrastinated with two more bites of his salad.

"It was given to me by someone who believed in fairy tales," he finally answered. "Fairy tales and magic. Sort of an anomaly in the twentieth century, don't you think?"

"A woman?"

"On a fifty-fifty guess"—Channing smiled—"yes. A *young* woman, as a matter of fact."

His features had softened somewhat, and a faint tremor underscored his words as if some long-forgotten emotion had just been aroused.

"How young is young?"

"Young enough," he replied, "to believe that people are capable of changing. Fortunately, maturity has a way of correcting that kind of optimistic vision."

Maggie waited for him to continue, not at all convinced that he actually would.

"Water under the bridge," he said at last. "Some things are obviously beyond the purview of wishful thinking. How's your salad? Change your mind about the pepper?"

"What was her name?" Maggie asked, resolute to keep him talking about the mystery girl who had conjured so vulnerable a show of reminiscence.

A sudden flash of icy contempt glittered in Channing's

eyes. "I don't think that her name is really any of your business."

A completely strange and baffling man, Maggie thought throughout the rest of their meal, wondering what kind of irreparable damage her curiosity had done to a relationship that was already guarded at best. That he could continue to talk pleasantly to her about a host of other subjects as if nothing had happened was far worse than the stony-faced silence she would have expected.

"Room for dessert?" he asked when she had finished her last bite. "I seem to recall a fondness you mentioned for chocolate mousse."

"You'd have to roll me home."

"What if I just roll you around the observation deck instead?" he proposed.

Maggie felt an unbidden heat steal into her face. He was the enemy, her conscience sharply reminded her, and a man who'd feel as little remorse in breaking a heart as he would in discarding the morning newspaper. Yet why, at that moment, did she also see him as something else—as someone who had suffered his own bout with injustice and could still be stirred to anger by it?

"Was that a yes or a no?" he asked.

Flustered that she had mumbled any sound at all, much less one that could be construed as an answer, Maggie replied that his suggestion sounded fine. "Unless you're planning to push me off," she added.

"Why would I do that?"

Maggie took a deep breath. "Because I owe you an apology."

"Well, that's not one of my usual reasons for pushing people off the Space Needle, but now I'm intrigued. An apology for what?"

"For invading your privacy by asking about—well, about someone you obviously don't want to discuss."

"Apology accepted . . . with one condition."

"What's that?"

He smiled as if enjoying a private joke. "I think I'll save it until later."

They went outside.

"Smells like rain tonight," Channing remarked, taking her arm as they strolled toward the metal railing for the sparkling night vista he had promised. "After a couple of seasons out here, practically anyone can predict the weather."

"What if they only stay one summer?"

"Then I'd say they were missing one of life's better opportunities. Seattle's a nice place to call home."

Even without looking at him, Maggie knew that his eyes were on her, analyzing her every reaction.

"That's a matter of perspective," she replied.

"I suppose." The maddening hint of arrogance about him had returned. "One summer's probably not long enough to decide."

Maggie leaned against the rail and stared out at the blanket of city lights that lay over six hundred feet below them. "So what's the condition you wanted to attach to my apology?" she asked.

The question hung between them for a moment as Channing lifted his squared jaw, projecting a majestic silhouette backlit by the glow of the observation tower. "Remember when we were talking about theater?"

"*Arsenic and Old Lace?*" Maggie nodded. "What about it?"

He moved away from the railing and was now standing close enough that she was sure he could hear her heart break its regular rhythm. With a look so galvanizing that it sent a tremor through her, he gently reached up to entwine his fingers in the curls at the back of her neck. The warmth of his breath fanned her face as he delivered the message he had been saving for reasons of his own. "I think it's about time to stop acting."

18

Too startled by his pronouncement to protest, Maggie dropped her guard just long enough for Channing to break her unspoken prohibition against a sexual advance from the enemy. In one swift motion he closed what little distance remained between them and pulled her forward as he turned her head to just the right angle.

Nothing could have prepared her for the explosion of his sudden kiss, his tongue parting her lips and tasting her with rough thrusts, trapping her senses somewhere between disbelief and desire. Possessively, the hand that had been on her hip slid around to the small of her back, pulling her tight against the hard, lean contours of his body.

Against all logic and common sense, Maggie found herself returning his embrace rather than fighting it, surrendering to the spontaneous crush of emotion that had drawn them together beneath the Seattle stars.

Even as her heart hovered over the fine line between love and hate, the tantalizing invitation to lose herself in his tightening grasp overrode any desire to escape.

When at last he withdrew to hold her at arm's length, Maggie's lips still burned in the breathless aftermath of his fiery passion. Confused by her own response, she lowered her eyes to keep from looking at him. Channing's hand tenderly tilted her chin upward, his blue eyes casting her an amused expression.

"I hope you're not going to be coy and ask me to explain why I did that," he said.

Maggie straightened. "I don't think 'coy' is the right adjective," she countered, "but I think I do deserve an explanation."

"Then consider it a two-parter," Channing replied. "The first part is because you're a beautiful woman and because I wanted to. Not that it's the first time you've ever heard a line like that from a member of the opposite sex . . ."

"And what's the second part?"

Channing gave her a wry smile. "You're awfully impatient to hear something that might burst your bubble about what I did—or rather, *we* did—just now. I wouldn't want you to jump in and attach the wrong meaning to it."

Maggie's face tightened in reminiscence of the words he had uttered just before he kissed her, the suggestion that it was time to stop acting. Unnerved by what the last sixty seconds had wrought, a disturbing premise suddenly leapt into her head. Perhaps Channing was not only keeping his business secrets from her but the existence of another woman as well. Why else, she reasoned, would her questioning have elicited such a response laced with guilt and bitterness? And why else would he want her living out at Lynx Bay, if not to satisfy some purpose other than work? Her response to his kiss was undoubtedly just the reaction he wanted.

"I think I'm well adjusted enough," she said calmly, "to handle anything you'd feel like saying."

He released his hold on her and resumed his earlier stance at the railing. "The other day you told me that you had inherited your penchant for shopping from your mother."

"What does that have to do with trying to seduce me?"

There was a trace of laughter in Channing's voice. "If I had been trying to seduce you, do you really think I would have chosen as public a place as this?"

Maggie let the question go unanswered.

"What I'm wondering," he continued, "is where you inherited your unflappable cockiness."

"Maybe it's an acquired talent."

"No, there are some things that are born into a person from the start. Ambition, resiliency . . . cockiness."

"Is there a point to this?"

"I just thought you might have inherited a trait like that from your father."

He was baiting her again, testing her to see if she would slip up and fall through the cracks in her own story. *He doesn't know anything,* her conscience insisted. He was only shooting in the dark in the hope of hitting something by accident.

"I have his sense of humor and his compassion for other people," she replied. "I think I've done well by both of them."

"Admirable qualities," Channing nodded. "Maybe that's what makes you different from a lot of the women I know."

Maggie couldn't resist a snappy retort. "And is that a fairly large number?"

Channing laughed. "I think I'd rather stick to talking about *you*."

"What's there to talk about that you don't already know?"

"Only one thing, really." Channing drew his lips in thoughtfully as if debating whether to share what was on his mind. "I guess I'm just curious about what the daughter of Clayton Price hoped to accomplish by coming to work for me."

Her mouth dropped open in shock.

"Take your time answering," he insisted, his voice disturbingly warm against the chill of distrust his question had just created. "You've obviously put a lot of work into the charade."

Maggie's mind raced for a way out. If he were calling her bluff, she reasoned, any admission would be feeding him information that could ultimately jeopardize the work of the Seattle police. If he *did* know what she was doing there, the question remained as to what action he'd take to ensure a swift end to her sleuthing. That he had brought her to one of Seattle's highest structures for a confrontation in the middle of the night did little to assuage her fears.

The unwelcome tension stretched tighter between them, compounded by Channing's outward show of total complacency.

Trying to regain control, Maggie opted for the one answer she hoped would catch her adversary off balance.

"Maybe I didn't want you to think you owed me anything," she said.

"I beg your pardon?"

Maggie met his gaze with a strength and determination she prayed was convincing. "I don't think you know how much I wanted to be a part of what my father was doing out here, of discovering things that could rewrite history." Maggie paced her reply carefully, injecting just enough wavering in her voice to attest to the supposed difficulty in saying it. "I wanted to come out while he was still alive, but he always told me it was too dangerous. Obviously, he was right." As the words began to flow, Maggie felt her confidence returning. "I thought maybe enough time had finally passed that, well, I guess it doesn't make any difference what I thought."

"That still doesn't explain what you're doing here now."

Maggie took a deep breath, pausing only a moment before the denouement she had fabricated out of desperation. "I wanted to work for you, but I didn't want you to feel any obligation to hire me . . . because of what happened."

Channing cocked his head. "And why should I feel any obligation? If I hired half my people out of pity or of guilt, I'd have a sorry excuse for a company, wouldn't I? I hire people because they've proven themselves, Maggie. And I keep them because they can do the job."

"I hadn't proven anything when you hired me," she reminded him.

"It's a good thing that you're not a betting woman, Maggie Price," he said with a smile. "You'd be so easy to take money away from right now."

"What are you talking about?"

"Wouldn't you rather ask me how I knew who you were?"

"Why volunteer it when you're as good as firing me on the spot?"

"Who said anything about firing?"

"Aren't you?" At least, Maggie thought, her extemporaneous ruse had protected Troy.

"I don't intend to let you off *that* easily. Besides, I have too many years invested in you."

"And what's that supposed to mean?"

"Let's walk a bit," he said, gallantly offering his arm. "The view's even prettier from the other side of the deck."

Reluctantly, Maggie joined him.

"So do you miss your old job back in Boston?" he asked.

"It'll still be waiting for me when summer's over," she said. "It's not as if I left it permanently. Why?"

"Just curious. By the way," he casually inquired, "did Bowman ever give you the skinny on how that commission is funded?"

"Grants," Maggie replied, perplexed by the question. "Everyone in Boston knows *that.*"

"And does everyone in Boston—or rather, you specifically—know who fronts some of that bountiful grant money?"

"Corporations," Maggie answered. "Corporations and—" the rest of the answer died in her throat, preempted by the satisfied expression on Channing's face.

"Yes, Maggie, whether you like it or not, you've been on my corporate payroll for the past four and a half years."

19

"*Your father was* a tremendous engineer," Channing said, "but, unfortunately, he had the sense of a radish when it came to things like life insurance. I knew that what he had taken out wouldn't last you very long, not with the job you were holding down when it happened. I also knew you'd never accept my charity."

Maggie's voice hardened. "Nor would I now."

Channing caught her arm as she wheeled to take leave of him. "The least you can do is hear me out."

Maggie attempted to wrench free, but his grip was too tight.

"You can think whatever you want about it, Maggie, but I *did* feel a sense of moral responsibility to see that you had things a little easier than you would have had on your own."

Maggie's temper flared. "I would have done just fine without you."

"Knowing you as I do now, I can see that. You've not

only got a brain in that head of yours, but the survival instincts to go with it."

"And yet you didn't think I could last for ten minutes without your so-called help."

"Oh, you would have lasted," Channing conceded, "but I felt you deserved better than that. You can't fault me for having your long-term interests at heart."

The condescension in his attitude only infuriated her more. "That job at the Commission happened to *mean* something to me," she said.

"There's no reason why it shouldn't."

"Isn't there? Now that I know the truth about where it—"

"I think you're reading this all wrong. It's hardly as if you were dead weight at the Commission or just part of some fine-print clause that they had to agree to." His voice became tender, almost a murmur. "Your boss and *his* boss both think the absolute world of you, young lady. And when Terrell called to tell me that you were taking a leave from your job for the summer—"

"Look," Maggie interrupted, "I don't see where any of this is going. I told you what I'm doing here, and if you're not satisfied with the answer, there's nothing more I can add to it."

"I happen to think that there is."

"Fine," Maggie snapped. "What?"

A strange look came into his eyes, and he hesitated a moment before replying. "Did you come all the way out here because you think that your father's death was my fault?"

Stunned by his bluntness, Maggie faltered in the silence that engulfed them.

"Do you?" he repeated, as if whatever action he might take next was contingent on her reply.

"I don't know," she said at last. "I honestly don't know what to think."

Channing's lips unexpectedly brushed her forehead. "I'll settle for that," he said gently. "For now."

Neither one said a word on the way back to the hotel. Owing to the mild evening, Channing had suggested they walk instead of ride. For Maggie, it only prolonged the amount of time she had to endure the confusing confines of his presence.

What on earth do you want from me? she wanted to scream. He had exposed her identity, patronized her with his wealth, and was now playing the martyred hero who wanted to win her trust. *And don't forget the other*, her conscience reminded her. Maggie forcefully shoved the memory of his bruising kiss into the darkest corner of her mind so that she could avoid dealing with it until she was good and ready.

The job at the Commission had been a timely godsend, Maggie recalled, annoyed with herself that she had never made what seemed now to be so obvious a chronological connection. Perfectly tailored to her education and background, the position had fallen into her lap, supposedly as the result of a referral from one of her college professors. That Channing had orchestrated the entire thing as recompense for her father's accident prompted a sourness in the pit of her stomach.

On the surface, of course, his intentions had all the earmarks of honor. Whether or not he had actually had a hand in Clayton Price's demise, some part of him had wanted to make it up to her. That she would never have accepted an open settlement from him was closer to the truth than she dared admit, for no amount of money could ease the pain of her loss. Then—as now—she would have seen it as nothing more than a generous payoff to pacify the bereaved.

It had taken every ounce of her willpower not to walk away from him at the Space Needle, much as she wanted to. Chagrined by the knowledge that he had known about her from the first day and that he had held the purse strings on her former livelihood, she realized she was a prisoner. The only bright spot in her predicament was that he had made no reference to her connection with Troy McCormick. At least she had not failed *him*.

"Now that our cards are out on the table," Channing had said when they emerged from the elevator to the street level, "I see no reason why we can't move forward and work as a team."

If only he knew, Maggie thought. *If only he knew*.

"Nightcap?" Channing offered when they reached the lobby of the hotel. "It's still early."

"I thought I'd just get a cup of coffee."

"Coffee sounds fine to me."

"By myself," Maggie clarified, indifferent to whether it sounded harsh or selfish.

To her surprise, Channing respected her wishes and bade her goodnight, yet not before adding that he had enjoyed their evening together. "And you really *are* beautiful in that dress," he complimented her. "It was an honor to be seen with you."

Not until he had strolled down the corridor and around the corner to the elevators did it occur to her that he had never given her the second half of his answer to the question of kissing her. Don't even give *that* incident another thought, her conscience advised her. Knowing Channing, it was probably already as good as forgotten.

In the hotel coffee shop she ordered a decaf, and then pensively stared out at the darkness, trying to assimilate all that had happened that evening. That Channing knew who she was at least cleared up some of the mysteries that had bothered her since her arrival. First of all, he had known where to send Brecht to collect her luggage. And then, his tight affiliation with Clive's boss would have enabled him to discount over half of the claims on her résumé. Had he enjoyed baiting her about her experiences in the Far East? For reasons of his own, Channing had chosen to perpetuate her myth for over a week, rather than expose her on the spot as a fraud.

It was this last that bothered her the most, raising a host of new, disturbing questions. Not once had he asked her how she had acquired the documents that identified her as Margaret Johnson, nor had he ever inquired how she had come to find out about the opening on his staff. Of course he could attribute both issues to resourcefulness on her part, but Maggie knew better than to believe that Derek Channing's curiosity about her had been sated. If anything, she would have to be even more careful.

Having reached this conclusion, she paid for the coffee and went up to her hotel room, looking forward to a steamy shower to relieve her tension after the evening of verbal gladiating. Inside, she kicked off both shoes, thankful for the respite from Channing's company. "Tomorrow is another day," she said out loud in her best impression of Scarlett O'Hara.

Too late, her glance fell on the shadow that stepped from behind the door, and its owner's hand swiftly closed over her mouth.

20

Maggie jabbed her elbow straight back, but her assailant's strength and expertise easily deflected the maneuver, pulling her tighter against him as a hot and husky voice reverberated in her ear. "It's me, Maggie," Troy whispered as she struggled to break free. "It's okay."

The sharp expletive that escaped Maggie's lips upon his release of her prompted an immediate, almost sheepish apology. "I just didn't want you to scream out," he said, rubbing the palm she had managed to leave faint tooth marks on.

"Wouldn't a simple knock on the door have sufficed?" Maggie asked, her heart still racing from the encounter.

"Only if we were dealing with simple circumstances. In this business, Maggie, you learn to grab opportunities when they happen."

Her annoyance was clear in the depths of her green

eyes. "Does that also extend to grabbing women you're supposed to be protecting?"

Troy took a deep breath and adjusted his smile. "I'd offer to come back when you're in a better mood, but—from the sound of it—I'd say I might have a pretty long wait."

"Look, it's just been a bad night, okay? You're obviously here for something important, and I'm keeping you from saying it."

"I like to think so, yes." Troy followed her to the edge of the bed but didn't sit down. "I got worried when you didn't check in."

"Slow waiters," Maggie lied. "I would have called you first thing in the morning."

"So consider I just saved you twenty cents with a personal visit." His expression grew serious. "What happened? Is something wrong?"

Maggie pressed both hands over her eyes. "Nothing and everything," she replied, at a loss as to where to begin.

Troy reached down to brush his fingers once across her cheek before landing them on her left shoulder and commencing a light massage. "That covers a lot of territory. Which part of it upset you?"

Maggie looked up into a face warm with concern for her well-being. "Channing knows who I really am."

Troy frowned. "How did he find out?"

"Maybe I should start from the beginning. . . ."

"I'm keeping you," Maggie murmured an hour later, astonished by the amount of time that had passed in her recounting—minus the kiss—of the evening with Derek Channing.

"No objection from this quarter. That's what I'm here for." Troy had seated himself on the floor at the foot of the bed with a pillow to cushion his back to listen to the whole story. "Doing any better?"

"I guess I just can't help feeling like I may have jeopardized things," she confessed.

Troy was quick to contradict her. "We all knew Channing was slick. In fact, I'd almost be disappointed in the man if he hadn't done some legwork."

"It's what he didn't ask me that's making me nervous."

"You mean about your phony papers and ID?"

"It just doesn't follow that he wouldn't bring it up."

"Unless he thinks you've got connections."

Maggie nodded gravely. "Connections that are going to lead straight back to *you*."

"We'll cross that bridge when we come to it, okay?" A half smile crossed his face. "I think you handled it just fine."

"You really don't see what this means, do you?"

"What I see is a beautiful woman who's letting herself get too upset about something that we both had an inkling could happen down the road."

"Down the road, yes," Maggie snapped. "Not just right after I started."

Troy shook his head. "None of that was your fault, Maggie. It's not as if he was suddenly bitten by a bug to go snooping on you because you looked at him wrong. As he said, you've been on his payroll for—"

"That's just it!" Maggie cut him off, irritated that someone as smart as Troy could be missing so salient a point. "Up until tonight, at least I had my old job to go back to. I could have walked away from this whole thing and gone home to Boston and never looked back."

"Which," Troy gently reminded her, "is exactly what I've been telling you all along."

"And how am I supposed to do that when the very job that meant something to me is controlled by the man I hate?" Maggie punched the bedspread in exasperation. "For all I know, he probably even owns the apartment building I live in!"

"Or at least sleeps with your landlady and half her friends," Troy quipped.

Maggie felt a brief shudder of humiliation, stirred by the memory of what had transpired on the observation deck. She was still not quite sure why she had omitted the incident of the kiss from her update to Troy.

"Did I say something?" Troy asked, conscious of her sudden discomfiture.

"No, I'm just punchy from lack of sleep. I probably should let you go."

Troy acknowledged her suggestion with a hesitant smile. "That may be a slight problem."

"What do you mean?"

He inclined his head toward the door. "Because there's a certain German who's cruising the hallway out there like a Doberman looking for someone to bite in the leg. Believe me, I had one helluva time getting *in* here in the first place."

"So you're telling me that you're going to stay on this side of the door?"

Troy winked. "I wouldn't be that presumptuous, Maggie, to make myself a guest without asking. Of course, if you'd rather have me go dangle by my ankles off a fire escape on the nineteenth floor and end up falling on my head, your wish is my command."

In spite of his intended humor, Maggie felt her pulse quicken. "It's just that—"

"You see that wingback chair over there in the corner? If it's not a problem for you, I'm going to park myself in it, watch you sleep, and slip out before the sun even hits the mountain."

"Watch me sleep?"

Troy's smile was boyishly affectionate. "It's a tough job," he said, "but *someone's* gotta do it."

True to his word, Troy was gone by morning.

In the gray shadows of dawn, Maggie rolled over to discover that the wingback chair was empty. To her surprise, she felt a slight pang of wistfulness at having missed the chance to say good-bye.

What a weird evening, she reflected as she replayed the details of everything that had happened. Overwhelmed by one man and—well, *under*whelmed by the other. That Troy had literally spent the night with her and not so much as tried to kiss her brought a smile to Maggie's face. *Chivalry still lives,* she thought, touched by the detective's caring and the unobtrusive way that he was letting her know she was important to him. *Maybe when this whole thing with Channing is over . . .*

Maggie pushed the speculation from her mind, disturbed by the knowledge that her association with the millionaire was without a foreseeable end. He controlled her present, he had influenced her past, and unless she started making some headway on what he was really up to in the catacombs, he could also try to determine her future.

Yet even more disturbing than the aura of danger he exuded was the burning sensation that he had branded on her in the space of a single, reckless moment. Hypnotized by his touch, she'd been swept by desire that obscured all common sense. That he could be so powerful as to squelch any rejection on her part made her aware that the biggest battle lay ahead of her. He was the enemy, her conscience reminded her. The man who had murdered her father. And yet she felt drawn to him somehow . . .

Impatiently Maggie flung the covers off the bed, resolute in her decision that Channing's brief stab at physical conquest would not enjoy a repeat performance.

So absorbed was her concentration on the new day that awaited that she didn't notice the note slipped discreetly beneath her door until after she had finished her shower.

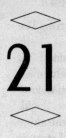

21

The broad, black strokes of Channing's handwriting neatly filled the middle third of the piece of hotel stationery. "Having some business associates for dinner tonight," it read, "and would like you to be present. Should be an enlightening experience and one that will add to your history of Elliott Bay. Try to wrap up with the Marquarts by three so we won't be rushed getting back. Formal attire—your black dress will fit the bill if you don't mind a second evening in it."

So now I've become his little resident hostess as well, Maggie thought, vexed with the liberties that Channing applied to the generic title of assistant. She wondered if he had even gone so far as to hint to his colleagues that she was providing him with more than congeniality and intelligent conversation. "I'll nip *that* one in the bud," she said out loud, envisioning the embarrassment she could generate by refusing to play along with his charade of domestic bliss. Maggie reread his directive about what to wear and felt her exasperation grow. The man was truly impossible.

It was his postscript, though, that accentuated her annoyance, along with a sense of her own vulnerability: "Kisses like yours shouldn't be wasted on the competition."

Her initial reaction that Derek Channing was decidedly full of himself was quickly replaced by the sudden apprehension that he was referring to Troy as a romantic rival. Certainly the fact that he hadn't mentioned the detective the previous night didn't discount the possibility that he or Brecht might have seen them together at some point since her arrival in Seattle. And once seen, it was probably only a matter of time before he discovered her friend's particular line of work.

They'd have to be careful, she decided. Very careful.

Cora Marquart opened the front door and greeted Maggie as if she were a long-lost niece. "It's simply been ages, dear," she said as she squeezed Maggie's hand and, with a thin arm around her waist, ushered her into the foyer. "How have you been?"

Maggie chose not to mention that it had, in reality, been less than twenty-four hours. "What a pretty dress," she said to her diminutive hostess after a brief exchange of pleasantries, the whole time not entirely sure whether it was Cora or Nora. "Is it new?"

"This old thing?!" Cora giggled, smoothing imaginary wrinkles from the flowered cotton bodice. "Oh no, it was one of Nora's hand-me-downs."

That the twins had ever enjoyed a period of physical size difference was almost as funny to Maggie as Nora's subsequent appearance in the parlor doorway wearing exactly the same style of dress.

"I hope my sister's not talking both of your ears off," Nora said. "Old people have a tendency to do that."

"No, not at all," Maggie insisted.

"Well, that's good." Nora smiled. "So how have you been, dear? It's simply been ages, hasn't it?"

Cora followed them into the study. "We really should have invited you to join us for breakfast," she said. "I don't remember if you said that you're a breakfast person or not."

Before Maggie could open her mouth, Nora said, "It would have to have been planned a day ahead, of course, because this morning we were porridged out."

Maggie suppressed a laugh.

"Which is why we had eggs instead," Cora added. "Not everyone likes eggs, you know. The cholesterol thing? Nora's is higher than mine these days, so she has to be careful with everything she puts in her mouth."

"My doctor says I have the body of a twenty-year-old," Nora snapped at her sister.

"Yes," Cora agreed, "and it's high time you return it before they file a missing person report."

Nora directed Maggie to the velvet settee and whispered, "Now don't you mind her. She's just a little pilled out from the excitement of you being here."

Maggie cleared her throat. "Well, shall we get back to what we were talking about yesterday afternoon? It was really interesting."

"Yes, it was, wasn't it?" Cora said. "What exactly was it?"

Maggie chose an innocuous opening that she hoped would eventually lead her back to her actual object of curiosity. "You were telling me all about the seamstresses on the waterfront," she said.

Nora pursed her lips. "Oh yes, the naughty ladies. Weren't they a stitch?"

Cora shook her head. "That line is getting so old, Nora. You're dating yourself. Aggie's going to think you're crazy."

"Oh, nonsense. My mind is like a steel trap."

Cora clucked her tongue. "Rusted shut from the rain. Now what were you saying, dear?"

"It's 'Maggie,' " Maggie gently corrected her. "And we were talking about the seamstresses." She opened her notebook. "I noticed from the town maps you had that none of the houses were identified."

Nora laughed. "Goodness no, but it didn't stop the menfolk from finding them."

"They just sort of set up shop wherever clients seemed to congregate," Cora added. "It made it easier to relocate if they had to."

"So there weren't any permanent brothels, then?"

Nora blushed at Maggie's use of the word. "Oh, a few, yes. There was that Italian one—what was the girl's name again, Cora?"

Cora bristled at her sister's question. "It's not as if I knew her personally."

"I never said you did."

"You *implied* it."

"Was it Gianecchini?" Maggie asked, recalling Channing's mention of the madam's name on her first trek to the underground.

"Yes, yes, that was it," Cora said. "A pretty girl, as I recall."

"You said you didn't know her," Nora reminded her.

"I knew *of* her. But then, so did most of Seattle. I understand she did very well for herself in spite of being such a mean-spirited little wench."

"But didn't the authorities come down on her if she was so easy to find?" Maggie asked.

"Oh, no. She had connections," Nora said. "That's how the ones like her stayed in business as long as they did."

"With the right connections," Cora added, "you could practically commit murder. That and any other kind of scandal."

Maggie snapped her fingers. "That reminds me . . ."

"Reminds you of what, dear?"

"That scandal out at Lynx Bay you were telling me about. Remember? The one where they had the—" Maggie pretended to be groping for the right word. "What was it again? It's on the tip of my tongue."

"Adultery?" Cora volunteered, then immediately looked embarrassed.

"If Mother were here," Nora said sharply, "she'd wash your mouth out with soap."

Elated that she had just led them into revealing something, Maggie continued cautiously. "Of course, there are two sides to everything. And without knowing the whole story—"

"Yes," Nora agreed, "but you have to wonder what kind of beast the man was that his own wife didn't want to live with him."

"I don't know that *I* could live on an island. All that water around you all the time." Cora shuddered. "I'd feel like a prisoner."

"So where *did* she go?" Maggie asked.

"Back to her own kind," Nora replied. "Not that he didn't put up a fight. Practically dragged her back by the hair."

"She's exaggerating," Cora said. "I heard he was very civilized about it. Very much the gentleman."

Nora sighed. "The one I felt sorry for was the child. Poor thing. Now *that's* where the real crime was."

22

Maggie's mouth dropped open in complete surprise. "There was a child involved?"

Cora eyed her suspiciously. "I thought you said you already knew that."

"My head's so full of facts and figures from my research, it's hard to keep them all straight. I guess I just forgot for a minute which incident we were talking about."

"Happens to the best of us although it happens to others much more than some." From the sly tilt of Nora's head, it was obvious that she counted her twin among the latter.

"I'd hate to have been the boy," Cora babbled on, oblivious to her sister's comment. "Being caught in the middle like that . . ."

"You can't help but feel sorry for the little guy," Maggie said, hoping that the mystery youth was within an age range to be categorized as "little."

"Oh, the boy understood plenty," Cora said. "A lot more than people around here gave him credit for. Why, the distance he kept from his father for the longest time—"

"Not that he was that fond of his mother, either," Nora interjected. "Now, I'm not sitting in judgment, mind you, but when a woman runs away from her responsibilities and takes up with some total stranger—" Nora shook her head. "It's a sad state of things when people can't sit down and talk out their problems, isn't it?"

"Sometimes you just can't," Maggie replied, surprising herself with how well she was maintaining her end of the conversation in spite of not knowing what it was about.

"Of course *nowadays*," Cora said, "no one would bat an eye about that sort of dirty laundry, would they? No, no, it's not like it was *then*. Not at all."

"Time does fly, doesn't it?" Maggie scrambled for a way to pinpoint a date. "Let me see, that would have been about—"

"Would you like some cocoa, dear?" Cora offered. "Then we can talk some more about those naughty ladies on the waterfront."

"We're cocoaed out," Nora said. "We do have a nice Earl Grey, though. Do you take tea, Aggie?"

"It's Maggie with an M, you goose," Cora corrected her. "And yes, why don't you go make a pot for us, Nora, since you're not doing anything."

Momentarily left alone with the remaining twin, Maggie refused to let the subject of the Lynx Bay scandal drop. "It must have been very hard on him when his wife left," she remarked.

"Hard on whom, dear?"

"You know, the husband."

"Goodness, yes. And then that shameless way she waltzed right back in? As if nothing had happened?" Cora leaned in to squeeze Maggie's wrist and whisper a confidence. "He was wise to it, though, and so was half the town. Especially since the baby didn't look like *him* at all."

Maggie's head was spinning at that point. "What do *you* think the real story was?" she asked Cora. "About the baby, I mean."

"Me?" The elderly woman pondered the question. "Well, dear, it's not my place to say, but I don't know how she ever expected to pass it off. Personally I think that Homer had the patience of a saint to handle it as civilly as he did. Most men would have wrung her neck and be done with the whole messy affair."

"Excuse me, but who's Homer?"

Cora laughed. "Where's your head, child? We've been talking about the poor man all morning! My, my, but you're getting to sound just like Nora."

"I hate to say 'I told you so,'" Troy remarked when Maggie told him on the phone that afternoon about the Marquarts' revelation, "but I don't think their elevators go to the top."

"But there must be *something* to it," Maggie insisted. "They were both going along at a pretty good clip. And if you ask me, it sounded damn convincing."

"It also sounds like the plot of a late-night movie. Or better yet, a daytime soap, coupled with a few nips of cooking sherry."

"We could at least check it out."

"I don't suppose this Homer character has a last name?"

"The name is superfluous," Maggie countered. "They had to have been talking about Derek."

"Homer. Derek. Derek. Homer. You're right—they sound so much alike," he teased.

"I'm serious."

"Yes, but aren't you forgetting something?"

"Like what?"

"Channing's never been married. At least not that *I* know of."

"But what if he *had* been? What if it was only for a short time and she wanted to break it off but he didn't and so she—"

Troy chuckled. "Your imagination just kicked into overdrive. Next thing, you'll be telling me that Brecht is the long-lost love child."

"Very funny."

"Listen, Maggie, it's a great story, but I think you're getting way off track with it. Besides, what does any of this possibly have to do with your father?"

"Okay, just hear me out a second."

"Only because I'll have no peace if I say no."

"Channing plays everything close to the chest, right?"

"An understatement if ever I heard one."

"Well, what if there was some payoff involved, some kind of blackmail? Channing would never want that kind of thing to get out for what it would do to his reputation."

"All the better to add to his mystique. For some women, that would be a turn-on, wouldn't it?"

Maggie reflected on the millionaire's sensuous attraction and her own disturbing awareness of it. "Let's just say that maybe my father found out something about Channing's past that he wasn't supposed to." Silently, she replayed the words of Clayton Price's last letter in her head. "Maybe that's the secret Dad was referring to, the one that Channing couldn't afford to have him walking around and knowing."

Troy was dubious. "I don't know that a domestic squabble and a paternity puzzle would merit cold-blooded murder—"

"But it's possible, isn't it?"

"Oh, yes. In this day and age, practically anything is possible."

The sky had become overcast by the time Maggie and Channing returned to the harbor at Lynx Bay, accompanied by a stir of north wind off the Sound.

"SkySet will have all the arrangements well in hand for dinner," he informed her as the bearded skipper eased the boat into its berth. "The rest of the afternoon is yours."

"What would you do without her?" Maggie remarked rhetorically.

To her surprise, Channing responded. "Hopefully, I'll never have to find that out. She's a good woman."

The sincerity in his voice only increased her misgivings about the pair's relationship. "Obviously, she's just as fond of you."

"Fond?" Channing repeated in curiosity. "What are you digging for now, Ms. Price?"

"I wasn't aware that I was."

Channing winked. "You were," he said. "And believe me, you couldn't be farther off the mark."

He was already sequestered behind the closed doors of his study when Maggie had changed into jeans and a

sweatshirt. Rather than interrupt him to tell him she
was going for a walk, Maggie let herself out, reasonably
assured that her actions were probably being monitored anyway, if not by Channing himself, then by his
bodyguard.

Back toward the mainland, the summer sky had
turned an ominous slate gray, threatening the city that
lay beneath it with rain. For a moment, Maggie
hesitated, debating whether to return for an umbrella
or risk a few sprinkles. Opting for the latter, she slowly
picked her way up one of the paths that led toward the
island's west side, a leisurely walk to afford her some
quiet time to contemplate what she had learned on
Queen Anne's Hill.

Mindful as she was of Troy McCormick's mission to
stick to the facts, a part of her rebelled at his continued
efforts to discount her own theories. Even his "I'll
check into it" closure when she hung up had left her
with a feeling that his heart was not truly in it.

Not that she couldn't pick up the slack herself. With
Channing's carte blanche for her to collect as much
information as she could about early Seattle, there
would be little—if anything—to stop her from extending her library work to a deliberate peek into her
employer's past. Indifferent as he was to the scandalous rumors, Troy needn't even know about her
extracurricular sleuthing until she could present him
with something tangible.

Pleased with her new plan of action, Maggie nearly
missed the flash of movement through the fir trees just
ahead of her as a cloaked figure moved away from her
and down the incline.

23

Hindered by the figure's advantage of an early start, Maggie tempered her desire to break into a run with the prudence of making as little noise as possible.

The soft earth deadened her footsteps as she followed, wending her way beneath low branches and past thick green ferns. Overhead, the wind sighed through the tops of the pines, echoing the rush of her own breath. She stopped to glance at the sky only once, dismayed to see that clouds had already swept in above the trees and engulfed them in a long, gray shadow.

Less worried about getting wet than about losing the chance to learn something, Maggie continued on her mission, conscious of the cool darkness that enfolded her as she entered the edge of the forest. Seemingly oblivious to being followed, the figure maintained its purposeful stride. Apparently he or she had taken this path many times before.

A "she" was more than likely, Maggie guessed,

though the speed and agility suggested the possibility of a young man. A young Indian man, maybe—a particular teenager minus the baseball cap?

Though Troy had casually dismissed her story about the Indian boy at Pioneer Square, the youth's startled face was still etched in her memory. She had not seen him again since that first day, but the nagging intuition that he had been spying on her—and perhaps still was—remained.

The obvious question was how anyone had gotten to the island in the first place. "You don't have to worry about encountering any snakes or wild animals on Lynx Bay," Derek had told her the first evening they went walking. "Most of them drowned in the swim coming over from the mainland."

And people? Clearly, if anyone could make it onto the island, it wasn't likely that their arrival would stay a secret for long. Channing and Brecht would both take care of that.

The murmur of a stream drifted through the silence and, in the distance, Maggie could see where it cut through a cluster of trees. As the figure deftly jumped across its narrow width to the other side, Maggie caught sight of a handful of flowers in his or her left hand. Maggie picked up her own pace, thoroughly perplexed as to what was going on.

The first drops of rain began to fall, pattering on the blackberry bushes.

Maggie cleared the stream as easily as her predecessor. Just beyond the clearing, she could see that the figure had come to a stop and was now kneeling down as if in prayer. Pine trees obscured Maggie's view, and there was no available cover for her to get closer without the risk of being seen.

Off to the right was a low pile of boulders clustered at the base of a cedar tree. If she could get to them, Maggie decided, she could crouch down and afford herself a better angle to see what the figure was doing. She would also be out of sight if the person turned around to take the same path back. *Slowly,* her caution warned her. *Very slowly.*

As she started to move, an accented voice behind her chilled Maggie to the bone. "That would not be wise, madam," Brecht said.

Derek Channing studied her across his desk with the amused expression of a school principal facing an incorrigible but entertaining truant. "You and Brecht seem to be at a constant state of cross purposes," he observed after listening to her version of what had happened.

"I don't think that pulling a gun and scaring me out of my wits was called for."

"A little extreme, yes," Channing conceded, "but in Brecht's eyes, you were trespassing where you weren't supposed to be."

"Then maybe you should mark off the island with yellow boundary lines," Maggie snapped. "I was under the impression that I was free to go wherever I wanted."

"Within reason."

"Meaning what?"

"Meaning exactly what I just said."

"Then maybe you should warn me in advance where the skeletons are, so I don't trip over them by accident.

With a tilt of his head, Channing indicated that Brecht should leave the room.

Maggie tried to sound defiant to hide her nervousness. "I think that you owe me an explanation."

"Excuse me, but why should I owe an explanation to someone who is as clearly in the wrong as you are?"

"I *thought* I was doing you a favor," she said.

"Oh? How do you figure that?"

"I was under the impression that we were the only ones living on the island."

"I'm sure that whatever conclusions you've drawn are accurate."

"Until today."

"Because you thought you saw someone?"

Maggie's temper flared. "I *did* see someone. An intruder."

"And you assumed he was dangerous?"

"Wouldn't you?" Maggie retorted, conscious that he had used the masculine pronoun in his reference.

"Not carrying a bouquet of flowers, no."

"I didn't see them until I got closer."

Channing steepled his fingers as he leaned forward. "Straight from the pages of Nancy Drew, Girl Detective. Most women would have chosen not to get involved."

"Like I said, I thought I was doing you a favor."

"And as you've already discovered—albeit unpleasantly—Brecht had the situation well under control."

"So you're admitting there *was* someone?"

Channing's voice shifted to an impersonal tone that stung more sharply than a display of anger would have. "I think we've taxed this conversation to its limits, Maggie. In the future, I'd like you to restrict your outdoor movements to where you can be seen from the house."

"Like a prisoner?"

Channing let the words hang for a few seconds between them, as if contemplating how best to answer.

"No," he said at last. "Like a woman I care for and don't want to see get hurt by her own curiosity."

Had there been a convincing way to excuse herself from the evening of company that lay ahead, Maggie would have taken it. Infuriated by Channing's remarks and determined to pick up exactly where she had left off at the clearing in the woods, the last thing she wanted to do was suffer a tedious dinner with three colleagues who were probably as egocentric as her host. The best she could hope for was that they would eat fast and leave early.

"So you're Channing's assistant we've heard so much about!" The round-faced man grinned, vigorously pumping her hand as she joined them in the foyer. Minus the glasses, Maggie thought, his cheerful countenance could have been the model for the "have a nice day" stickers. "Pete Barstow," he introduced himself. "Channing and I go way back."

Maggie turned her attention to the elegant Asian woman whom Barstow was helping off with her coat. "My wife, Lynne-Mae," he said, "and, of course, I'm sure you've already heard of Twylar Zarzy."

"What was that again?" Maggie asked as the third guest—a thin man with the look of ingrained snobbery— took her hand the moment Lynne-Mae released it.

"Twylar Zarzy," the thin man repeated, displaying a gap-toothed smile that seemed contradictory to an overall image of perfection and aloofness. "Zarzy International Exports?"

"Oh yes," Maggie said, taking a cue from Channing's nod over Zarzy's shoulder that protocol required a white lie of recognition. "It's nice to finally meet you."

Zarzy beamed his approval.

"I'm afraid our coats are awfully wet," Lynne-Mae said. "Just that short walk up from the pier—"

"No problem," Channing assured her. "Maggie will hang them up for you out in the mudroom. They should be dry after dinner."

"Allow me to help you," Zarzy volunteered. "I'd hate to see you ruin such a lovely dress. Is it silk?"

Puzzled but flattered by the newcomer's attentiveness, Maggie led the way to the back entrance of the house and the tiled room that doubled as a laundry and storage area for umbrellas and galoshes.

"Fabulous house he's got," Zarzy remarked. "You must love living here."

"It's just for the summer," she replied, lest he assume her arrangement with Derek Channing was of a permanent nature.

"Not if Channing can help it," Zarzy said. "He's quite impressed with you, you know."

"Thank you for mentioning it."

"Nothing I'm sure you haven't heard before." He reached up for a hanger. "So you're from Boston?"

It took a moment for his question to register, her attention suddenly riveted on what was already hanging from the upper rod to dry.

24

Zarzy seemed not to notice that she didn't reply. "We have a lot in common," he said.

Maggie's eyes kept returning to the dark cape, its folds still damp from the afternoon rain.

"You're from Boston, too?" she distractedly inquired.

Zarzy chuckled. "No, but the headquarters offices of two of our biggest insurers are. You've probably heard of them. . . ."

It was an explanation he managed to extend all the way back to the living room, where the others had convened for drinks and hors d'oeuvres.

"So how do you like Seattle?" Lynne-Mae asked as Maggie joined her on the couch.

"Well, I haven't exactly hit all the city sights. The project has been keeping me busy."

Barstow clucked his tongue in dismay. "Can't keep a pretty girl like this underground all day, D.C. You oughta let her out now and then to explore and have adventures."

"Oh, I think she has all the adventure she can handle," Channing replied with a wink in Maggie's direction.

As the conversation shifted to Zarzy's latest acquisition of a textile mill, Maggie studied Channing's guests, wondering whether their knowledge of the man who employed her went beyond the professional. Certainly Barstow's comment about their friendship going a long way back suggested him as a potential resource, should she ever have a chance to talk to him alone.

Barstow seemed to be at least ten years his wife's senior, and his ample girth suggested a fondness for food and a total indifference to health and longevity. A monkish fringe of brown hair circled the back of his head, a shade almost too dark for his pale complexion. He looked to be a badly preserved fifty, Maggie guessed, wondering if his tenure on the city council had aged him prematurely. That someone as odd-looking as Barstow would be linked with so stylish a woman as Lynne-Mae only affirmed the adage that opposites indeed attracted.

From her brief sojourn to the mudroom with Zarzy, she had learned that Lynne-Mae was assistant curator for the Emerald Gallery, one of Seattle's more prestigious museums dedicated to Chinese artifacts. Though she barely reached Maggie's shoulder—even including her upswept black coiffure—Barstow's wife carried herself with a sense of authority and grace that made her seem much taller. Periodically, she glanced in Maggie's direction, projecting a warmth that almost seemed to reverse the women's true roles as hostess and guest. Not until much later in the evening did Maggie realize how much she had missed female companionship ever since her arrival in the Pacific Northwest.

It was Twylar Zarzy, though, who intrigued her the most. Decked out in a tux, the exporter constantly crossed back and forth between being an elitist and being a puppy eager to please. His lanky frame was without an ounce of spare flesh, and he seemed to be of an indeterminate age—older in years than Channing, and yet worlds younger in spirit than Barstow. Even Channing hadn't failed to notice the way he ingratiated himself with Maggie, pausing with verbal asides to patiently explain things to her that must have been common knowledge to the others. A potential ally? It was too early for Maggie to tell.

"To the new venture," Channing said, lifting his glass in a toast.

"Enough about me," Zarzy insisted. "I'd like to hear more about what you've found down there."

It was Channing's turn to take the lead. "Well, as I'd mentioned, we're looking to open up Marion Street by the end of summer, permits notwithstanding."

Barstow whistled. "That far north? Not too likely, is it?"

"When we're talking city fathers," Channing declared, "no stone's being left unturned."

"He's got a point," Zarzy said. "Their influence wasn't as limited as we'd like to think. In fact, that theory about the prostitutes—"

"Maggie's been working on exactly that," Channing interrupted, his voice underscored with pride. "Maybe I should let *her* tell it."

"I'm really the rookie here," Maggie said, surprised that Channing would thrust her into the spotlight with his peers.

"Don't let her fool you," Channing told the others. "She knows a lot more than she'd like you to believe."

"You give me too much credit," she replied, well aware of his comment's double meaning.

"Credit where credit is due," Lynne-Mae said. "From what I've heard, a woman's intuition is exactly what this project has been needing. Go right ahead."

Barstow paused to dab his mouth with his napkin between bites of London broil and anecdotes of Seattle history. "Yesler Way used to be Mill Street," he explained. "Ox teams used to skid the logs on it to Yesler's Mill in the Sag."

"Which is why they also called it 'Skid Road,'" Lynne-Mae added.

Barstow sighed. "She always spoils the punch line."

"So that's where the expression came from?" Maggie asked.

Barstow nodded. "The Place of Dead Dreams. As many times as they renamed it, Skid Road is the one that earned a permanent niche. And, you see, it also divided the territory between Doc Maynard and Carson Boren, the south side being the seamy part you didn't want to visit at night by yourself."

"Unless, of course," Zarzy interjected, "you were *looking* for the kind of trouble in question."

"A century hasn't really even changed that," Channing said, referring to the contrast between the district's newer high rises and the waterfront facades that housed adult movies and bars of questionable character.

"I'm not sure I like the idea of your assistant spending so much time there," Zarzy said, draping an arm over the back of Maggie's chair.

"Oh, we keep a good eye on her," Channing assured him.

Before Maggie could respond, Brecht entered the dining room, withdrawing a note from his pocket and handing it to Channing.

"If you'll excuse me for a moment," Channing said as he slid back in his chair, his face betraying no clue as to the note's contents. "Please go on with your meal."

With militaristic precision, Brecht followed him from the room.

"You don't like him much, do you?" Zarzy remarked when the two were gone.

"I beg your pardon?"

Across the table, Lynne-Mae was engaged in a quiet conversation with her husband about how many helpings he had taken of au gratin potatoes.

"Helmar," the thin man said. "Although I guess you know him as Brecht."

Surprised to hear that the man went by more than one syllable, Maggie smiled. "Is my dislike that obvious?"

"He rubs most people that way, truth be told. Kind of a cold fish, isn't he?"

"Absolutely frigid."

"Are either one of you going to have more vegetables?" Barstow cut in, already pushing back his cuff that he not dip it across his plate.

"Pete—"

"You can't fault me for the vegetables, Lynnie," he said. "My system could use the vitamins."

"No, you go right ahead," Zarzy said when Barstow asked a second time. Then he returned to Maggie. "You were saying?"

"He just gives me a creepy feeling, especially the

way he keeps showing up when you least expect him."

"Yes, but you have to admit he's devoted to Channing like nobody I've ever seen." Zarzy shook his head. "That kind of loyalty is hard to come by these days."

"So where does it come from?"

"His loyalty?"

Maggie felt her adrenaline surge at the possibility of unlocking another facet of Channing's personality. "There must have been a million people that Channing's money could have hired," she replied. "Why Brecht?"

"Your chronology needs a little bit of enlightenment, dear," Zarzy said. "You see, at the beginning, it was Brecht who first hired *him*."

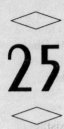

25

Zarzy seemed to enjoy her confusion. "Have I surprised you?" he queried.

"To say the least!"

"Maybe we should continue this at some other time."

Across the table, Lynne-Mae had abandoned her battle with her husband and was turning her attention back to the others.

"Do you get out for lunch?" Zarzy continued. "Or do you prefer to brown-bag it with the crew down in the sewers?"

Maggie laughed. "Believe me, I come up for air as often as possible!"

"It's settled then. Have you been to the Pacific Crabhouse yet? Closest you can get to a view of Elliott Bay without getting your feet wet."

"Sounds great. Did you have a particular day in mind?"

Channing's return preempted Zarzy's reply.

"Not bad news, I hope," Lynne-Mae said as he took his seat.

"Nothing that a few phone calls and some action on the stock exchange can't resolve by morning," Channing assured her. "Did I miss anything?"

"Just Twylar putting moves on your assistant," Barstow said with a smile. Lynne-Mae punctuated his comment with a gentle elbow to his ribs.

Channing arched a brow. "Oh, really?"

"Not that she needs your permission," Zarzy said, "but I don't think you feed her nearly enough. Any problem with me spiriting her off to someplace expensive for lunch?"

"So soon after finishing SkySet's London broil? My housekeeper will be disappointed."

"I'll talk to her personally and explain," Zarzy offered. "Besides, it won't be until after I get back from Anchorage. For that matter, I'll take your housekeeper to lunch, too. She's the only one who laughs at my jokes."

"That *is* coming up, isn't it?" Barstow asked. "So when do you shove off to go commune with the Eskimos?"

"Day after tomorrow, unless the board calls an emergency meeting."

"Sounds like a great trip," Maggie said. "How long do you get to stay?"

"Two weeks," Zarzy replied. "I'll call you for that lunch date when I'm back in town."

Two weeks. For the frustration she felt at coming so close to more answers, it may as well have been two months . . . or two years. Troy, of course, would have reminded her that anything worth having was worth waiting for. Either that, or he'd tell her that the root of Brecht and Channing's association wasn't relevant to the case at hand. More likely, the latter.

They had adjourned to the living room for coffee, though Maggie's mind was having a difficult time focusing on the conversation at hand. Something else that Zarzy had said—something so simple as to almost seem insignificant—still remained with her. Disturbed that she'd have to wait two weeks to follow it through, Maggie tried to come up with some innocuous way to bring up the subject before the exporter took leave of Lynx Bay.

"I'm not sure," Lynne-Mae was saying, "that the redevelopment project didn't create a larger problem than existed before."

"But what about all the jobs?" her husband argued. "There were plenty to be had for those who wanted to work."

"Plenty if you could meet the qualifications and could give a permanent address. Not to mention getting the information to begin with."

"They had a similar problem down in the capital of California," Channing interjected. "Once they revitalized the old part of town, it forced all the transients up into the business district."

"And right under the legislators' noses," Barstow added. "Not that it made any real difference. You've got the same problem as you've got up here with the Indians—all displaced and nowhere to go."

"Are they still getting into the tunnels?" Lynne-Mae asked Channing. "You told us last time it was an ongoing problem."

Maggie was suddenly alert.

"Cleveland's had to chase a couple out now and then," Channing replied. "Harmless for the most part, disoriented for the rest. Some of them are kids just looking for a new place to deal drugs."

"All the more reason for you to be careful," Zarzy advised Maggie.

"What worries me," Channing continued, "is that we're going to get one in there someday where it's not buttressed, and we could be looking at a major lawsuit."

"And *I'll* be looking at an eight o'clock directors' meeting tomorrow morning without any sleep if Pete and I don't call it a night," Lynne-Mae said, consulting her watch. "Would you mind, Derek?"

"Guess that means me, too," Zarzy said, "since we're all in the same boat." The exporter stood up to stretch. "As usual, Channing, you've outdone yourself."

"Sounds like the mountain will be out tomorrow," Barstow said, cocking an ear toward the window. Maggie regarded him with a puzzled expression. "I see you haven't taught her all of our local colloquialisms yet," he remarked to Channing.

It was Lynne-Mae who provided the interpretation for her. "'The mountain's out' means that it's a clear day," she said. "If Pete's right that the rain has stopped—"

"Of *course* it stopped," Barstow insisted. "At least an hour ago."

"I'll get your coats," Maggie offered, hoping that Zarzy would accompany her again. To her dismay, however, Channing had already engaged him in a conversation about the upcoming trip to Alaska. With time running out and no opportunity to talk to him privately,

Maggie found herself taking slow steps to the mud-room, hoping that inspiration would strike her.

To her relief, it did.

When she returned to the guests with their coats, Lynne-Mae's perfectly sculpted brows dipped together in a frown. "I'm afraid that's not mine," she said, indicating the dark cloak in Maggie's arms.

Maggie feigned embarrassment. "You're absolutely right. I swear I don't know where my head was when I grabbed this one off the rack. Sorry about that."

"Oh, I don't know," Barstow said. "You might start a new trend, Lynnie. We could call you the Caped Crusader of Chinatown."

Maggie laughed. "I don't think the owner would give it up that easily, do you, Derek?"

Though his expression was one of nonchalance, there was no missing the lethal glint in his blue eyes. "No comment," he replied.

"It'll just take me a second," Maggie said, as she turned to take leave of them, satisfied that she had least proven to Channing that the figure in the woods hadn't been a figment of her imagination, and furthermore, that it was someone who resided in the house.

"We'll have to do this again soon," Lynne-Mae said after Maggie brought her the correct coat. "Maybe you can come by the museum on one of your free days and I'll loan you those books I mentioned."

"Bring along a couple of strong flunkies to carry them back for you," Barstow advised. "This lady has a library that won't quit!"

Zarzy kissed the top of her hand. "Lunch after Alaska," he reminded her. "Don't forget."

"Oh, speaking of forgetting, what was it again that you wanted me to tell SkySet for you?"

Zarzy look puzzled.

"Something you talked about at dinner," Maggie said, "but I don't remember exactly what it was."

The exporter shrugged. "That makes two of us."

"It'll probably hit you at three in the morning," Barstow said. "If it does, don't call and tell us."

"Just tell her for me that dinner was fabulous as usual," Zarzy said.

Maggie smiled. "I'd be happy to, Twylar."

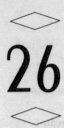

26

Almost three days passed before Maggie could relate the story of the dinner party to Troy. Whether vexed by her irreverence or dependent on her clerical skills, Channing kept her on a short leash that made it virtually impossible for Maggie to touch base with the detective any earlier.

"I was worried about you," Troy said. "When you go too long between these phone calls—"

Maggie interrupted to reiterate that she was only exercising the very caution he himself had advised. "The man was watching me like a hawk."

"All the same, babe, I think you're antagonizing him more than learning anything we can actually use. That stunt after dinner was damned dangerous."

"I proved a point, though, didn't I? Two points, if you want to get technical."

"Because you found a wet cape?"

"Because it proved to him that I really *saw* someone."

"I'm sure he never doubted it for a minute, Maggie. Unfortunately, you'd probably be less at risk if you *hadn't* seen anyone."

"So why didn't he just shrug it off and say that it was SkySet out for a walk? Simple question, simple explanation."

"Because a man like Derek Channing doesn't give explanations," Troy replied. "Haven't you worked for him long enough to figure that out yet?"

"So what about the other thing I proved?"

"What other?"

"Have you always had this short an attention span?" Maggie teased him. "I was referring to Twylar's confirming that SkySet speaks English. Just as I thought all along."

Troy sighed. "Well, in the first place, dear, I'm not sure I'd put a lot of stock in someone with such a ridiculous name. How do you know it's not phony?"

"Oh, honestly. If it were something else, do you really think he'd change it to Twylar Zarzy? It's not the sort of name you just make up out of the blue over breakfast."

"So you're saying that you met him just once, chatted over steaks, and he's suddenly a pillar of integrity? He's a close friend of Channing's, remember? He probably even writes bad checks to cover the rent."

"He can't be that close a friend if he's willing to confide a few secrets over lunch."

"The only thing *that* tells me is that his vision is good enough to recognize a beautiful woman when he sees one and stake a claim. Friendship and fair play be damned."

"Jealous?"

"Not unless you start favoring his company over mine."

Maggie couldn't resist a dig at Troy. "You haven't exactly been constantly by my side," she said. "Maybe I'd pay more attention to you if I felt like you hadn't sent me into a den of thieves by myself."

"You seem to be holding your own, Maggie Price."

"I'll take that as a compliment."

"And well deserved. So do you think I should have Zarzy checked out?"

"No, but I thought maybe you would. You don't seem to think I should trust him."

"I'm a cop, Maggie. I don't think you should trust anyone just because he hovers like a lovesick moth and can make the housekeeper laugh."

"Which proves," she reminded him, "that SkySet knows English."

"Or that he can tell jokes in Snohomish. You're reading too much into this."

"Are you sure you're not just a little annoyed that I was right?"

There was a long pause at the other end of the line. "Just in case you are, do us both a big favor."

"And what's that?"

"Don't talk to her."

Ken Cleveland held up the broken loop of metal with tweezers and examined it as if it were the Hope Diamond. "What do *you* think?" he consulted Maggie.

"Part of a belt maybe? A buckle?"

"Looks like it went through the fire," he said before carefully sliding it into a plastic bag. "Let's hope we don't also find the guy who was wearing it at the time."

In spite of the gruesome image his comment conjured,

Maggie laughed. "Only in a Stephen King novel," she added.

The weeks of working together had established a rapport between the two of them with which Maggie felt comfortable, though she had yet to draw out of him anything further on the subject of his predecessor's death. It was evident from his ease with her that Cleveland considered her a peer, a friend with whom to share his extensive knowledge of engineering, archaeology, and Seattle trivia. Even after her formal training under him had ended, his willingness to include her as often as possible in what he was doing rather than leave her behind in the workroom was flattering.

"Must have been some blaze that day," he remarked. "Wild enough to melt your socks off, I bet."

"So who did they blame it on? A cousin of Mrs. O'Leary's cow?"

Cleveland shook his head. "A batch of hot glue and a floor soaked with turpentine."

"Almost sounds like arson."

"Nope. Pure accident, far as they could tell. Seems that a pot of glue boiled over up at the woodwork shop and caught fire, and it spread fast. Well, the smoke was so thick, the firemen had a passel of trouble just figuring out which building was on fire. Next thing they knew it spread to Dietz and Mayer's Liquor Store and blew up about a hundred barrels of whiskey." Cleveland withdrew a bandana from his back pocket to wipe the grime off his hands. "Now that's when things got really bad, if you ask me. A body couldn't even drink the nightmare away."

By day's end, Cleveland explained, the inferno had consumed over a hundred and twenty acres, leaving nothing to show for almost half a century of habitation.

Every wharf, every mill, every business worth its salt was gone. Martial law was instituted to halt the outbreak of looting.

" 'Course it brought out the enterprising side of folks, too," the foreman said with a chuckle. "The waterfront girls didn't waste any time setting up shop again the day after and working out of canvas lean-tos. Running joke was 'How's business?' and they'd reply, 'In-tents.'"

If there was a positive aspect of the disaster, though, the foreman went on, it was the way that Elliott Bay's locals pulled together to rebuild themselves. While many cut their losses and moved south to Oregon and California, those who remained served as inspiration to new immigrants. Eventually the city was reborn on a better base than before—one of brick rather than wood.

"Must've been a damned sight to the Indians," Cleveland concluded, "to see so many white men building a new city right on top of a crappy old one."

"Probably just as confusing as their descendants seeing Pioneer Square turned into something they didn't recognize."

"Got that one right. Lot of 'em used to sleep down here and in the buildings up at street level. Sleep and drink hooch. Nothing else to do, I guess."

Though she already knew the answer, Maggie played the innocent. "They don't ever get down here now, do they? I mean, everything is pretty much sealed off, right?"

Cleveland shook his head. "I wish. See, the problem is we don't know how many places up there still got cellar access. You got cellar access, all it takes is a couple loose boards and you're in. Especially kids."

"Really?"

"It's the skinny ones that are a pain the rear," he continued. "Not that they're all bad. Just curious. I remember this one kid who was always getting in. Never said anything, just hung back and liked to watch us. Got to the point we used to bring little extras for lunch and leave 'em out—you know, like you'd do for a cat or something? Anyway, we nick-named him Wolf Boy, 'cause he looked like that's what he'd been raised by."

"Does he *still* come around?" Maggie asked, wondering whether it was the same youth she had seen her first day on the project.

"Not as much as he used to," Cleveland replied, "and, of course, the boss is a lot stricter on that kind of thing these days. Too much liability."

"Yes," Maggie nodded, "I can imagine."

"Back about—oh, five years or so, though, the boy used to be here all the time. Couldn't get rid of him." The foreman shrugged. "Must've lost interest. You know how it goes with kids these days. Can't keep their attention on anything unless it's loud, takes quarters, or has to do with sex."

It was his mention of five years, though, that locked in Maggie's head. Five years since the death of her father. And—farfetched as Troy might call the idea—the existence of a possible witness.

27

"Maggie!" Lynne-Mae exclaimed, rising from behind a desk of glass and black lacquer. "What a wonderful surprise!"

"Your secretary said it was okay to just come in." Maggie shifted her purse to the opposite shoulder so she could shake hands without knocking anything from the desk's meticulous surface. "I probably should have called first."

"Oh yes, I wish you had." Lynne-Mae sounded disappointed. "I've already made some plans for lunch."

Maggie was quick to reassure her that it was just a spontaneous visit sandwiched in between her morning trek down to the tunnels and an afternoon at the county records office. "Besides, I'm not really dressed for lunch," she added, suddenly self-conscious of her jeans and camp shirt in contrast to Lynne-Mae's russet brown silk suit and delicate cream-colored scarf.

Lynne-Mae laughed. "Nonsense. You'd be lovely if

you were wearing a paper bag and rubber thongs."

"Fortunately, my salary isn't *that* low."

"May I offer you some tea? I have about half an hour before my appointment arrives." The scent of ginseng moved with her as she leaned forward.

"Tea would be great, thanks."

As Lynne-Mae pressed the intercom button on her phone to summon her secretary, Maggie took a glance around the elegant office, marveling at how perfectly it suited its occupant. Just like the desk, the long credenza, bookcases, and visitor chairs were polished black lacquer, as were the narrow picture frames that featured stylized egrets and pastel-colored tropical fish.

Rice-paper screens, instead of conventional curtains or miniblinds, covered the tall, vertical windows, supporting the illusion that one had stepped into the heart of China rather than the sixth-floor suite of a cosmopolitan office building. Across the room, a five-panel folding screen depicting Chinese courting scenes in cloisonné and mother-of-pearl separated Lynne-Mae's private office from a conference area with table and chairs.

"My home away from home," Lynne-Mae said, reading Maggie's thoughts. "It's the one place Pete always knows he can find me."

"You both seem to enjoy your work," Maggie commented, still finding it hard to imagine that the two of them could have much in common.

"We're fortunate that way, yes. Although I'd really like to see my husband make this his last year in government."

"Oh?"

"He's not in the best of health," Lynne-Mae confided. "And with some of the new blood that's been introduced recently to the city council—well, enough about politics. That's not what you came to see me about, is it?"

"Actually, I wanted to take you up on that offer of a few books. You made it all sound so interesting at dinner last week."

"Interesting is just the tip of the iceberg." Lynne-Mae looked up to acknowledge the young woman entering the room with a wicker tray containing a black porcelain teapot and two cups. "And working with Derek," she added, "must be absolutely addictive."

"It's a challenge," Maggie replied, for lack of a better response.

Lynne-Mae winked. "Many women would trade places with you. And not just to play archaeologist."

"It's strictly professional." Maggie wondered even as she replied why she felt any need to explain herself or her relationship with her employer.

Across the desk, Lynne-Mae smiled. "He's an attractive man, though, don't you think?"

"I try not to mix opinions like that with my work."

Again, the enigmatic smile. "So have you heard anything from Twylar yet? A postcard, at least?"

Puzzled by so presumptive a question about a man she had met just once, Maggie only commented that they'd be having lunch when he returned from Alaska.

"I think he was taken with you," Lynne-Mae said. "Although that's not surprising. You're a very pretty girl."

"So have you known him long?"

"Twylar?" Lynne-Mae shook her head. "We met him through Derek a few years ago," she said. "Actually, Pete met him first. Extraordinary, well-read man, but rather on the lonely side. You probably gathered that from the other night."

"He did seem to enjoy talking a lot, but I hadn't put it down to loneliness."

"He lost his wife in a car accident in France about ten years back. The man absolutely worshiped her. Pete says he's been roaming the earth ever since, looking for someone to take her place." Lynne-Mae caught the flash of discomfiture on Maggie's face. "Oh, but don't worry, he's smart enough to know forbidden fruit when he sees it. Twylar will be perfectly safe around you."

Before Maggie could open her mouth to protest, Lynne-Mae had deftly changed the subject to the museum's latest acquisition of Ming vases from a gallery in Chicago. "But, of course," Lynne-Mae concluded, "*nothing* we have will compare to what Derek digs up right in our own city."

"Do I hear a little bias in that?" Maggie teased her.

"Because Derek's a wonderful man? Or because the Chinese community here in Seattle is entitled to its heritage? Right on both counts, Maggie. I can't tell you how honored we are that he chose The Emerald to reap the benefits of all his work."

"But what if he doesn't find what he's looking for?" Maggie asked, amazed at how successfully Channing had conned a woman as intelligent as Lynne-Mae into believing he was really looking for Chinese artifacts. "After all, it's been over a hundred years."

Lynne-Mae blinked in surprise. "There's no stopping a man and his ambition. If it's still down there, I have every faith he'll be the one to discover it."

A knock on the door preempted any continued discussion of Channing's talents.

"Oh, come in," Lynne-Mae said, issuing a gracious smile to someone behind Maggie's back. "We were just talking about you. . . ."

◇ ◇ ◇

It shouldn't have bothered her, Maggie told herself, and yet it did. While Lynne-Mae was entitled to have a lunch date with whomever she wished, it seemed duplicitous for her not to mention the party's name until he literally walked right into the middle of their conversation. Furthermore, that she had assumed Maggie's interest in Channing had already transcended the professional level was disturbing. Maggie wasn't sure which state of affairs bothered her more.

"I made reservations at our usual place," Derek told Lynne-Mae as his lips grazed her cheek in greeting. "Any objection?"

"To a plan of yours?" Lynne-Mae laughed. "Never."

"I really should be going," Maggie murmured, disturbed by the casual intimacy of their friendship. "I have a lot to do today."

"The books!" Lynne-Mae suddenly remembered. "Let me get them for you."

"That's okay. I wouldn't want to hold the two of you up."

Over Lynne-Mae's insistence that it was no problem, Channing came up with a suggestion of his own. "If we have time after lunch," he said, "I'll take them myself."

Lynne-Mae's laughter floated through the room like an echo of expensive crystal. "The *last* time," she reminded him, squeezing his arm, "we ended up closing the restaurant. . . ."

They barely seemed to notice that Maggie left. Annoyed that their obvious ease with each other would even affect her, Maggie rode down the elevator and walked through the marble lobby toward the revolving door. What should it matter to her whether Derek

Channing could beguile women from L. A. to Vancouver or lived the life of a monk? It was hardly worth a second thought. Besides, Lynne-Mae was happily married. Their friendship—and their lunch date—was really none of her business.

Startled by how bright the sun had become while she was inside, Maggie paused for a moment outside the museum to rummage in her purse for sunglasses— just long enough to catch sight of a teenage boy who was watching her from across the street.

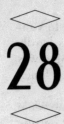

28

"I hope you don't think I'm cynical for saying so," Troy said across the table, "but don't they all sort of look alike?"

Maggie took offense to his remark. "Indians?"

"Teenagers. I mean it's gotten to the point where sometimes you can't tell the guys from the girls."

Maggie pushed aside the remains of her sandwich. "It was definitely a guy, and I'd also bet my next paycheck it's the same one I told you about before."

Troy pushed his fingers through his hair before addressing her with a half-grin. "Save your money. It's summertime, Maggie."

"So?"

"So school's out. The entire district is swarming with kids—probably hundreds of kids—just like the one you saw."

Maggie felt her temper rise. "Why do you discount

everything I say? I thought we were supposed to be a team."

"And half of this team is going to get me in trouble with the brass if I keep chasing false leads."

"I only mentioned it as a point of interest."

"And because you want me to do something about it."

"It doesn't bother you that he's following me?"

"You don't know for certain that he is. Channing was in the same building, too, wasn't he?"

"Why would he be following Channing?"

"Hell if I know. Listen, a lack of sleep is no excuse, but it's the best one I can give you for my mood."

"How come you're not sleeping?"

The taut outline of his shoulders strained against the fabric of his shirt as he stretched, and for a moment she caught herself wondering what he'd look like without it. Smooth, tan, probably the same light shade as coffee after she had added enough cream to her liking. The restless energy of his movements made her curious about what he did to work off the lunch he had just consumed, whether he belonged to a health club or simply let the demands of his job burn up any excess fat.

Guiltily she looked away from him to concentrate on the last of her soda, knowing that she had only conjured such romantic fantasies because she was so frustrated with Channing.

"Shouldn't I have said that?" Troy asked.

"I'm sorry. Said what?"

"So much for laying my heart on the table," he replied. "Womp! You just set the ketchup bottle down on top of it."

"Troy—"

"Okay, I forgive you," he said. "If you can forgive me for saying what I just did. It was completely out of line."

"Considering that I didn't hear it at all—"

"Insult to injury," Troy sighed. "Maybe I should have just stuck to *showing* you instead. Ready to go?" Mystified by his comment, Maggie followed him to the cash register, then out to the street.

"This way a sec," he said, taking her hand and leading her down a narrow alley next to the café.

"Where are we going?"

"Just something you need to see before you go back."

At the end of the alley, Troy told her to close her eyes.

"I thought I was supposed to see something."

"Just close them," Troy insisted. "And you will."

It was the taste of his lips, though, and the unexpected sensation of his arms locking tight around her midriff that she experienced next. Before she could recover from the initial shock, he tilted his head and deepened his kiss, brooking no resistance. Maggie's hands clutched his shirt to keep from falling backwards, her equilibrium disrupted by the intensity of his embrace and the rough skate of his hands down her back.

When at last he released her, his breathing was labored, his voice starkly uneven. "It goes against all the rules, but I couldn't let you go another day without knowing."

"Knowing what?" Maggie was still reeling from what had just happened, and she was ill-prepared to accept what she was afraid he'd say next.

"Conflict of interest. If I get tempted to take any more liberties like I did just now, I'm afraid one of us will have to go off the case. In a nutshell, Maggie, I'm nuts about you."

"Troy—"

"Okay, so it's premature, but every minute you spend out there with Channing is a minute away from—" Troy left the sentence unfinished.

Maggie offered to finish it for him. "You?" she said.

"Let's just say I think maybe you're getting a little too close."

"Isn't that the whole point? To have someone on the inside?"

Troy slid his fingers up through her silky hair. "Just promise me that if I tell you to get your buns out of there in a hurry, you'll do it?"

Before she could reply he pulled her into his arms and kissed her again, his tongue urgently probing her mouth.

"Promise?" he said once more before they parted. Too perplexed by conflicting emotions to argue, Maggie nodded, eliciting a broad smile from the detective.

"There's more where that came from," he whispered as he pressed his fingers to her lips and then slipped on his dark glasses.

"More where that came from," she repeated to herself after she watched him disappear around the corner, unsettled by the intrusive reminder of the *last* kiss she had received from a man she hardly knew. A man named Derek Channing.

And in that awful moment of reflection, Maggie could already see which of the two kisses had reached the greater depth to her soul and left its indelible mark.

"I didn't expect to see you back until tomorrow," Cleveland said. "Weren't you off at the—uh—"

"County records office," she finished for him.

"Oh yeah. How did that go?"

"Like looking for the proverbial needle."

For the foreman's benefit, she had fabricated a story connected to the descendants of Seattle's early merchants. In reality, of course, it was little more than a cover to learn more about her enemy and his origins. Frustrated by what amounted to an exercise in futility, Maggie blamed her disagreeable mood on a recalcitrant clerk and a reading room without air-conditioning. "I'll go back where I left off tomorrow," she told Cleveland.

His brow furrowed. "Could it wait? We got a full day coming and you oughta be here for it." He related the next day's agenda of excavation with unrestrained enthusiasm.

"I suppose," Maggie said. "Let me check with the boss and see where he wants me."

"Oh, that reminds me. He called about an hour ago and left you a message about your going back to the island."

"Change in the time?" she asked. In the weeks that passed, they had fallen into a fairly regular pattern of arrivals and departures.

"He said to go ahead and go back by yourself," the foreman replied. "He's going to be spending tonight in the city."

29

Maggie found it impossible to shake the image of Lynne-Mae and Channing from her mind, an image disturbingly accompanied by a vision of luxuriant, black satin sheets and tapered candles that smelled of ginseng.

That silvery laugh of Lynne-Mae's, that smoldering look of his that he reserved for special people. She had seen that same expression in his eyes herself, Maggie remembered with a stab of jealousy. Enough to recognize it when it was directed to someone else.

Then her conscience cut in, reminding her that Channing's love life wasn't any of her concern.

Love life. For the entire, interminable trip out to Lynx Bay, Maggie kept replaying every comment, every glance, every nuance between the woman she had tried to cultivate as a friend and the man she already knew to be an adversary. Certainly the coincidence of Channing opting to spend the night on the mainland after a long lunch with Lynne-Mae fueled the fires of speculation about whether he'd be spending it alone.

For all of the semblance of a comfortable marriage, it was not beyond reason that Lynne-Mae's undisguised admiration of Derek was only the surface of something deeper. And, his obvious appreciation of her beauty and respect for her intellect gave rise to the notion of reciprocal favor, not to mention the credibility her museum lent to his underground project.

Had the allusions she had made in her office been part of a sly test to see if Maggie was competition? Or were they instead just the optimistic projections of a concerned acquaintance who wanted to see her favorite bachelor married off to a worthy match?

It was too early to tell either way, Maggie decided, her head already crowded with enough confusion about the other man in her life.

The kiss in the alley had caught her off guard, though in retrospect it now seemed the logical culmination of a steady build of romantic interest on Troy McCormick's part. Despite his curt manner with her when discussing her mission, he seemed concerned about her and sensitive to the pressures that tugged at her from all directions. His very presence affirmed that knights still existed in the twentieth century, and had she rebuffed his advance, Maggie mused, she probably would have seen his soft gray eyes begging forgiveness.

And yet, for all of his bold and chivalrous promises to protect her, there was another side to the Seattle detective that Maggie had trouble dealing with. Quick to dismiss her theories, he had appeared to Maggie on more than one occasion to be decidedly sexist. Was it her bias on the case that elicited his flippancy? Or just the fact that she was a woman?

As the island slowly came into sight across the water, Maggie's thoughts turned back to Channing. She was startled at how much more she actually knew about her reclusive enemy than about her demonstrative peer.

Channing's roots lay in wealth and prestige on the East Coast; Troy had the golden looks of a middle-class Californian but had never mentioned his birthplace or parents. Channing's mission in life had been dictated from childhood: to manage and expand his family's extensive holdings in commerce and industry. Troy had made the grade as detective on the Seattle police force but had not shared anything with her about what he had done before that, much less why he had chosen a career in law enforcement. Even Channing's reference to his dabbling in theater at school was more than she knew about Troy's hobbies or interests.

Nor could she overlook that there had been a significant woman in Channing's past life, a woman whose mention could still cause him anger or pain. Troy, in contrast, had seemingly sprung straight into adulthood with nary a scratch of a prior broken heart. If pressed for an answer, would he regale her with wit and poetry and profess that true love had never touched him until the first day they met in Boston? Or, like Derek Channing, was his work the ultimate salve for bitter feelings that neither time nor another woman could mend?

Only one thing was certain in Maggie's mind: to completely trust *either* man right now would be about the dumbest step she could take.

Brecht was nowhere to be found.

While Maggie wanted to take delight in his apparent absence from the house, experience had taught her that he was only exercising his infamous proclivity for melting into the wallpaper. She also knew that summoning him again would be as easy as opening a forbidden drawer, picking up a telephone receiver, or traipsing through the woods after a cloaked figure. All she had to do was make a show of "trespassing" and Channing's stern-faced bodyguard would soundlessly materialize to advise her that she was breaking some unspoken law.

The previous week's encounter with him in the forest still rankled her, rekindling her suspicions that the truth behind her father's death was somehow connected more strongly to Lynx Bay than to any of his work on the mainland. Why else, she wondered, would Brecht have been prepared to threaten her eavesdropping with something as drastic as a bullet?

Though Troy might dismiss it, Channing's subsequent decision to set parameters on her island exploration was a strong enough argument in Maggie's book that he had something *outside* those parameters to hide. Something . . . or someone.

With at least an hour and a half remaining until dusk, the desire to pick up where she had left off was a temptation too strong to ignore.

There was still no sign of Brecht as Maggie let herself out the back door of the mudroom. SkySet, quietly mending a quilt in one of the upstairs bedrooms, had paid her no notice.

Not that *she* could be trusted, either, Maggie reminded herself. At least twice since the dinner party she had bit back the urge to address the Indian woman in English, just to see her reaction. Now, warned by Troy to continue to play dumb to the housekeeper's secret, it was as if an even wider chasm of noncommunication existed between the two women than before. Maggie had never felt more isolated in her life.

As much satisfaction as she might derive from confronting the housekeeper with what she had learned from Twylar, however, there was wisdom in Troy's advice to bide her time and stay silent. "As long as they think you haven't caught on," he had said, "they might be careless enough to slip up."

Careless? It was hardly a word that fit Derek Channing's habits or attitude. If anything, Maggie thought, the millionaire had created a coded script impervious to all of their attempts to break it. Even her conversation with Lynne-Mae, she reflected, might have been nothing more than just a well-rehearsed scene to keep her off balance.

She thrust the thought of Lynne-Mae and Derek out of her head as she hiked deeper into the woods, pausing every few steps to listen for the sound of Brecht. Twice she even stepped off the path to crouch down behind bushes, purposely waiting for him to slink by wearing his three-piece suit and grim expression of disapproval.

Both times, Maggie eventually came out and continued walking, reconciled to the notion that either she had successfully escaped the house without his notice or he was already lying in wait somewhere just ahead, amused by her juvenile attempts at hide-and-seek. What story would he tell Channing, she wondered, if he actually did shoot her? Would Channing condone such an action and be thankful to have neatly rid himself of an employee who was proving herself a troublemaker?

When at last she reached the stream and the clearing, her mind tried to reconstruct where she had been standing the previous week. A few more paces and her orientation was restored. She passed by the tree and the outcropping of rocks, looking back only one more time to see if Brecht was behind her.

Relieved—and puzzled—to find herself alone, Maggie proceeded to the spot where she had seen the figure kneeling down. The ground's surface was broken by a narrow slab of dark marble that the tree had obscured from her view the last time she was there.

A wave of apprehension swept through her as she approached the crude grave site that Channing had not wanted her to discover. With a quick intake of breath like someone about to plunge into icy water, Maggie leaned forward to read the chiseled inscription.

30

Try as she might to let sleep overtake her, the name and date on the grave marker refused to leave Maggie's memory.

Seven years past, the body of Fiona Lindsay Channing and her baby son had been laid to rest on the island that Derek called home. The inscription indicated that she had been only a month shy of twenty-two when death had claimed her, and no label of beloved wife, sister, or daughter had been carved in the stone to establish her formal tie to Channing. Yet even without the requisite words beneath the young woman's name, the dull ache in Maggie's stomach affirmed what her intuition had suspected all along.

It was his wife's room that Maggie was staying in, she realized, not just guest quarters that had been coincidentally decorated to accommodate the taste of a female visitor. It was an elegant room that Fiona had slept in, dressed in, and perhaps taken quiet refuge in behind books and letters and music. The very room and bed in which she might also have made love to Derek . . . or someone else.

Doubtless it was also Fiona's lipstick that had rolled into view the first day Maggie opened the bathroom drawer, a lipstick that had inadvertently been missed when all that had once belonged to her was removed. Had Channing cleaned out the bedroom himself? she wondered. She tried to picture it, tried to imagine the state of vulnerability to which a man as strong as Derek Channing had been reduced by the loss of both wife and child on the same day.

Or had he instead turned the painful task over to SkySet? Certainly his mention of how long the housekeeper had lived on Lynx Bay placed her on the premises at the time it—whatever "it" was—had happened. Even more telling was the respect still paid to Fiona's memory seven years later by SkySet herself, if indeed it was the latter who had taken fresh flowers to the grave.

Brecht, as well, had surely been a party to Channing's domestic crisis, Maggie decided, though the measures he took to guard Fiona's place of burial struck her as extreme. Was it his employer's order he was simply carrying out? Or was Brecht's own connection to the dead woman much deeper than it appeared on the surface?

Had she been a brunette, Maggie wondered, or a blond like herself? Had she been tall or short? Athletic or fragile? A girl who had come from origins similar to Derek's, or a poor but winsome Galatea to whom he could play Pygmalion and mold into the ideal wife?

Maggie found it impossible not to harbor fantasies about Fiona Channing, particularly because of the Marquart sisters' hints of scandal and deception. There was a major discrepancy in their testimony about two children involved—a boy who was old enough to foster resentment toward both of his parents, and a baby whose looks were convincing enough for an entire community to be suspicious of its parentage.

Had Fiona's baby boy been stillborn, he would not have been seen by enough people for such an opinion to take root, much less look drastically different from any other baby. Could the Marquarts have been that wrong in their recollection of what had transpired at Lynx Bay?

Senility, she could almost hear Troy whisper to her through the darkness. What else could she really expect from two spinster loons who couldn't even remember which one of them was five minutes older? Still, Maggie had known other women just like the Marquarts in her life—doddering seniors who couldn't remember what they had eaten for lunch two hours before but could recite in vivid detail what they had been doing the day the stock market crashed, or who was wearing what at the opening race of the Kentucky Derby thirty years before, or what it was like to pass through the bewildering immigration lines at Ellis Island.

Though Cora and Nora's story of adultery and illegitimacy had been convoluted in the telling, Maggie was not yet ready to discount that there was also an element of truth in it, a truth confirmed in part by what she herself had discovered in the woods: the existence of a wife and a baby.

Fiona. Fiona. Fiona. The name echoed in her head like the hollow gong of the downstairs clock, its distant tone indicating that the night had already started its edge into morning.

Unbidden, the bruising memory of Channing's kiss at the Space Needle crept back to haunt her. Had he kissed Fiona that way, she wondered, consuming her with a savage intensity that left her knees weak and her head spinning? Moreover, had his bride returned his lust or merely endured it until she could make good her final escape to the arms of someone much kinder, much sweeter?

Escape had clearly not come to Fiona Lindsay Channing as she must have planned it. That she had been buried—possibly in secret—on the very island she had been so desperate to escape sent a chill of irony down Maggie's spine. Fiona's husband still controlled her, even now—the same way he was trying to control Maggie.

Maggie shuddered as she tried to imagine what had happened, for somehow a simple death in childbirth seemed far too innocent against the backdrop of duplicity she had sensed thus far at Lynx Bay. An accident? Murder? Maggie's mind hovered on the last and remembered the heavy-handed manner in which Brecht had ordered her back to the house, brandishing a gun to ensure her cooperation.

Channing had something scandalous to hide, of that she was certain, something that the ever-vigilant Brecht was sworn to protect. And more than ever, Maggie feared, it could well be the same secret that had cost her father his life.

Restlessly she turned her pillow over to its other side and felt its coolness against her neck, wondering whether she was the first woman who slept in that bed to have insomnia. She recalled the crystal and Derek's brief intimation of Fiona's philosophy. Did his reaction then mask a deeper pain, or did it reflect a cruel satisfaction at having won the final quarrel?

Whichever the answer, it was clear in Maggie's mind that neither she nor Fiona was anywhere close to his thoughts *that* evening. His attention and his heart were undoubtedly consumed by a black-haired lover who smelled of ginseng.

The irritability caused by her lack of sleep did not escape a casual mention by Channing when she met him for coffee at the waterfront the following morning, an invitation/order dutifully passed on to her by Cleveland.

"Did you wake up on the wrong side of the bed?" Channing pleasantly inquired, wearing the look of a man who had just gotten all that he wanted.

"At least I woke up on my own," Maggie replied, not caring how it sounded.

"Should I be insulted or flattered that my sleeping habits intrigue you?"

"They don't."

Channing buttered his biscuit. "Then I don't suppose that was you who phoned the Barstows' last night and hung up?"

"Why should I do that?"

"You shouldn't, especially from what you know about me."

Maggie held her tongue.

"I *was* there, by the way," he added. "Pete and Lynne-Mae don't mind putting me up in their guest room when I stay overnight in the city."

"How nice of them," Maggie replied. *And how convenient for his mistress*, she added to herself.

"Lynne-Mae really likes you," Channing continued. "Which reminds me, I have those books you wanted to borrow. She said you can keep them as long as you like."

"Tell her thanks the next time you see her."

"She also mentioned something you had said yesterday."

"What was that?"

Channing poured himself some more coffee. "The county records office. It seems to have become a favorite haunt of yours. That and the library reference room."

"We talked about that, didn't we? My looking up descendants?"

His smile held a disturbing spark of eroticism. "I would have thought your interest was a little more"—Channing paused—"personal."

"Meaning?"

"What exactly is it that you want to know about me, Maggie?"

Unnerved by his ability to follow her every move, Maggie faltered for a convincing reply.

"Why don't I just save you some trouble?" he said. "I'm forty-one, I was born on May fourteenth in West Virginia, my favorite color is orange, my net worth is over—"

"Why are you doing this?" she interrupted.

"Because every minute you spend snooping about my past is a minute that I really shouldn't be paying you for, should I?"

"I was working on the project," Maggie insisted, "which is where I should be now instead of in this ridiculous conversation."

"So your curiosity is satisfied?" he asked. "There's nothing else you're dying to find out?"

The cool condescension in his voice pushed her past

any decision she might have made to just let the matter drop.

"Only one thing," she said.

"Which is?"

"Have you ever been married?"

He shot a commanding look at her, a look that made Maggie almost wish she could retract the question, for certainly she had just betrayed her previous day's discovery. Wordlessly, she waited for his reply, wondering if he'd even give her one or just leave her at the table.

At last he spoke.

"No," he said firmly. "No, I never have."

31

"You probably don't remember me," the male voice said on the telephone a week later, "but I'd like to take you to lunch."

"How was Alaska?" Maggie asked upon recognizing the caller, sinking into the chair beside the extension that Brecht had told her to pick up.

"Laboring under a freak summer storm," Twylar replied. "And from the looks of the sky this morning, I brought some of it back with me."

"The rain's been off and on for a while, so I don't think you're guilty."

"Fortunately, the place we're going for lunch is indoors. Will you be on the mainland today, say about one-thirtyish?"

"Not on the agenda. How about tomorrow?"

It had been a peculiar week, underscored by an aura of strain ever since her coffee conversation with Channing. Whether she had truly breached their friendship or he simply sought to clip her wings for the time being, they had spent the majority of it apart, Maggie remaining behind on the island with a mountain of paperwork. As if the intermittent rain showers were not enough to keep her indoors and occupied, Brecht had managed to keep within convenient earshot of every move she made, including each trip to her bedroom.

"It would have to be after two," Twylar said. "No, wait, I think I can cancel that. Let's see—eleven? Eleven-thirty?"

"Eleven-thirty would be fine."

"Let me give you a central meeting place then. Do you know Doc Maynard's at First and Yesler?"

"The crew goes there for beers sometimes. It's not that far from where I'll be."

"Perfect. I'll pick you up there at eleven-thirty."

As she hung up the phone, Maggie felt an odd sense of relief, almost optimism. Even after only one meeting, her intuition about Twylar Zarzy was that he could be trusted. Troy's remarks aside, the widower had a candor that put her at ease and an obvious insight into Channing that he had no compunctions about sharing. Just twenty-four more hours, Maggie thought, and she'd have another piece of the puzzle.

"You know what I could really use for all of this?" Maggie said out loud as she sat cross-legged on the floor of the study a few hours later, surrounded by manila file folders. Outside the tall windows, silver rivulets of rain raced their way down the glass, casting wavering shadows across the carpet.

Brecht glanced over at her as he methodically fed papers into the fax machine, obviously treating her question as purely rhetorical and, thus, in no need of a reply on his part.

"Some archives boxes," Maggie said in answer to her own question. "The kind with lids so you can stack them?"

Brecht went on with his task.

"You're a big help," Maggie muttered under her breath, pulling the top of the felt pen off with her teeth.

To her surprise, Brecht spoke. "I was considering your question before misleading you with an answer," he replied.

"Sorry," Maggie said. "I thought you were just ignoring me until I committed my next transgression."

"Perhaps you can tell me when that will be," Brecht remarked without looking at her, "so I might synchronize my watch."

From her viewpoint on the floor, it was hard to tell for sure, but the hidden side of Brecht's profile could have been suppressing a smug smile.

"That's the kind of thing your boss says," she pointed out. "His influence must be rubbing off."

"*Our* boss," Brecht corrected her.

Maggie combed her hair back with the fingers of both hands. "Do you realize we're having a conversation, Brecht?"

"Are we?"

"Maybe we should call the press. I think this is more than you've said to me the whole time I've been here."

"Perhaps," Brecht countered as he programmed the next phone number, "it's because we have only one thing in common."

Maggie eyed him critically. "Your opinion or his?"

"You'll find the kind of boxes you need in the attic," Brecht informed her.

"You're actually going to trust me to go up there all by myself?"

Brecht regarded her with his usual expressionless look. "The good silver is kept down here," he replied.

Maggie resisted the urge to ask if Channing's family skeletons were as securely locked away.

If there was one thing to be said about Brecht, Maggie thought as she climbed the stairs to the attic, it was that at least she always knew where she stood with him. Conscientious and loyal to a fault, he seemed to regard Channing as some kind of god and everyone else as merely pawns whose purpose was to appease him.

Time and again, Twylar's cryptic reference to their former roles of employer and employee had come back to her, exhausting her imagination with theories and hunches of how such a liaison might have come about. Further, why would Brecht have stayed on after such roles were reversed?

At least by tomorrow, part of the mystery would be cleared up.

She was thankful, of course, that Twylar had possessed the good sense not to say anything about it on the phone. Mindful of Brecht's sneakiness and SkySet's secret knowledge of English, the possibility of being overheard was a strong one. All she needed, Maggie realized, was for one or the other to report back to Channing so he could squelch her plans.

With a start, she suddenly remembered something.

Twylar's remark about Brecht had been made at dinner while Channing was out of the room, but there had remained at least one pair of ears that could have been tuned in to their dialogue.

Lynne-Mae.

Maggie's mood veered toward anger at how gullible

she had been in her initial impression of Barstow's elegant wife, how enthusiastically she had perceived Lynne-Mae as a potential new friend. Had it not been for Channing's arrival at her office that day . . . Maggie pushed the consequences out of her mind, oddly grateful that the situation that had made her so upset had also prevented her from pursuing a real friendship with Lynne-Mae.

Trying to forget about Lynne-Mae for the time being, Maggie opened the attic door and stepped inside.

Like the rest of the house, it had an ordered appearance that seemed almost unnatural. Well-swept and tidy, it was a far cry from the kind of attics that Maggie had encountered as a little girl. No headless black dress forms teetered precariously against rusted birdcages, and no open trunks revealed sloppy yards of vintage fabric, stuffed animals minus their button eyes, or old books and clay crockery.

Illuminated by three slanted windows in the roof, the loft before her was further testimony of Channing's zeal for neatness. Even the spare furniture—bentwood chairs, teak end tables, and a Victorian daybed—had been grouped for livable occupancy rather than stacked on top of each other or callously dismantled and shoved into a cobwebbed corner. Even more peculiar was that there weren't any visible cobwebs.

In spite of the rainy day, there was enough natural light from above to make flipping the switch inside the door unnecessary. Intrigued by the sight that greeted her, Maggie crossed the room and scanned its contents for the boxes that Brecht had indicated were there.

Just as promised, she found half a dozen of them—disassembled to save space—next to a cabinet whose glass doors revealed orderly stacks of china and crystal. In a brief glance Maggie noted that Channing's cast-aways were finer than most people's Sunday best.

She could probably carry all six down in one trip, but the opportunity to spend more time exploring in the attic was tempting. Not that she'd find anything of major consequence. Certainly if anything incriminating had been stashed there, Brecht would never have let her set foot in the door.

As she picked up three of them, her glance fell on something that her own shadow had previously obscured—the corner of a dark wooden picture frame poking out from behind a Victorian quilt rack draped with crocheted afghans encased in protective plastic.

Expecting little more than a seascape or a still life, Maggie set the boxes aside and, with a cautious tug, pulled the hidden canvas into view.

32

Even in the shadowed shafts of light from the rooftop windows, it was obvious that the woman in the portrait was beautiful. Her aristocratic oval face glowed with pale gold undertones. It was perfectly framed by wavy ash-blond hair swept back just enough to show garnet earrings the same shade as her strapless evening dress. With gloved hands neatly folded in her lap, she exuded the regal certainty of someone who knew her place in the world, with her dove gray eyes peeking out from beneath long lashes.

Maggie stared at the picture, transfixed by what the painter had so effectively captured on canvas—an enchanting goddess about to rise at any moment from her velvet wingback chair and join her handsome husband in the next room, taking his arm for escort to the opera or ballet.

Fiona?

For reasons she couldn't quite fathom, Maggie had

come to assume over a week of speculation that Channing's wife had possessed long dark hair and the fiery spirit of a gypsy, a girl untamed by the responsibilities of marriage and at odds with the protocol of his peers. The woman in the portrait, however, seemed to fit her role of wife and society hostess as if it had been tailor-made for her.

Maggie looked harder, puzzled by the existence of visual discrepancies that were at odds with her first guess about the mystery woman's identity. The dress, for instance, was the trademark of an earlier age, as were the elbow-length gloves. So, too, were the hair and makeup—glamorous imitations of a look made popular by film actresses long retired from the spotlight.

Also, there was the woman herself to consider. Even if the portrait had been painted in Fiona Channing's last year of life, there was a self-assured maturity to the woman that one would not expect of a subject at the age of twenty-one.

More bothersome to Maggie at that particular moment, though, was the nagging feeling that the portrait was somehow familiar. It seemed impossible, considering that she had yet to discover a single female subject among Channing's art collection, which was dominated by oils and lithographs of nature as well as the unyielding visages of his male ancestors. Maggie impatiently searched her memory but found nothing to explain her sense of déjà vu.

Did she dare draw it out further for a closer look, or, better yet, turn on the overhead light? Before she could decide, the sound of a footfall on the stairs startled her into pushing the picture back into its hiding place, knocking over the flattened boxes as she did so.

"Thank goodness you're here!" she gasped as

Brecht's silhouette filled the doorway. "These things are more cumbersome than they look. Want to give me a hand getting them downstairs?"

From the corner of her eye as she let herself out of the room, Maggie caught him checking the attic for evidence of disruption. She could only hope that he would not notice the frame had been moved.

"I understand you're having lunch tomorrow with Twylar," Channing remarked, pouring himself a snifter of Rémy Martin and extending the one already poured to Maggie.

Outside, the summer storm had intensified, making Maggie feel even more tense for some inexplicable reason.

"Are you clairvoyant," she asked, "or do your spies rival the CIA?"

Channing smiled. "Nothing quite that impressive. "Twylar called me about something else, and your name came up in the conversation."

Maggie felt herself stiffen, already anticipating that Channing had once again outfoxed her. "Good or bad?"

"Definitely good," he answered. "Very flattering, in fact."

"The man hardly knows me."

Channing regarded her over the top of his glass like a gem cutter studying a diamond. "Maybe some things a person just recognizes at first sight."

Disconcerted by his sudden scrutiny, Maggie changed the subject. "So what's been keeping you on the mainland this week?" *Besides Lynne-Mae*, she added to herself.

"Business. As you're already aware, I have more pies on the rack than just the one on the table."

"I haven't heard that one before."

"Old Virginia expression."

Channing settled into the sofa across from her. In his jeans, tennis shoes, and a beige broadcloth shirt open at the throat, it was the most casual she had seen him since her arrival at Lynx Bay. His relaxed and cavalier look somehow redoubled her determination to remain distantly formal. Even his black hair—still damp from the rain just half an hour before—had been roguishly stroked by the whims of the wind, an errant lock dipping above his right brow.

"I keep forgetting you grew up back there," she said. "It's hard sometimes to picture you living anywhere but Lynx Bay."

"We all have our roots, I guess. Mine just happen to be east." The faint drawl in his voice tempted her to ask more.

"A happy childhood?" she asked.

"Privileged. Not always as happy as I would have liked."

"What would have made it happier?"

To her surprise, he answered her question instead of evading it. "Both parents in the same state might have helped." Channing winked. "But I assume you can relate to that?"

Given the knowledge he already had of her father's predisposition to follow adventures wherever they led him, Maggie nodded in agreement, seeing no need to defend it.

"I suppose there were advantages to being shuttled back and forth at that age," he continued. "Gave me a taste of two worlds . . . exposed me to travel . . . got me to see my parents as separate individuals instead of as a couple."

"You make it sound almost as if being a couple was a curse in their case."

"Not at the beginning, but bad enough at the end to not wish on your worst enemy." He thoughtfully sipped his drink. "Seattle was a little too 'heathen' as far as my mother was concerned." Channing shook his head. "I think she'd be shocked to see what a gem this city's grown into."

"Is she still—"

A resounding crash of thunder drowned out Maggie's last word, and then the living room plunged into pitch darkness.

"It's okay," he quickly assured her, reaching across to touch her hand and making contact with her knee instead. "We've got a generator—Brecht'll have us back in business in a few minutes."

Through the French doors, a brilliant streak of lightning illuminated the south balcony and the trees beyond.

Channing's hand did not leave her knee. Maggie shifted slightly to dislodge it.

"Do thunderstorms bother you?" he asked.

"Not as long as I'm inside where it's safe," she replied, wishing almost immediately that she had dropped the last three words. *Safe.* How could she possibly imagine herself safe when she was less than three feet away from a man to whom lies, deception, and possibly murder came so easily? A man to whom she was also so dangerously attracted . . .

"Take my hand a second," Channing murmured through the darkness.

When she hesitated he added, "I don't want us falling over the furniture like a couple of clowns. There's a little more light and less to run into if we're closer to the window."

"We could always stay put, too," she countered, glad

for the shadows that hid her apprehension.

Channing chuckled. "Suit yourself." She could hear him stand up and start to move.

"Okay," she said, deciding that she'd rather know where he was than sit in the dark waiting for something dire to happen. "Shouldn't the lights have come back on by now?"

"And spoil such a spectacular view?"

With fingers tightly entwined in hers, Channing led them through the obstacle course of furniture until they were standing a few feet from the French doors, its panes slick from the rain that had been steadily pelting them all day and into evening. As her eyes grew accustomed to the darkness, Maggie marveled at the intermittent fireworks igniting the Pacific Northwest sky so dramatically that it resembled the negative of a photograph. "I won't fight *that* argument," she said, tilting her head to address the man by her side.

Nor could she fight the combustible passion of Derek Channing as he suddenly pulled her flush against him and bracketed her narrow waist with both hands as he kissed her with the urgency of a man too long deprived of the intimacy of another's touch.

Before logic and reason could intervene, she felt herself returning his crushing kiss, consumed by a savage harmony that burned all other memory in its path, obliterating her resistance. With lips damp and parted, there was a catch in her breath as she tried to say his name, conscious that his mouth had finally left hers to seek the smooth hollow of her throat.

"Shhhh," he whispered as a sizzle of light was reflected for only an instant in his blue eyes as they roved over her face with an unquenchable warmth, and an unquestionable desire. "Shhh . . ."

33

Beneath her fingertips on his broad chest she could feel his heartbeat, could savor the sensual heat that emanated through his skin and through the thin fabric of his shirt. Like dry kindling at the mercy of a hungry flame, Maggie saw the last of her willpower disintegrate under the strength and magnetism of the very man she had declared for the past five years to be her worst enemy.

As he drew her higher and closer to him, her body willingly responded to his, acknowledging at last the primary source of the feverish discontent she had felt for the past two weeks. For in spite of the doubts, in spite of the lies, in spite of everything she believed about Derek Channing, she had never before wanted a man as much as she now wanted him.

Mindless of the storm that set thunder to reverberate across the breadth of Puget Sound and sheets of rain to mercilessly splash against the windows, they imprisoned each others' limbs in a web of growing arousal, an exploration punctuated by low murmurs that defied translation.

Tentatively at first, her fingers toyed with the buttons on his shirt, working them free one by one and stroking with her knuckles the coarse mat of dark hair that lay beneath. Intoxicated by the very scent and nearness of him, she worked her way toward his belt, ardently pulling free the shirt's remaining inches and caressing the warmth of his bare skin as she locked her arms around his taut midriff, arching back ever so slightly that his moist mouth might descend and claim what was no longer forbidden.

Channing's tongue darted and danced over hers, and he groaned her name as his hands traversed the length of her back, pausing only a moment before sliding a hot palm beneath the waistband of her jeans to cup the smooth curve of her derriere and pull her hard and tight against the juncture of his legs. Rhythmically, his mouth throbbed a passionate message back and forth between her wet lips, a message interrupted only by his insertion of a verbal one. "Think maybe we could find our way upstairs?"

The sudden return of the living room to a state of full light jarred both of them apart, a move that might have been seamless had Channing's Rolex not accidentally caught on the back of Maggie's belt in his hand's rapid withdrawal. In the space of a second, their guilty eyes made contact and the impulse to burst out laughing struck them both at the same time, setting Maggie to plummet back into his arms and muffle her giggles against his chest.

"Damn that Thomas Edison!" Channing cried in melodramatic anger as he kissed the top of her head. "At least it answers the question about our ability to find our way upstairs." He extricated his watch and playfully slapped her behind. "We'd be morons *not* to."

The sound of a telephone ringing in the next room distracted her. Channing's fingers reached up to trace the line of her jaw and gently redirect her chin so that she was facing him. "Whoever it is has terrible timing," he said.

Conscious of their dishevelment and the libertine spontaneity that had caused it, Maggie found the voice to share her foremost concern. "Do you think our own timing is any better?"

Channing raised a brow. "Because you work for me?"

Maggie hesitated, disturbed by the reality that there was no way she could articulate the dark barrier that loomed between them without jeopardizing the fragile display of trust that their brief intimacy had just generated.

In the absence of a reply, Channing reacted to what he guessed her answer was going to be. "If that's the only problem, I could fire you and then reinstate you next Tuesday."

"Why Tuesday?"

Channing smiled. "Because if I said 'tomorrow morning' instead, you'd feel seduced and abandoned, wouldn't you? And that's not what I want you to feel at all, Maggie."

At the base of her throat, a pulse beat and swelled as though her heart had risen from its usual place, a condition that only affirmed her desire in spite of the truth she sought.

"Did I say something wrong?" he asked, concerned by her silence.

Whatever she might have replied was preempted by Brecht's appearance in the doorway. "Excuse me, sir," he said, "but Mrs. Barstow is on the line."

She knew he was going to take the call even before he excused himself with a quick, apologetic kiss to her cheek. Brecht's arrival on the scene always spelled some harbinger of evil. That the latest one should take the form of a woman who might well have been enjoying Channing's physical favors for all of the past week was a blow too strong for Maggie's dizzied senses to handle. She had wanted to see her worst speculations proven false, and one phone call had brought them all crashing back.

When he discovered her missing from the living room upon his return and knocked on her bedroom door fifteen minutes later, the eager response he had assumed would be waiting for him was unexpectedly replaced by the eyes and the stance of a cautious stranger.

"A problem at the museum," he said, "although it probably could have waited until morning."

"Did you take care of it for her?" Maggie asked, conscious of the subtle bite in her words and curious as to whether Channing even noticed the change in her tone.

"That's what friends are for," he said, cocking his head in puzzlement at the way her body blocked the bedroom doorway. "Are you going to invite me in?"

Maggie inwardly summoned the strength to dismiss her tremors at the recollection of his kiss and his touch and the compelling strokes of his hands only moments before. "I'm not sure that's such a good idea," she replied, hating the way it sounded.

"Neither one of us was putting up much resistance to the idea when we were downstairs," Channing reminded her. "What changed in the last few minutes?"

In retrospect, there were a dozen other things she could have told him, a dozen answers that might have been closer to the truth and not inflicted the flicker of pain she saw in his face on the heels of her most accessible lie.

"I'm afraid that there's someone else in the picture," she said, thinking that it was a clever allusion to Channing's own illicit involvement with Lynne-Mae as well as a credible escape from an emotionally and sexually charged situation she was not ready to deal with. What she hadn't anticipated was Channing's reaction.

There was a cold edge of irony in his voice, a malevolent cousin to the same voice that, just moments earlier, had huskily groaned intimate promises in her ear.

"I hope you know what you're doing, and who you're doing it with."

He was gone before she could say another word.

That Channing was absent from breakfast the next morning didn't surprise her. Nor did she find it odd that his daily list of assignments for her hadn't been left out in its usual place. Whether her lie had wounded his heart or his ego, the bottom-line message of the firmly closed door to his study was clear: he didn't want to see her, a punishment he no doubt felt suitable for denying him access to her bedroom and to her body.

What disturbed her more, though, were the parting words he had used when he took leave of her, words that had kept echoing through her dreams throughout another restless night. Was it a warning not to cross him? Or a snide way of telling her that he knew more than he let on about her meetings with a certain fair-haired detective?

Maggie felt herself shudder, not knowing at that moment which interpretation was the lesser of two potentially explosive evils.

34

With twenty minutes to spare before Twylar picked her up, Maggie slipped her change into the pay phone at Doc Maynard's, thankful that the tavern wasn't crowded enough to make talking and listening difficult. Only the bartender, a waitress, and a handful of early diners peopled the vintage gathering spot.

"I had a hunch it would be you," Troy said after her first hello on the recording. "Did you survive that killer storm last night?"

Maggie took a deep breath. "Storms have never bothered me," she replied, not daring to tell him that rougher conditions than the weather were currently assaulting her heart. "How about you?"

Troy considered her question for a moment. "I think they're more enjoyable when they're shared . . . especially in front of a fire."

His tone of voice left no doubt in her mind that the desired object of his sharing was her. That she couldn't reciprocate such thoughts made her feel sorry that she had returned his kiss, sorry that she wasn't able to return the detective's obvious interest. Regardless of her suspicions about Channing, his—and not Troy's—was the spell that still held her, a spell she had to break before even considering another man's affection.

"So what's the agenda today?" Troy asked her.

"Twylar is back from Alaska. He's picking me up for lunch in a few minutes."

"Not to be nosy, but do you know where you're going?"

"Sounds pretty nosy to me," Maggie teased, nonetheless appreciative that he was only asking out of concern for her safety with a stranger. "It's a place called the Pacific Crabhouse."

Troy whistled. "On *my* salary, I'd be lucky if I could afford to eat the coasters."

"Damn," Maggie muttered, "and I left my tiara back in Boston."

"Well, all I can say is that it sounds like the competition is getting pretty stiff."

"What competition?"

"I'm glad you just said that," he replied. "Gives me hope that your head's not turned by money and that I've got a shot to convince you I'm not such a bad catch."

She hadn't intended to bring up the subject, but it almost seemed cruel not to. "I've been thinking about last week," she said. "About what you told me in the alley."

"And you think maybe the train's moving too fast?"

"A little, yes." Though she was relieved by his intuitive remark, it didn't lessen the difficulty of the words she still had to say. "I just think that until this whole thing with Channing is over, that until I've finished working with you officially—" Maggie hesitated, conscious of the real reasons that lay behind what she was saying. "I don't think that being involved is such a good idea for either one of us."

With staid calmness, Troy responded to what had to have been a disappointment. "I hope that doesn't mean what it sounds like from *this* end."

"What does it sound like?"

"You're not feeling something for Channing, are you?"

Maggie masked her guilt behind a laugh. "Of course not. I just don't want any outside distractions to come between me and my mission."

"I'd hope," Troy said, "that we're both professional enough that it wouldn't interfere." There was a long pause, a pause that Maggie hoped wasn't the prelude to another declaration of love. "Whether or not you and I have a chance," he finally said, "I don't want to lose our friendship."

"Neither do I."

Seemingly satisfied with her response, Troy inquired whether she had learned anything new in the past week.

"I've been mostly busy with paperwork," she replied, determined not to divulge her latest discoveries until she knew their complete connection to Channing. "What about you?"

"Well, I've been following up on a couple of your ideas."

His revelation surprised her, because of his prior resistance to her theories. "And?" she prompted him.

"Well, it's not your fault, Maggie. You just have to realize that I probably hear dozens of ideas every day.

Most of 'em lead to dead ends, hard as you work your tail off to prove otherwise. After a while, you just learn to stop getting excited and concentrate on what's solid."

"So, was there anything to what the Marquart sisters said about the scandal?"

"That's what I wanted to tell you. That mystery guy named Homer?"

"Yes? The one I think was Derek?"

"Not unless he was moonlighting as the Marquarts' gardener back in 1955. *His* name was Homer."

"I hope you brought your appetite with you," Twylar said as he escorted Maggie into the elegant brass and glass restaurant. Reminded of Troy's remark about the coasters, Maggie smiled as the hostess led the way to a window table with a harbor view that could just as easily have been New England.

The polished oak floors and brilliant brass banisters reflected light from the high chandeliers, and on a refectory table to the right of the steps was a dazzling display of desserts. Maggie gave it only a quick glance, certain that even inhaling would add unwanted calories.

The melodic strains of a string quartet were punctuated only by the clinking of crystal glasses and the murmur of hushed voices. It was definitely not a cop hangout, Maggie decided.

"This was one of my wife's favorite restaurants," Twylar said, after ordering them both drinks. "Of course, it used to be 'The Flying Dutchman' back then, you know, as in Wagner? The owners were opera buffs, and that's all you used to hear. On Thursday nights, they even had an open mike for some of the locals to get up and sing." Twylar parted his lips in a gap-toothed grin. "Am I boring you already?"

"Not at all," Maggie assured him as she opened her menu, nonetheless impatient to hear what he had promised to tell her two weeks ago. "So what do you recommend for lunch?"

"Well, to each his own," Twylar said, "but I've always been partial to the Scampi Maison."

"Scampi Maison? Sounds like a character in a Damon Runyon story. A French gangster, maybe."

Twylar laughed and pointed to another one of the items. "'Scarlett Scallops,'" he read with a raised eyebrow. "Obviously a woman with a past. Maybe the girlfriend of 'Crab Legs Malone.'"

"Or 'Mussels Alexander.'"

The silly game reminded Maggie of her father, who had always been a quick wit and a master of puns. Twylar's unexpected similarity endeared him to her all the more.

"So how do you like working for Derek?" he asked, offering her the basket of sourdough bread. "Is it all that you expected?"

"I'm not sure that I was expecting *anything*," Maggie replied. "I just wanted a change of pace for the summer, and this job seemed to offer it."

"Not to speak out of turn," Twylar said, "but I think it might lead to even more than you think."

"I beg your pardon?"

"Derek. He hasn't stopped talking about you."

"I'm sure he talks about a lot of women." Maggie wondered what had possessed Twylar to broach so personal a subject with her.

"Well, you'd have to know him for as long as I have to recognize when he's met his match. I know it's not in my place to say it, but you're a prime contender."

"Too bad, then, that I'm not contending." Maggie took a sip of her drink. "So how long have you known him?"

"Oh, too long to keep track of. Sometimes when you've shared the worst together, it seems as if you've known a person forever." A wistful look came into Twylar's eyes. "He was a godsend, you know, when I lost my wife."

Maggie recalled what Lynne-Mae had said about the accident that had taken place ten years ago. Twylar must have known about Fiona then. The challenge, of course, was finding a casual opportunity to drop her name and gauge his reaction.

"He had his own hands full enough as it was," Twylar said, "but you know, he was on a plane to Paris almost as soon as we hung up that day. Made all the calls, took care of all the arrangements. . . . I could never have handled it without him."

Maggie seized the chance to bluff, hoping it wouldn't backfire. "It must have been a comfort having both of them fly over."

Twylar seemed puzzled. "Both of them?"

"Didn't he bring Fiona?"

35

From what she could tell, Twylar's reaction of astonishment was genuine.

"Fiona? Now where did you run across *that* name?"

Maggie concentrated on buttering her bread to avoid meeting his eyes. "It came up the other day."

"From Derek?"

"Who else?" Maggie recognized that she had just touched a nerve.

"Well, I suppose that it's good he's finally talking about it," Twylar murmured. "It's certainly been enough years. Excuse me, but what was it you just asked me?"

"Only if she went to France with him."

Twylar shook his head. "Oh, Fiona wasn't officially in the picture until almost a year later. And besides, I don't know that she would have done much good under the circumstances."

"What do you mean?"

"Oh, she was such a slip of a girl, and very sensitive. One of those free spirits that you could picture cavorting barefoot with fairies and throwing rune stones to tell the future. Not of this earth, if you know what I mean."

This was definitely at odds with the image of the woman in the portrait, Maggie thought.

Twylar sighed. "Well, at least he's finally coming out and talking about her again. Those were pretty black days he went through with her toward the end. I didn't envy him the lot he was cast on *that* one."

"I'm sure you were a help to him," Maggie said, hoping he'd volunteer the details she was dying to ask.

"Not as much as Brecht, I'm afraid." Twylar brightened. "I owe you a story on that, don't I? I'd almost forgotten."

Maggie smiled in spite of her frustration that they were leaving the intriguing topic of Fiona.

"You know he's German, of course?" Twylar asked.

Maggie nodded.

"Did you also know that his family was supposedly thick with Eva Braun?"

"Hitler's mistress?"

"The same. Actually, to hear Brecht tell it, they were more like the kind of neighbors who watch your flat when you're gone. Not bosom buddies by any means, but you know how ugly rumors get started."

The arrival of their salads interrupted Twylar's story.

"I hope you didn't mind my ordering the peppercorn dressing," he said. "It was my wife's favorite, but you can certainly send it back if you don't like it."

"Delicious," Maggie murmured after a hasty bite. "As you were saying?"

"Well it was a friendship that no one apparently batted an eye about until well after the war was over. That's when the Nazi-hunters really came out of the woodwork and decided to ferret out anyone with connections to the Third Reich. Took them over thirty years, but they finally caught up with Brecht's father. You might have even read about it. Made all the major papers."

"Refresh my memory."

"A baker in Wiesbaden. Harmless little old man who'd give a moth its freedom rather than kill it. At any rate, Brecht had married, had two little boys, and was still living in Germany when his father got hauled off for interrogation."

The story sounded vaguely familiar to Maggie, though she had not paid much attention at the time. The very idea that Brecht had a family of his own was enough of a surprise to her.

"Anyway, to make a long story short, Brecht was pouring out his story in a Wiesbaden bar one night to a young American financier with a reputation for backing underdogs." Twylar winked. "I don't suppose I have to tell you who *that* was."

"Derek?"

"Brecht was desperate. He'd spent every cent trying to buy good defense for his father, but the case was going down the tubes. At that point, of course, he'd already lost his wife and his children. Apparently the media harassment was too much for her, and she took the boys back to her parents in Austria, never to be heard from again."

"So what could Derek do that German lawyers couldn't?"

Twylar smiled. "I guess it just gets back to the adage

that money talks. One thing you have to know about Channing, Maggie, is that he'll go to any lengths when he thinks he's right. And in Brecht's case, he thoroughly believed that the old man was innocent, and it was worth his time to prove it."

"But how did Brecht expect to pay him if he'd already spent everything he had?"

"Maybe with the only thing he had left. Himself."

"Sounds like he sold himself into slavery."

Twylar shook his head. "You'd have to understand Brecht and his sense of honor," he said. "Clearing his family name and seeing his father exonerated from charges of atrocities he didn't commit was the only thing that mattered to him."

"And did he get what he wanted?"

Twylar dabbed at his mouth with his napkin. "A bittersweet ending, unfortunately. Channing's lawyers were able to garner enough evidence that the charges were dropped after almost two years in trial."

"Why is that bittersweet?"

"Prison isn't easy on anyone, and we're talking about an old man who was already in poor health." He paused for a moment, lost in reflection. "He lived to enjoy less than a month of freedom before succumbing to a stroke."

For the first time, Maggie felt empathy for the man she had always regarded as little more than a heavy.

"I guess that makes their relationship a little easier for me to understand," she said at last.

"Well, like I said back at dinner," Twylar reiterated, "that kind of loyalty is hard to find these days. There's not a thing in the world that Brecht wouldn't do if Channing asked him."

Including murder? Maggie wondered. But the question went unasked.

Throughout the rest of lunch, Maggie tried to reroute the conversation back to Fiona, but it was clear that Twylar wasn't going to fall for it. Intent on telling her his favorite anecdotes about the export business, he monopolized their talk with stories of people Maggie had never heard of and issues that were of little interest to her.

"Dessert?" he offered. "I hope you saved room."

"Thanks, no, just coffee."

Twylar inclined his head a moment toward the direction of the music. "You hear that?" His fork kept time to the melody. "Pachelbel's *Canon,*" he said. "It was my wife's favorite piece of music, especially this part coming up. Dum—da-da-dum—da-da—dum-a-dum-a-dum-a-dum-a—"

"You must miss her a lot," Maggie commented.

"A place like this brings back memories, yes. You would have liked her, I'm sure. So vibrant, so full of fun. I'm rambling, though," he apologized. "Forgive me."

"No, I think it's nice. You were lucky to have had each other."

"You're too kind. Not many people have what we did, that's for certain."

"Do you think . . ."

"Do I think what?" Twylar asked when she hesitated.

"I was just wondering whether Derek had that same kind of feeling for Fiona."

Twylar scowled. "Fiona? I shouldn't think so. Why?"

"Just something you said earlier, about him finally being able to talk about her again."

"Only because of the way things happened." Twylar shook his head. "Terrible when someone dies that young and with so much still to offer."

"And to lose the baby, too," Maggie added. "It must have devastated him."

"Oh, it did. He couldn't have been more crushed if it had been his very own. . . ."

36

"*Did I say* something that upset you?" Twylar asked.

Maggie recovered from her open-mouthed startlement with the first thing she could think to say. "I guess I'm just surprised that you knew. About the baby, that is."

"Derek would never condemn a child just because of its father," Twylar replied. "That wouldn't be like him at all." An odd expression flitted across his face. "What surprises me, of course, is that you knew."

Maggie's head was now thoroughly spinning with confusion. "I don't really remember how it came up in the conversation," she said. "A weak moment, I guess."

"It would have had to be," Twylar said. "Derek's not given to that sort of thing. Weak moments, I mean."

She shrugged. "What can I say?"

Twylar studied her across the table. "Why all of this interest in Fiona?" he asked, his voice underscored with a trace of suspicion that hadn't been there before.

"No particular reason."

"No?"

"Why should there be?"

"There shouldn't," Twylar replied. "Which makes me all the more curious."

There was no graceful avenue for exit save the very one to which Twylar had alluded when they first arrived. "Well, actually, Twylar, maybe there is."

"Care to share it?"

"Only if you promise not to repeat it."

His face broke into a wide grin. "A secret? Secrets can be dangerous."

"This one would be more on the order of awkward. I'd really prefer that you not say anything, especially to Channing."

"Then consider my lips safely sealed. What is it?"

Maggie took a deep breath as if the disclosure pained her. "I guess I just wanted to know what my predecessor was like. Seeing as how you had known her, I thought—"

"Predecessor?" Twylar chuckled. "I don't mean to correct you, Maggie, but don't you have the wrong word there?"

"Do I?"

"Well, not unless you were planning—" the rest of the answer died on Twylar's lips as he was suddenly distracted by something over her shoulder.

"What is it?" she asked, failing to see what had caused so dramatic an interruption. "You look like you just saw a ghost."

"If you'll excuse me," he hastily apologized, scooting back his chair and nearly colliding with the waiter directly behind him. "Something I need to take care of. I'll only be a minute. . . ."

Perplexed by what had caused such a state of anxiety, Maggie turned her head to watch him go.

"More coffee here, ma'am?" the waiter asked.

Maggie nodded distractedly. By the time she looked back, Twylar had already disappeared into the restaurant's foyer.

When nearly ten minutes had passed and Twylar had not returned, Maggie decided to go look for him.

"Excuse me, ma'am?" the same waiter said, glancing down at the unpaid check.

"Oh, I'm coming right back," she quickly assured him, nonetheless struck by the potential absurdity of being stiffed for a lunch that easily cost half of her weekly paycheck.

She spotted Twylar in the foyer before he spotted her, his back turned toward her as he held a phone receiver up to his left ear and gesticulated with his right hand.

Instead of stepping out of sight before he could turn around, Maggie decided to *let* him see her.

"Is everything all right?" she casually inquired.

Obviously startled by her presence, Twylar had cut short his call. "No rest for the wicked," he said, "and I don't get any either. Thank goodness I passed by a phone or I would have forgotten to check in with my office."

"So is everything all right?" Maggie repeated.

"Oh, fine, except that I'm afraid I'm going to have to get you back to Pioneer Square." He stole a look at his watch for emphasis. "Duty calls."

He followed her back to the main part of the restaurant to pay for their lunch, acting for all the world as if nothing peculiar had happened.

Maggie was annoyed that she could have misjudged him so poorly. Something, or someone, had certainly set Twylar off and broken his entire mood of chumminess.

Troy's words came back to haunt her. "Don't forget that he's Channing's friend and not yours," he had said of Twylar.

Challenging Twylar about his bolt from the table or his subsequent phone call would do no good, she realized, nor was he likely to continue being a wellspring of gossip about Channing.

Was it Channing he had been talking to so earnestly when she discovered him? Maggie's intuition told her it was. What she couldn't figure out was *why*.

The drive from the Pacific Crabhouse passed largely in silence, Twylar occasionally breaking it with observations about the weather or the upcoming election for mayor.

Only once did he murmur anything that seemed out of place. "So did you know anyone out here before you came from Boston?"

On the surface it seemed to be an innocuous remark, but Maggie's guard shot up nevertheless. "Not a soul," she replied, wondering just how much Channing had told him about her background. "I'd heard good things about the city from people who had visited, though."

"It does have plenty to offer," Twylar agreed. "You've probably met a lot of new friends *since* then?"

The comment wavered halfway between a statement and a question. Maggie treated it as the latter.

"Work keeps me pretty busy," she said. "Why do you ask?"

"No particular reason."

She had promised Troy a call if time permitted, which it did since lunch had been truncated. Mindful of the clouds that now hinted at afternoon showers, Maggie slipped back inside Doc Maynard's to contact him before returning to work.

What she had to report from the encounter with Twylar, however, almost made such a call seem a waste. Insightful as the story about Brecht and his past had been, it wasn't going to raise Troy McCormick's suspicions of Channing's bodyguard. Nor would he find anything tangible in the confirmation that Channing had been married to someone who had been unfaithful. *Stick to the course,* Troy would tell her, reminding her that extraneous material wasted their valuable time.

"If you're there, pick up," she said on the recording, puzzled that Troy wasn't around to answer. "Hello? Hello?"

"Not calling *me*, are you?" said a familiar voice just behind her. Startled, Maggie turned to see the towering presence of Ken Cleveland.

37

"Just leaving a message for the boss," Maggie improvised, hoping the foreman wasn't aware that Channing didn't have an answering machine. "Guess we'll touch base later."

"Is that telepathy or what?" Cleveland said in response to her answer. "You know he called you right after you left this morning? I told him that he just missed you by a nose."

"Oh, really?"

Cleveland shrugged. "Well, you know what they say—great minds run in the same circles."

His use of one of her father's favorite phrases sent an unexpected shudder down Maggie's spine.

"Buy you a beer?" Cleveland offered.

"No, actually, I was—"

"Didn't you have a lunch date today?"

"That's why I changed clothes," Maggie explained. That the foreman had never seen her in anything other

her working attire probably accounted for his unabashed staring at her navy challis dress and heels.

"You're kinda dressed up for Doc's, aren't you?" Cleveland said. "Not that it's bad or anything." Before she could respond, he was already tossing her another question. "Your date didn't go and stand you up, did he?"

"Just dropped me off," she said, in spite of the fact that it was really none of his business. Her glance absently fell on the half-empty mug of beer in front of him. His garrulous manner hinted that it wasn't his first drink that afternoon. "Did I miss anything downstairs while I was gone?"

"Nothin' to write home about." He nodded toward the beer. "Just stopped in for a cold one."

"Well, I won't keep you from it." She had already done a quick scan of the tavern and discovered that Cleveland was alone, which surprised her for someone who seemed to enjoy the company of his crew. "See you back at work."

"Sure you don't want one yourself?" he asked again. "No hurry for us to scoot. We got all day and then some."

Coming from the man who kept everyone's nose to the grindstone under Channing's orders, it struck her as an uncharacteristic remark. "I've missed a lot this past week," she said. "I really should get going."

"Then let me finish up and I'll walk you back. Protect you from the riffraff."

Maggie smiled. "Are they traveling in droves today?"

"Rain brings 'em all out. Sorta like worms on the sidewalk. Can't hardly miss 'em."

"Then I'll consider myself in good hands."

The matter settled, Cleveland straddled one of the

barstools and motioned her to take the one next to it. "Been meanin' to ask you a question anyway."

"And what's that?"

"Things goin' okay? You haven't been around much."

"Demanding boss," she replied, "but I'm fine. I tend to work well under pressure."

"*Damn* well."

"Thanks."

"I mean it," he insisted. "Couple of us had real doubts about it back at the start."

"Doubts?"

"Your bein' a woman 'n' all."

Maggie felt compelled to take issue with so sexist a remark. "Maybe if you'd hired women on the crew before this," she said, "you would already have found what you were looking for."

Cleveland gave a hearty slap to his thigh. "You got yourself a spunk that won't quit, Maggie."

"I like to think so, thanks."

"I mean that. It's like black 'n' white between you and that other one."

"Other one?"

"Real looker," he continued, "but a real ice maiden."

"Excuse me, but I'm a little confused. I thought you told me that there hadn't been women on the project before."

"Wasn't *on* the project. Just came down with the boss now and then to check it all out, see what we were doin'."

Maggie watched the level of his remaining beer descend and wondered whether she should encourage him to order another. Anything to keep him talking freely.

"This was last year you said?" she asked.

"Oh, hell no." Cleveland wiped his mouth off with the back of his hand. "Back when I was still assistant."

Maggie felt her heartbeat quicken. "Did *you* think she was pretty, Ken?"

He shrugged. "Seen prettier. Real classy, though. Real expensive. Bite your head off if you sneezed wrong, though. You know the kind. Anyway, we used to tag these nicknames on her that—well, I won't repeat in mixed company."

"So what was her *real* name?"

A deep crease furrowed its way across Cleveland's forehead. "Asian chick," he finally said. "All their names sound alike if you ask me."

"Lynne-Mae?"

"Yeah, that's it," he said. "That or Mae-Lynne. You know her or what?"

Maggie nodded. "It's hard to imagine someone like her in the tunnels, though."

"Ain't *that* the truth!" Cleveland guffawed. "Like a fancy diamond in a pile of manure. Pardon my French."

"So does she still visit the project?" Maggie asked, surprised that she had never run into her nor heard her presence discussed among the crew. Someone like Lynne-Mae would be hard not to notice, much less talk about.

"Not anymore. Used to go down real regular with the boss. Sometimes twice a week."

"Well, she and Channing *are* good friends."

"Oh, I wasn't talkin' about *him*," Cleveland said. "I meant *my* old boss. Clayton Price."

Maggie was shocked. Having made a split-second decision to stay at the bar and hear what else Cleveland had to say, she began to cough uncontrollably.

"Hey, are you okay? Sure you don't wanna drink?"

"Well, okay. Maybe just one."

Maggie managed to nurse that one mug to the foreman's three in the hour that followed. Excited by the new information she was learning, she could hardly wait to find a quiet place to assimilate all of it.

"Can't twist your arm?"

Outside, a light rain had started to fall on the sidewalks of Pioneer Square. "If I had a second one," she replied, "I'd be out like a light."

"Hard to swim you back that way, all passed out," Cleveland remarked, alluding to her residence on Lynx Bay. "You like it out there?"

"The commute's a hassle, but otherwise, it's fine."

Cleveland eased off the barstool in preparation to leave Doc Maynard's. "Some people got all the perks, I guess."

From the way he said it, Maggie thought she detected a tinge of resentment. "Do you think it bothers any of the others?" she asked. "I mean, the fact that I'm living out on the island and the rest of the crew—"

"Oh, hell no. Nobody's business what sorta deal you two got cookin' in private. Long as you get your job done."

His earlier remarks about her being a woman edged back into Maggie's thoughts. "Mind running that by me again?" she asked sharply as she followed him toward the door.

The foreman suddenly stopped in his tracks, so abruptly that Maggie nearly ran into him. "Well, I'll be damned!" he muttered.

Then he was bounding toward the door before she could even ask why.

38

For *a man* of his size, Cleveland moved with surprising speed, reaching the curb just as the traffic light turned from yellow to red and sprinting across the street. Maggie held back, certain that she was too late to beat the traffic.

From where she stood, though, it quickly became obvious what had prompted Cleveland's spontaneous pursuit. A slender youth with long black hair was zigzagging his way through the other pedestrians. It was the Indian boy, Maggie realized with a rush. She was startled to see him again and somewhat relieved to affirm that he wasn't a figment of her imagination, that the foreman had seen him, too. Anxiously, she waited for the light to change again so she could try to catch up with them both.

Although the number of times that the boy's path had crossed hers could still be counted on one hand, the coincidence of his loitering just outside Doc

Maynard's as they were exiting that afternoon was suspicious.

More worrisome, of course, was the realization that—like Brecht—he could well have been stalking her from the beginning. Certainly Troy's earlier assumption that it was probably Channing and not Maggie who interested the amateur spy fell by the wayside in light of the boy's unexpected reappearance. It had to be her, Maggie thought, for surely he would have had no reason to be spying on Ken Cleveland.

But if indeed he was the Wolf Boy, as Cleveland had said they'd nicknamed him, his ready access to the underground would facilitate any snooping at his own discretion. To hang around as public a place as Pioneer Square just didn't make sense.

It was the foreman's own reaction, however, that made even *less* sense. Why bolt for the door and lend chase to a scrawny teenager who looked like any other, whose motives at being near the popular Pioneer Square tavern may have been completely innocent?

Maggie broke into a run the moment the light changed to green, thankful that Cleveland was at least wearing a bright shirt that stood out in the crowd.

Of all the days to be dressed up, she thought in dismay, her agility encumbered by her narrow skirt and heels. When at last she caught up with Cleveland almost five blocks later, he was breathless and less than pleasant.

"Damn Muckleshoots!" he muttered, his irritation level increased by the splash of mud he had just acquired on the bottom of his jeans.

"Muckleshoots?" Maggie repeated.

"Fastest thing on two moccasins. Whole damn tribe's like that, y'know. Couldn't catch 'em if your life depended on it." Cleveland glared at her as if she were personally responsible for the Muckleshoots' speed.

"The hell with 'em," he cursed, doubly annoyed by the fact that his loss had been witnessed by a woman. "Damn tunnel rat."

"So what was that all about?" she asked.

"Nothin' important."

"From the way you were running, I'd say it was." Maggie wondered whether she could squeeze any more information out of him before sobriety returned. "I assume he's someone you know?"

"No big deal. Long gone by now, anyway."

"What about those buildings over there?" Maggie pointed to a row of dilapidated brick and wood structures that had seen better days. Imagining herself in the role of a boy on the run, she decided that it was a likely place for one to take refuge.

"What about 'em?"

"Do you think that's where he could have gone? He might have thought that maybe—"

"Who the hell knows what they think?" Cleveland snapped. "Come on, let's go back."

"No way," she replied. "I've run this far with you, I want to find out what he's up to."

As she started to step away from him, however, Cleveland's hand shot out to grab her upper arm. "Don't get messin' in stuff that's none of your business, Maggie."

Maggie's gaze traveled from his hand to his eyes. "I think if it's about the tunnels, it's not only my business but Channing's as well."

At the mention of their mutual employer, Cleveland lightened his grip but did not let go. "You go chasin' after that kid on company time, Channing's not gonna like it."

"Do you think he'd like it any better, if I were spending my company time at Doc Maynard's instead?"

It was a low blow, but one that hit the mark she intended.

"No law against it," he muttered in defense of his liquid lunch, but his voice had lost its earlier swell of bravado.

"No law against satisfying curiosity, either," she replied, "which is what I intend to do."

Now free of the hand that had restrained her, Maggie turned away and started walking in the direction of the brick buildings. There was no point in running, she decided. The boy had either put a couple dozen blocks of distance between them already or was safely biding his time in an alley.

"You're gonna get me in real trouble," Cleveland said, traipsing alongside of her.

Maggie didn't break her stride. "For what? Picking up where you left off? He's already got enough head start."

"You got nothin' to do with this."

"How do I know that if you're not going to tell me anything?"

"Can't. I got my orders."

"Suit yourself," Maggie replied. "I'll just have to find out on my own."

Cleveland glowered in anger. "He's not gonna like it. You go catchin' hell from Channing, don't come whinin' to me."

Maggie stopped and faced him squarely.

"Why would I catch any hell from the man I'm living with?"

It was not exactly a lie, she told herself. In light of the erroneous conclusions that Cleveland and the crew had already drawn about her association with Channing, there was probably nothing to lose by going along with it if it served her purposes.

Her remark visibly ruffled him, and in his expression of discomfiture Maggie now saw two things very clearly. The first was that he was about to give her the answer she wanted. The second was that she had just acquired an enemy.

"Kid's a damn thief," Cleveland muttered. "I'm just doin' my job."

"By chasing him away?"

The insolence in his reply was apparent. "By catchin' him like the boss told me to."

39

Cleveland's statement smacked of just enough falsehood that, in that very instant, Maggie was actually glad the boy had gotten away.

"Has Channing reported the thefts to the police?" she asked, wondering what kind of fool Cleveland took her for.

Cleveland muttered a reply about third parties only getting in the way.

"I'd just think with all the equipment down there—"

"Look, Channing's got it under control and it's none of your damn business, okay?"

"Maybe so," she replied, conscious that the rain had started to come down a little bit harder. "It seems a little strange to me, though, that you would have run this far after him and then quit. From where I was, it looked like you almost had him."

It was an argument Cleveland chose not to defend, which gave subtle credence to the new theory that was spinning in Maggie's head.

When the foreman had first run from Doc Maynard's out into the street, the thought had obviously not occurred to him that Maggie would do anything besides wait in the doorway for him to come back. That might account for the look of annoyance on his face when she caught up with him, which she had mistakenly attributed to his messy splash through the puddle.

Had she not been following him, Cleveland might have seen his chase through to its desired conclusion. Collaring the boy in her presence, however, would have been awkward. For whatever reason, he had intended his pursuit and capture of the young Indian to be a private affair, a plan that her own tenacity had just squelched.

The blunt intrusion of the foreman's voice on her speculations jolted Maggie back to reality.

"I'm gettin' out of this rain," he snapped. "Do whatever the hell you want."

What Maggie *wanted*, of course, was to find out who the boy was, why he was following her, and most of all, what Cleveland's business with him was. Surely the foreman had to be acting on Channing's direct orders.

Without Cleveland accompanying her, however— Maggie stopped herself in mid-thought, struck by the irony that while his hulking presence might keep her safe from unseen attackers, she certainly might not be safe from Cleveland himself.

If Channing wanted the boy that badly, Maggie thought with a chill, there could only be one logical reason why.

To her relief, she and Cleveland managed to keep their contact with each other minimal upon their return to the tunnels for the rest of the afternoon. Even her usual announcement that she was taking a short break upstairs failed to elicit his usual offer of company.

"Please be there this time," she anxiously prayed under her breath a few minutes later as she waited in the phone booth for Troy's answering machine to pick up. "Please . . ."

"So how was the big lunch date?" he asked when he came on the line. "Did you save me a coaster?"

In light of all that had transpired to distract her since she left the Pacific Crabhouse with Twylar, it took Maggie a moment to recognize that the detective's levity was a result of their previous conversation, to convince her that they could be just friends.

"Lunch was okay. Listen, I don't have a lot of time." Indifferent as Cleveland had been to her leaving he still could decide to take a trip up to street level himself. "Can you do something for me?"

"What's wrong?"

"I'm not sure, but there's something I need you to check out right away."

"About Channing?"

"No, it's about that Indian boy I told you I keep seeing, the one who's been following me?"

"What about him?"

Maggie repeated what had happened at Doc Maynard's, ending with the address of the building where the boy had disappeared.

"He probably just cut through an alleyway to the other side," Troy said.

"Or back down to the tunnels."

"Either way, it sounds like you wouldn't have caught up with him. I'm not sure what you want me to do."

"Would you laugh if I said trust my intuition?"

"I think you know me better than that, Maggie. I'd never laugh at anything that you thought was serious."

"I think it could be serious enough to get him killed," Maggie said. "And I don't believe for two seconds that it has anything to do with a couple of tools missing from the tunnels."

"What *do* you believe?"

Maggie took a deep breath. "I think he saw something five years ago that he wasn't supposed to. Why else would Channing want him caught?"

"I hope," Troy said, "that you didn't repeat that theory to your burly buddy."

"Of course not." Maggie felt herself fidgeting, impatient for the detective to take the ball and run with it. "So what do you think?"

"At this point? Unfortunately . . ." he trailed off.

"Another wild goose chase?"

"That, and not enough hours in the day, babe. Unless you've got something a little more substantial to go on, I could be looking for Indians from now until Christmas. He's not exactly the only one running loose in Seattle, in case you hadn't noticed."

"In other words—"

"In other words," Troy said with a sigh, "tell me again what the kid was wearing. Maybe one of the patrol guys saw him and can help me out on this."

"I thought you just agreed it was a wild goose chase."

"Let's just say I don't want to see your own get cooked," he replied. "And you're getting damned close enough for that to happen."

Whatever it was that had prompted Channing to call her that morning was obviously not critical enough for him to try a second time. As she returned to Lynx Bay late in the afternoon, it occurred to her that she didn't even know whether he had been to the mainland or stayed behind on the island all day, cynically nursing his wounds of rejection from the previous evening.

His whereabouts and his feelings, of course, were not of primary concern to Maggie at that moment. Anxious to be alone and to assimilate what she had learned that day, she took the steps to her bedroom two at a time.

As her hand touched the knob, however, the sound of a drawer sliding shut on the other side warned her that the room wasn't as empty as she had left it.

40

From Maggie's viewpoint, the most disconcerting thing about the intruder's reaction to her arrival
was the total lack of fear or embarrassment at being
caught. Anyone else, she thought, would have at least
exhibited some outward show of guilt—a blush or a
stammering explanation.

"Mind telling me what you were doing just now?"
Maggie demanded, seething with anger that truly nothing was safe from Derek Channing's pervasive nosiness
and sense of control.

SkySet merely smiled at her and proceeded to cross
toward the door, her secret business with Maggie's
dresser drawers obviously concluded.

That the room was impeccably tidy and not strewn
with overturned furniture and piles of ransacked
belongings did not lessen the disturbing reality that
Maggie's privacy had been violated. And it had to
have been at the behest of the man whose advances

she had rejected less than twenty-four hours ago.

"I wouldn't be in such a hurry to leave if I were you," Maggie said, standing in the doorway to SkySet's departure. "I want to know what you were looking for."

The housekeeper regarded her with a look of puzzlement.

"That's a pretty convincing act," Maggie said, her tone still relatively civil in spite of her escalating emotional level. "Unfortunately, I think we both know that that's all it is—an act you've perfected for my benefit."

There still remained no reaction on the Indian woman's leathery, age-lined face.

"I already *know* that you can speak English," Maggie went on. "So why don't you give me an answer in it and save us both some time?"

Had he been there to say something, she knew Troy McCormick would have disapproved of the current tack she was taking. Showing all her cards, he had already warned, would leave her without any aces down the road when it really counted.

The fact remained, though, that Troy wasn't there to advise her in times like this, much less to protect her when she felt she most needed him. It was more her own judgment than his resources that kept her safe and just steps ahead of a ruthless enemy.

"I'll stand here all day if I have to," Maggie told the housekeeper. "Are you going to tell me or not?"

The next voice to speak, however, wasn't SkySet's.

Oddly enough, Maggie sensed that he was behind her even before he said anything.

"Is there a problem, madam?" Brecht curtly inquired.

Maggie felt her composure slip for an instant, though it was not from the man's silent arrival nor his intercession on the housekeeper's behalf.

As she turned to address him, Maggie's thoughts were pulled back to what Twylar had shared at lunch about the bodyguard's life before Derek, freezing on her lips what would ordinarily have been a snappy retort in response to his question. *It's just Brecht being a snoop again,* she reminded herself. And yet it was not the same Brecht she had been watched by since the start of summer.

That he had ever been anything other than Channing's loyal servant would not have occurred to her prior to the exporter's story, nor would she have fathomed on her own the peculiar circumstances which had brought the two men together as lifelong friends. Accustomed as Maggie was to his one-dimensional role as the resident heavy, his past now seemed to contradict all her expectations of him in the present. For difficult as it was to accept, Brecht's personal claim to sorrow seemed even deeper than her own, and his true vulnerability must have been hidden behind the polished guise of a professional bully.

With his next words, however, the familiar persona of a man in full control returned.

"This seems to be your day for confrontations," he said sharply.

"And it seems to be SkySet's day for being in the wrong room."

Brecht inclined his head toward the housekeeper before murmuring a string of words that Maggie didn't understand.

"I've already asked her in English," Maggie informed him.

Brecht arched a brow. "And what was her answer?"

"That's what I've been waiting for."

"Unless you speak her language, I should think you'd have a long wait."

SkySet cast a quick glance at Maggie before answering Brecht in her native tongue.

Satisfied with her response, the bodyguard offered a translation. "She laundered your clothes," he said. "You'll find them in the proper drawers where they belong."

"And what will I find missing?" Maggie challenged them both, in spite of the fact that the housekeeper's hands were empty and her dress contained no visible pockets.

"Perhaps you should take up your concerns with Mr. Channing."

"Fine. Just let me know when he gets back."

Brecht's impenetrable expression unnerved her. "You'll find him downstairs. I came to tell you he's been waiting for you."

As she approached the closed double doors to the room where she and Channing had first met, Maggie was already replaying every past confrontation with him in her head. A disturbing pattern was evident, one that seemed designed to keep her perpetually off balance.

Time and again, she had challenged his authority and attempted to cover her tracks with elaborate lies. "You're going to get yourself fired," Troy had warned her, cautioning her that the only way she'd be able to learn anything would be if she lived by Channing's rules and suppressed her zeal to be the next Nancy Drew.

Time and again, however, the man had done the opposite of what one would expect. Instead of firing her for her duplicity, he had chosen to bring it to her attention and then let it go. That he knew her real identity and even hinted at why she might be in Seattle was even more perplexing.

"You're sure he doesn't know you're working for us?" Troy had asked her recently, reminding her that the loss of her cover would put her in more danger than she could imagine.

"How could he?" Maggie had said. "I'm being careful."

With a man like Derek Channing, though, she already knew that one could never be careful enough.

She knocked on the door twice and entered the room without waiting for an answer.

Channing glanced over at her from where he leaned on one corner of the partners desk, his lips parted as if he had just been about to respond to the knock.

Maggie's eyes, though, were instantly riveted on the woman who occupied the chair in front of him, casually withdrawing her jeweled hand from Channing's knee.

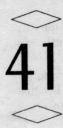

41

Lynne-Mae's lilting salutation seemed as phony to Maggie as Channing's air of detached innocence. Was it a deliberate flaunt of their relationship, she wondered, or did they really believe that she was still oblivious as to how things stood between them?

The sour remembrance of what had nearly happened the previous, stormy evening in Derek Channing's arms was only made worse now by the irony that it was his mistress' phone call that had preempted anything further—the same mistress who was occupying a place at his desk as if she owned it . . . and him.

"We were just talking about you!" Lynne-Mae exclaimed through red lips as exquisitely perfect as the tailored suit that matched them in shade.

"Then don't let me stop you," Maggie replied with as much cool grace as she could muster.

Channing's resonant voice stopped her before she could retrace even one of her steps to the hall.

"Is something wrong, Maggie?"

Aware of the dull ache of memory that his very nearness conjured, all she wanted at that moment was to be as far away as possible from Lynx Bay and everything associated with it. Of course, Channing probably knew that and relished the fact that his backstage maneuvers in her life had put him in complete domination of it.

"Nothing that can't wait until later."

"If the two of you need to be alone—" Lynne-Mae started to offer, but Derek was already responding to Maggie's statement.

"Not the way you just burst in," he said. "You look like you've either got wild bears after you or the house is on fire."

"If the house were on fire," Maggie answered, "I'm sure Brecht would have been here already to tell you." And if bears were after her, she added to herself, Channing probably couldn't have cared less, as his concentration was occupied elsewhere.

Lynne-Mae gracefully uncrossed her right leg and leaned forward as if to rise from the chair. "I really should be getting back, Derek," she said. "We can always continue this some other time."

"Oh, don't leave on my account," Maggie insisted, hating them both for continuing their calm charade. She hated herself as well that it should even matter to her that Channing and Lynne-Mae were lovers.

"Nonsense," Channing said to Lynne-Mae, before looking back at Maggie and delivering an unexpected bombshell. "Anything you have to say, I'm sure you can say in front of my partner."

It took her a moment for the last word to sink in. "Partner?" Maggie repeated.

The word apparently surprised Lynne-Mae as well, though not in the same way. "You hadn't told her?" she asked Channing.

"Watching Maggie play detective and discover things herself is far more amusing," Channing replied. "Obviously, this wasn't one she already knew."

Maggie was as irritated by his tone as she was apprehensive about his use of the word "detective." Exhibiting a candor she didn't feel inside, Maggie chose to take the offensive.

"So what's this big secret I'm in the dark about?" she countered. "That you and Mrs. Barstow are more than just friends?" Her emphasis on the title "Mrs." conveyed no doubt as to the assumption she had drawn about the two people in front of her.

Channing's folded arms and half-smile only exacerbated the situation.

"As a matter of fact, we are," he replied. "Although I think the conclusions you've jumped to about us could stand for a little enlightenment."

"Derek and I have been business associates ever since the project began," Lynne-Mae said, resting her hand on the desk just inches from Channing's thigh. "The support of my museum was what he needed to get the final clearances to proceed."

"Which," Derek added, "makes the museum the recipient of whatever I dig up."

They're lying, Maggie's intuition warned her. She kept glancing at the other woman's hand, imagining where it would travel if Lynne-Mae and Channing were alone.

"My own reputation is on the line for this, Maggie," Lynne-Mae continued. "Not even my own husband thought this was a very wise investment of time or money."

Not to mention the daily involvement with a man as sensually lethal as Derek Channing, Maggie added mentally. That they could both sit there and feign a casual and chaste relationship in front of her was an insult to her intelligence.

Channing seemed to be reading her mind. "If I'd known we were also having an affair," he said to Lynne-Mae with a wink, "I would have called you more often when Pete was out of town."

The woman's serious reply caught Maggie off guard. "I don't think that this is something to joke about, Derek, especially under the circumstances."

Channing nodded. "I defer to your judgment on it, then." Obviously Lynne-Mae held a power over him that Maggie had never imagined anyone could.

"By the way," he said, turning back to Maggie, "what was it you were going to say when you came in? You never did get around to it."

"I just caught your housekeeper going through my things."

Channing arched a brow. "Oh?"

His one syllable response irritated her. "I feel I'm entitled to some degree of privacy while I'm here."

"A reasonable request," Channing agreed, "in spite of the fact that you have yet to show any reciprocation of it."

Maggie felt herself color, embarrassed that his comment not only rang with truth but that he had said it in front of a third party.

"So is anything missing?" he inquired. "I assume that you're making an accusation of theft against SkySet?"

"I . . . haven't had a chance to check," she replied, conscious of how many notches her bravado had slipped since she first came into the room. Impulse, she realized, was about to cost her another admonishment. "Brecht interrupted before I had any opportunity to look for myself."

"The plot thickens," Channing said with a smirk. "So Brecht is implicated in this, too?"

Maggie's anger was returning, fueled by his indifference to her complaint. "He asked her what she was doing there," Maggie snapped. "Obviously, my English wasn't clear enough for the woman to understand."

"Oh, I think we've already established that she understands everything and then some," Channing replied. "How and when she chooses to speak our language is entirely up to her."

"Because of me?"

Channing's eyes narrowed. "You flatter yourself, Maggie. Your arrival here has done nothing to change our routine except to introduce disruption."

Lynne-Mae touched Channing's forearm as if to warn him from saying something he might regret.

"If SkySet dislikes English," he continued, rising from the corner of the desk, "maybe it's because it's the language of the men who raped her when she was a girl."

Stunned by his revelation, Maggie was unable to think of anything to say.

"As for anyone searching your room," he went on, sliding open the center drawer of the opposite side of the desk, "I think that finding *this* already told me everything I needed to know."

He was holding her father's letter.

42

Maggie paled. The damning evidence of her true reason for being at Lynx Bay was now in the enemy's possession.

"I assume that you recognize this," he said, fixing his icy blue gaze on her.

Neither a denial nor a confession would vanquish the fear that gripped her. Like a cobra poised to strike, Channing was waiting for her to say something, relishing his own act of triumph.

"You do recognize this, don't you?" he asked, seeming hardly aware that Lynne-Mae was even in the room.

Maggie met his accusing eyes without flinching. "Yes," she replied. "I recognize it."

She knew that within the next few seconds he was going to demand an explanation of the words her father had penned before his death. And he would demand to know not only how she had come by it but what she intended to do about it now, five years after the fact. Maggie could only stare, dumbstruck, at the manila envelope she had taken such pains to hide on her first evening at Lynx Bay. She had not even known until that very moment that it was missing. Because of Brecht's vigilant watching of her every move, she had been wary of constantly checking on the letter to decrease the chances of being observed.

Troy, of course, had advised her against taking it with her to Lynx Bay in the first place. "I'll hold it for you myself," he had offered. "You're as good as dead in the water if Channing or his lackey runs across it."

For reasons purely superstitious, however, Maggie had declined, viewing her father's last written words as a talisman to protect her in an unfamiliar environment. In retrospect, Maggie realized that Troy knew their enemy better than she did, and that it had been a mistake to keep the letter anywhere in the house. What disturbed her further was just how long Channing had kept the letter's discovery to himself.

"I suppose," Channing said, "that I should give you credit for being clever. Most people wouldn't have chosen a place quite that inaccessible."

Maggie cast a glance at Lynne-Mae, though she knew better than to expect any helpful intervention from the woman. Channing's exotic visitor probably wasn't hearing anything she didn't already know.

"Most people," he continued, "have probably also never experienced a housekeeper as thorough in her work as SkySet. Just because an armoire is too tall for someone to see the top of it doesn't mean that it shouldn't be as well dusted as the rest of the furniture."

Maggie finally found the voice to issue the only retort she could think of. "Good help *is* hard to find."

The line of Channing's mouth tightened a fraction. "So are people that you can trust."

Maggie braced herself for what she knew was coming, knowing that she had no ready lie or excuse. For all of the scenarios and Plan Bs that she had carefully rehearsed in her head, this—unfortunately—had never been one of them.

Neither was what Channing did next.

"I'd better see to SkySet," he announced, tossing the envelope on the surface of the desk and moving toward the open doors. "I'm sure your accusations have upset her."

Just short of Maggie, he stopped.

"For a smart woman," he remarked, "you have an uncommon knack sometimes for missing the obvious."

He was gone before she could ask him what he meant—if indeed she could have forced the question from her lips at all—closing the doors behind him and leaving her alone with Lynne-Mae.

Stunned by his bluntness and the awkward situation in which he had just thrust her, Maggie wished herself invisible.

Lynne-Mae's voice—reserved and elegant— delicately broke the silence.

"That was handled very badly," she said.

The understated but nonetheless certain chord of censure in her voice reminded Maggie of their roles in the triangular relationship.

"On his part or mine?" she asked.

Lynne-Mae contemplated her for a minute. "While my friendship with Derek is obviously the longer," she replied at last, "it doesn't blind me to his treatment of other people. There were better ways that he could have broached the subject with you. I apologize that he didn't use one of them."

"I assume, then, that I'm the proverbial last to know?" Maggie asked, unable to dispel the belief that Lynne-Mae was Channing's mistress.

Lynne-Mae was serene and totally unflappable. "If I knew what you were really asking, Maggie, perhaps I could answer what you want to know."

Maggie slowly crossed toward the desk and stared down at the envelope before leaning forward to retrieve it, unable to fathom why Channing had left it behind instead of taking it with him.

"Did he show it to you?" she asked.

Lynne-Mae nodded. "Almost three weeks ago."

Three weeks. "Why did he wait so long to say something, then?"

She wasn't expecting an answer, of course. Anyone who knew Derek Channing to any degree knew that the pace he set was entirely predicated on his desire to keep the opposition guessing.

The Asian woman issued a half smile. "One might ask you why you waited five years to come to Seattle."

Had the letter truly fallen into Maggie's hands five years ago, she would have caught the first plane to the West Coast and not left until the investigation laid to final rest all the questions behind her father's accident. But the police themselves hadn't known of the letter's existence until its anonymous mailing just months ago.

"Why *did* you wait so long?" Lynne-Mae asked.

"I guess we all have our reasons," Maggie replied, still wary of telling Lynne-Mae the truth.

"I'd just think that when he had mailed it to you, you would have been out here much sooner to square the record."

"What makes you say that?"

Lynne-Mae's dark eyes glinted. "Because great minds run in the same circles."

43

To hear her father's echo in the voice of strangers twice in one day was almost more coincidence than Maggie could reasonably handle.

"An original philosophy of yours?" she asked.

"Borrowed from an old friend," Lynne-Mae replied.

"Oh?"

"An original thinker very much like you, in fact. Always ready to take a different path and defy convention, yet keep returning to the issues and values that really matter."

"I'd take that as a compliment except for one thing."

"And what's that?" Lynne-Mae gracefully rested her arm on the polished surface of the desk as if she had no immediate plans to return to the mainland, much less to her husband.

"This is only the third time that you and I have even met," Maggie said. She thought of what she had just learned from Ken Cleveland a few hours before, that

Lynne-Mae had not only known Maggie's father on a professional level but had spent quite a few weeks at his side down in the tunnels.

"Only the third?" Lynne-Mae repeated, a delicate black brow arched in astonishment. "It seems like I've known you much longer."

"Not nearly long enough," Maggie continued, "to really know what I'm like."

"Perhaps I should rephrase that, then," she said. "I've known *about* you much longer."

"From Channing?"

"No. From your father."

Maggie's mouth dropped open, and Lynne-Mae smiled enigmatically but said nothing for a few minutes. Then she began to explain.

They had first met at a commission meeting, to which he had accompanied Channing to demystify the aspects of engineering for lay people whose influence could facilitate the project's future.

"He never liked making presentations, though," Maggie said, puzzled by Lynne-Mae's sudden willingness to open up.

"It was being the center of attention, I think. But for Derek, he would have done anything."

Anything, Maggie thought, *except sit back and watch him break the law*.

"I don't think I'd ever seen someone quite so swept up in a goal as your father," Lynne-Mae went on. "Or quite as awed by the man he was working for." She smiled wistfully. "A lot of people try to curry favor with Derek by feigning admiration. Your father wasn't one of them, Maggie. Just one look at him and you could tell that his respect came straight from the heart." Even her husband, she added, had noticed that.

As Lynne-Mae continued her story, Maggie's thoughts flitted back to the various letters and calls she and her father had exchanged during his first months in Seattle. Indeed, she recalled, it was as if her father had found gainful and happy employment on Mount Olympus as a water boy to the gods. It was always "Derek this" and "Derek that" to the point where he even hinted that Maggie should fly out and meet the resident Adonis who lived on his very own island.

Much to her father's disappointment, however, she had always declined, saying that she couldn't take time from her job or other commitments. In truth, of course, she wanted no part of his matchmaking, not to mention that it might have had ramifications on the association of the two men themselves.

Of course, Clayton Price had undoubtedly been just as busy selling her good points to his boss as he'd been pitching Derek to her. When she had voiced this concern to Troy he had assured her that Channing took little interest in the private lives of his employees. "If he knew your dad even had a daughter," he said, "I'm sure it's been long forgotten after all this time."

Maggie turned her attention back to the present, conscious of the brooding portraits of Channing men who surrounded her in the study.

"Your father had a way of explaining technical things," Lynne-Mae was saying, "that made them easy to understand." While well versed in the Chinese history and culture that was being unearthed beneath the streets of Pioneer Square, her knowledge of the excavation process was lacking until Clayton's invitation to see it firsthand. "Pete, of course, was aghast when I told him about my new obsession."

For an instant Maggie wondered whether she was referring to her sewer treks or her blossoming friendship with the lead engineer. And perhaps, she speculated, if it were the latter and Pete had been jealous . . .

Lynne-Mae's undisguised enthusiasm for the tunnels cut into Maggie's inner dialogue.

"It doesn't seem like your kind of place," Maggie remarked, recalling Cleveland's own description of her as the "ice queen."

Lynne-Mae acknowledged her remark with a tilt of her head. "To use your own words, this is only the third time you and I have spoken. There's a great deal about me, Maggie, that you don't know." The fringe of her lashes cast shadows on her cheeks. "There's also a great deal you don't know about Derek."

They were returning to territory in which Maggie felt uncomfortable, and Lynne-Mae's remark triggered a host of memories that she would have preferred not to have. Memories of desire that couldn't be reconciled with her escalating suspicions. Memories of Lynne-Mae's silvery laugh and the meaningful glances exchanged between her and Channing. Even if his relationship with the enigmatic Mrs. Barstow was as platonic as he claimed, there still remained his lies about the other woman who had shared his last name and whose body lay buried on the island.

"I may be out of place to say so," Lynne-Mae continued quietly, "but I've known Derek a number of years. We've seen each other through difficult times in the past, and—"

"Please!" Maggie interrupted her. "Whatever you were going to say—"

"I *am* going to say it," Lynne-Mae firmly insisted

without raising her voice, "because I think you need to hear it from someone who knows him as well as I do."

"Hear what?"

"Derek isn't the cold-blooded monster that you seem to think he is."

"And what about *this*?" Maggie challenged, indicating the envelope in her hands. "If Derek Channing were such a saint, why would my father have written the opposite?"

Lynne-Mae's answer came without hesitation. "I have no reason to believe that he *did* write that letter, Maggie. And neither should you."

44

"*Are you saying* that I don't know my own father's handwriting?" Maggie shot back.

"The man *I* knew," Lynne-Mae replied, "would never have turned that way against Derek."

"And how well was that?" Maggie demanded, dreading to hear confirmed what Cleveland had implied, that it had been a rich woman's dalliance with a convenient stranger to ease the boredom of life with a husband whose passions were limited to politics and food. While she could forgive her father his weakness and attraction to a woman as appealing as Lynne-Mae, the notion of the latter using him as a diversion or a catalyst for jealousy made Maggie angry beyond words.

Lynne-Mae's right hand was gracefully poised on top of her left, camouflaging the subtle act of rotating her wedding band.

"How well *did* you know my father?" Maggie repeated.

"Well enough to know he was totally incapable of such hateful accusations."

Their conversation ended there—cut short by Lynne-Mae's need to return to the mainland—and it was this final, peculiar exchange that remained at the forefront of Maggie's memory almost an hour and a half later.

To say that nothing made sense to her anymore was an understatement. Predispositions she had carried at the beginning were being twisted left and right, altering reality into a carnival funhouse mirror in which nothing was true or recognizable, save for the enduring fact that her father was dead and buried.

Even Troy McCormick—the alleged hero who was only a telephone call away—harbored secrets, the biggest one being why his research had not revealed some of the very things she had literally tripped over as an amateur detective.

Her puzzlement about Troy was overshadowed by the mystery of how much more Channing still knew and had not yet revealed. Based on his pattern of revealing his knowledge only when it suited him, it was not beyond reason that he had known from the very start that Maggie was working for the police—and moreover, that he suspected her motives to implicate him in the murder of Clayton Price.

What didn't make sense, though, was why he would continue to keep her close to the Pioneer Square operations and to his personal life. Even their last altercation in the study—witnessed by Lynne-Mae—had not closed with the outcome she had expected, of her being told to collect her belongings and leave Lynx Bay immediately. Until otherwise advised, she had to assume that she was still a full-paid employee.

Were his lies so seamless, she wondered, that he feared no repercussions from her or anyone else?

Or was he a man who truly had nothing sinister to hide?

Maggie shuddered at the latter possibility. She was as overwhelmed by its capacity to refute her bitter assumption of five years as she was anxious to validate that her father's esteem for Derek Channing had not been grossly misplaced.

At odds with virtually all of the household and possessing no appetite for the dinner whose aroma was curling its way upstairs from the kitchen, Maggie grabbed a sweater and flashlight and set out on a walk, resolved to let physical exertion wipe out the stress of too many taxing mind games against players who were obvious pros.

While a number of paths crisscrossed their way along the shoreline and into the island's interior, it did not take Maggie long to realize that she was following the same one she had taken with Derek on her first evening at Lynx Bay.

Vexed that, even absent, he was exerting influence on her power of choice, she purposely stepped off the path and onto the flat gray rocks whose surface was dusted with deposits of sand and slimy kelp offered up by the Sound with each tide.

True to the weather report's prediction, the sky carried a renewed threat of rain. Maggie sighed. Another storm. Another night of wondering where exactly her life was taking her.

If only the next island weren't so far away. And if only she had never come to the Pacific Northwest to begin with.

Troy's arguments, of course, had been persuasive. "We'll get Channing eventually," he had assured her. "But we'll nail him faster with your help."

There was also no denying that investigation of the matter was what her father would have wanted. Hadn't he implied as much in the letter, the last words that he had written before the accident?

"Where did you get this?" she had asked Troy back in Boston, incredulous that the wayward correspondence had taken years to reach its intended destination. "It's dated the day before his death."

"It was sent in a separate envelope to the Seattle P.D. a couple of months ago," Troy had explained. "No return address. Only a King County postmark. Doesn't tell us a damn thing except that it was mailed locally." Even that, he had told Maggie, could have been a ruse to throw them off.

"So where has it been all this time?"

Troy had hesitated in his response, a hesitation that—upon reflection—she now recognized as his reluctance to cause her any more pain.

"Your father," he'd said at last, "must have entrusted the letter to someone else—maybe a good friend, or someone he worked with—to mail to you in the event that—well, in case anything happened to him."

The supposition had disturbed her when she'd first heard it and disturbed her even more now, having met the diverse characters who had peopled her father's world. That someone had been trusted with such incriminating evidence against Derek Channing and then had broken the promise to deliver it was difficult to stomach.

"Channing's influence can buy whatever he wants," Troy had said. "Obviously it bought someone's silence."

"That doesn't make sense, though," Maggie had protested. "If Channing knew the damn thing existed, how did it ever get mailed to the police five years after the fact?"

Troy didn't have an answer for her.

"All we can assume," he finally said, "is that a guilty conscience finally caught up with whoever it was your father trusted with that letter. Either that, or they got screwed by Channing for something unrelated and want to nail him now as much as we do."

Troy's reply pounded in her head as she headed into the woods.

Brecht and SkySet were obvious candidates she could eliminate from the list of people who might have mailed the letter. So, too, was Lynne-Mae. While her actual association with Clayton Price remained undefinable, her loyalty to Derek was certainly unquestionable.

Pete Barstow, on the other hand, could be an adversary of the millionaire. Hadn't he opposed Lynne-Mae's support of the project, citing it a foolish risk? If he *did* harbor resentment for the time she continued to invest in Channing's enterprise, a police investigation would not only threaten to shut down the project but also complicate the charmed life of a man his wife so clearly admired.

Ken Cleveland? He had worked under Maggie's father and perhaps been privy to the older man's secrets. If his promotion after Clayton's death had been enough to buy his silence, though, what had then prompted him to break it five years later and tip off the police? His pursuit of the Indian boy at Channing's behest was another mystery, unless Cleveland had switched loyalties again in midstream and was newly pledged to protect his boss.

Twylar Zarzy was an enigma as well. His eagerness to talk to Maggie and his obvious gratitude to Channing as a friend weren't the fodder of any long-standing feud. Had Clayton Price entrusted him with the letter, it would have been with faith that Twylar would not disappoint him. Maggie scowled when she remembered that, to her knowledge, the two men had never even met. If they had, her father had never deemed it important enough to mention to her.

As she looked up, a deeper furrow creased her brow. Too absorbed in her speculations to pay attention to where she was going, she discovered that her feet had taken her into the forest clearing and just a few paces from the grave of Fiona Channing.

Maggie stiffened when she saw that someone else was already there.

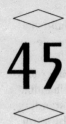

45

"*I had a feeling* you might come this way," Channing said.

Just like you know about everything else, Maggie wanted to retort, but she held her tongue.

With his hands thrust deep in the pockets of a light parka that matched his eyes, he tilted his head as he studied her. "I also had a feeling—obviously unfounded—that you might catch the boat back to the mainland with Lynne-Mae."

"Like a prisoner escaping Alcatraz?"

"From what I've read about it, their success rate for seizing freedom wasn't very high." He frowned. "Is that really the way you see yourself, Maggie? As a prisoner?"

Maggie glanced down at the grave and then back up at Channing. "Did *she?*"

"What do *you* think? I'd be interested to hear what kind of farfetched conclusions you've come to."

"Dull, I'm afraid, compared to your own caliber of fiction."

As her response brought a tightening to his jaw, Maggie suddenly felt conscious of the isolated surroundings and the imminent danger that his presence now posed. She had gone too far, her conscience warned her, her insatiable curiosity trespassing on more than just the burial site of someone he had loved. A man like Channing, she realized, would never stand for being called a liar to his face. But since it was too late to retract her reply or say anything to appease his ego, she could only wait and see his reaction.

"Fiction?" Channing repeated as if it were a foreign word he'd never heard before. "Care to be more specific?"

They stared at each other across the grave. "You're standing in front of evidence that disputes *one* of your claims," she finally found the voice to say.

"Meaning?"

"You said you'd never been married."

"You have an odd fixation on my marital status," Channing observed. "Why is the answer so important for you to know?"

Maggie chose not to address his hint that a personal attraction on her part was behind her probe of his background.

"Well?" he pressed. "Why?"

"Because if you'd lie about *that*, I suspect you'd lie about anything else." For an instant, her mind flashed back to her father, back to his mission to bring the two of them together for a happily ever after. Not once had he mentioned that Channing was a widower, she recalled. Was it because Channing had never shared it with *him*? Or because, as Channing himself maintained, a marriage had never existed?

By quick calculation Maggie realized that Fiona would have been dead only six months when Clayton Price took his position as foreman. Even if Channing had never broached the subject of her death himself, Maggie thought, six months would have been fresh enough in the minds of the underground crew for someone to have mentioned it in passing. And yet, if they had, surely her father would have told her.

"What makes you so certain that I've lied to you at all, Maggie?" Channing asked, his face bathed in the shadows.

"The name Channing isn't obvious enough?"

"There are other ways that she could have come by the same surname than being my wife. I don't suppose that possibility has occurred to you?"

"How? By being a kid sister you've conveniently never bothered to mention?"

"No," Derek replied. "By being married to my poor excuse for a brother." Before Maggie could respond, he went on to deliver the equally startling balance of his long-kept secret. "Fiona was SkySet's daughter."

After Maggie recovered from her initial shock, Channing proceeded to tell her SkySet's story.

Pregnant from a brutal rape by one of the mainland gangs, SkySet had found herself as victimized by the judicial system as by her attackers. Inaccessibility to medical care, compounded by the shame she had brought to her people and her family, had left the Indian woman fearful and desperate. She had even contemplated suicide, deeming herself unworthy to live any longer.

It was the unborn life she carried inside of her, however, that had ultimately made her decision. Certain that the spirits would never forgive the selfish taking of a soul so innocent as a child's, she had forced herself to go on.

"A lot of women in her predicament would have crumbled by their first trimester," Channing said.

Maggie was reminded of an earlier comment he had made, praising SkySet as a good woman. "Faith can pull people through a lot," she said, "even when it's the only thing left to hold on to."

"SkySet was fortunate," Channing continued, "to have a Caucasian ally to hang on to as well."

"You?"

"No, our alliance began much later," he replied. "Her real friend was a volunteer at the Settlement House." One of several programs offering meals and counseling to Indians, he explained, it had attracted the generosity of several prominent Seattle matrons, among them a woman who had befriended SkySet from their first day of meeting.

"While her husband wasn't keen on the idea of her getting so personally involved," Channing went on, "he also wasn't about to stand in his wife's way—that's how much he adored her. By the time SkySet's baby was born, he had even agreed to let her use his wife's maiden name as a surname on the birth certificate."

"What about 'Fiona'?" Maggie asked, conscious that a light rain had just started to fall. "You'd think that at least the first name—"

"—would be Indian?" Channing finished her sentence. "SkySet had experienced enough prejudice in her own life that she wanted her daughter to assimilate to life in a white man's world as easily as possible. 'Fiona,' as I understand it, was the name of the heroine in a book her benefactress was reading at the time."

Channing tilted his head toward the ominous sky. "We should get back."

Maggie nodded, wondering whether it was the rain that concerned him or the eeriness of discussing someone who lay buried only a few feet below them.

"So what happened to these people?" she asked.

"Up until about ten years ago, she was *their* housekeeper," he replied. "Fiona—for her own good—had been sent to a boarding school."

"For her own good?"

"You find that strange?"

"I'd think she'd want to be close to her mother instead of off at school with strangers."

"SkySet was doing what she thought best, although in the end I'm not sure it would have mattered one way or the other. There was also the fact that Fiona was a handful to begin with."

The distant rumble of thunder made them both pause. "As usual," he commented on her lack of an umbrella, "I see you're not prepared."

"A little rain never killed anyone."

They made their way in silence down the hill toward the beach.

"So what happened ten years ago?" Maggie asked, vaguely recalling that a decade was how long Channing had once mentioned the Indian housekeeper had worked for him.

"Ten years ago," he replied, "the woman who had given SkySet more hope than she had ever dreamed of was killed in an automobile accident in France."

Maggie's mouth dropped open, astonished by what Channing had just revealed. "Twylar's wife?"

"Yes," he said. "Twylar's wife."

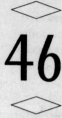

46

Maggie recalled Twylar's remarks at lunch about the young girl whose education and upbringing he and his wife had financed. What was it that he had said? Something about Fiona not being in Channing's life at the time he flew to France?

Though she couldn't recall the exact words, she did remember the tone in which it was delivered, which now made sense in the context of a guardianship he had entered against his desire. Absent a wife with a fondness for attaching herself to strays, Twylar must have wanted to free his life of painful reminders. SkySet and her daughter had obviously been two of them.

"Looks like we're due for another good one tonight," Channing commented on the approaching storm. "Thank goodness one of us has the sense to come in out of the rain."

Maggie ignored his dig. "So how did *you* get SkySet and Fiona?" she asked.

"A solo arrangement to begin with," he answered. "Twylar was closing up the house and had no more need of a housekeeper's services. I took SkySet on the condition he'd make other plans for her if she didn't work out to my satisfaction."

"Obviously she did."

"A man would be a fool *not* to be pleased with her," he said.

"And Fiona?"

"SkySet kept her over on the mainland the first year until—well, until she decided it would be better to put her into other surroundings."

"What was the problem?"

Even in the darkness, she could sense that Channing was amused. "Are all of these questions a ploy, Ms. Price, to keep the focus off of some unresolved issues between you and me?"

"You continue to answer them," Maggie pointed out.

"So I do," he said. "What was your question again?"

"Fiona. What was wrong that SkySet wanted to move her?"

"Peer influence. The last year of formal school had turned the girl into a flake. Not to mention a flirt. There had already been suggestions on the part of the faculty that she didn't have the grades to graduate. SkySet was understandably upset."

"And so you brought her out here?"

"Whatever the girl's proclivity for mischief, her mother and I both knew the kind of trouble she'd be headed for if she stayed on the mainland."

They were almost in sight of the house.

Before she could ask her next question, Channing was already supplying the answer.

"How could I have known, that more trouble than

any of us could have imagined was already here on the island?"

Maggie hesitated a moment before venturing what the trouble might have been. "Your brother?"

In the darkness, Channing's voice had taken on an icy tone. "You'll forgive me if David's not my favorite subject. Why don't we change it?"

No! Maggie wanted to scream, irritated that the rug kept being pulled out from under her every time she got close enough to learn something of value. "I didn't know that you even *had* a brother," she said.

"Perhaps," he proposed, "you were too busy discounting my claim that I didn't have a wife."

Maggie was thankful for the darkness that hid her rush of color. "So your brother's name is David?"

"Like I said, he's not my favorite subject." Channing suddenly halted, distracted by the frenetic bob of a flashlight just ahead of them.

"What's that?" she started to say, but Channing was already quickening his pace to meet the approaching party.

"Excuse me, sir," Brecht said, "but there's been an incident in the tunnels. . . ."

Even if she had been able to keep up with them, the firm shutting of the study door was a definitive message that neither Channing nor Brecht wanted her included in their conversation.

Incident? It had to be some kind of code between them, Maggie figured. A word that would have profound meaning to Channing but absolutely none to her.

As she climbed the stairs to her bedroom to change out of her damp clothes, her mind was racing with possibilities. A break-in? A breakthrough? A brawl? The latter conjured the image of a drunken Ken Cleveland picking a fight with his peers.

Maggie dismissed the last scenario as quickly as it had come. The crew had all but vacated the tunnels by the time she had left that afternoon. It wouldn't have been like Cleveland to remain behind on his own. No doubt he had returned to Doc Maynard's to drink off the grudge he harbored against the female population in general and Maggie in specific.

As she pulled off her sweater, Maggie's glance gravitated toward the armoire, its great height reminding her of how clever she had fancied herself in concealing her father's letter. *Nobody is that good a housekeeper,* she thought, certain that the letter's discovery had been the result of a purposeful search and not a routine dusting.

Now that Channing knew about it, of course, there still remained the issue of what he'd do next. Fiona— not Clayton—had dominated their talk in the woods, almost suggesting that he had put the controversy aside to the point of forgetting about it.

No, her inner voice argued. A man like Derek Channing never forgot anything.

That he also didn't forget his friends was a character trait that, curiously enough, nearly moved her to tears. Both SkySet and Brecht had been revealed in a short span of hours to have had a lion's share of tragedy. And they had both emerged as thoroughly devoted allies of Channing.

Twylar Zarzy, as well, had said that he could never have handled his wife's death without Derek. Even the enigmatic Lynne-Mae, Maggie sensed, could have had her own host of troubles made lighter by Channing's intervention, thus accounting for her deep loyalty now.

Maggie reminded herself of the flip side that such altruistic acts could be hiding. Once indebted to the man for a favor, it was only a matter of time before he would return to collect on it. For those who already regarded him as a heaven-sent knight, the perpetuation of a well-placed lie would not be that heavy a price.

She had just stripped out of her jeans when a sharp knock at the door made her hastily grab them up off the bed. "Yes?" she replied, not expecting the door to open in response to her acknowledgment.

Derek's eyes locked on hers after making an inevitable sweep of her only partly clad body.

"I'm going to need you to get dressed right away and come downstairs," he informed her, exercising willpower to not let his glance fall below her face.

"Is something wrong?" Even as she said it, the irony occurred to Maggie that almost everything that had transpired that day fell under the category of being wrong.

"There was a problem in the tunnels tonight," he replied.

The *incident*. "What kind of problem?"

"We'll discuss it when you come downstairs." He was starting to pull the door closed behind him.

"Animal, vegetable, or mineral?" she asked, annoyed with his vagueness.

Channing paused a moment. "Human," he said.

"That's all you're going to tell me?"

His eyes met hers again. "Oh, there's *one* other thing," he added. "Someone from the Seattle Police Department is on his way out here."

47

Whatever Channing read into her startled reaction he kept to himself. With any luck, he'd assume that her bafflement was in response to his announcement that something was wrong at the tunnels, not that the long arm of justice was about to span Puget Sound.

"Why are they coming out in a storm?" she asked. Outside her window, the now persistent pelt of rain affirmed that she and Channing had returned to the house in just the nick of time. "Doesn't the Coast Guard discourage that kind of recklessness?"

"Apparently," Channing replied, "they don't seem to think it will keep until morning."

What the hell is going on? Maggie wanted to scream, furious with his secrecy as he closed the door firmly.

Maggie went into the bathroom and splashed cold water on her face, hoping that it would snap some sense back into a head run amok with anxiety. But the sense of uneasiness at the bottom of her heart made it impossible. As she reached for the hand towel her eyes met their reflection in the bathroom mirror.

"What have you gotten yourself into?" she murmured, recalling that she had asked the very same thing of her father's photograph on her desk back in Boston. She was no closer to an answer tonight than she had been that first afternoon when Troy came to see her.

The Seattle Police Department, she kept reminding herself as she dressed, was made up of more than one person. The likelihood of them sending the one person she happened to know was remote. Maybe they'd send just an ordinary guy to ask ordinary questions about what the crew was doing under Pioneer Square and advise that they please try to keep the noise level down. Or maybe it had something to do with export laws, she thought.

Incident. The word hammered inside her head. *Incident.* It wasn't the kind of word that one associated with a pleasant social call, conjuring instead quite the opposite. Something had happened in the tunnels that merited police involvement. Something that they were expecting Derek Channing—and possibly her—to answer for. Something that—in spite of a storm—couldn't wait until morning.

"It won't be Troy McCormick," she kept repeating under her breath, thinking back to how many times she *had* wished for his presence on the island. This evening, in contrast, he was probably the *last* person she wanted to see. Not now, anyway.

Too much had happened to her that day. Too much that she had to sort out before she could even think of facing the detective again and telling him that maybe they were wrong and had been wrong from the very beginning. Maybe Derek hadn't been involved, she'd say. Maybe the truths that she had held about the man for the past five years were the result of an adversary's well-crafted scheme to topple the Channing empire.

She could already hear McCormick's reply, the road-weary response of a policeman who had spent too many years seeing the bad side of human nature and doubting the existence of anything good.

"He got to you, too, didn't he?" he'd remark, reminding her that Channing's deadly charisma was as potent as the Midas touch. "He got to you just like everyone else. . . ."

Maggie anticipated that once he was finished telling her that she was letting emotion interfere with her judgment and responsibility, he'd take her off the case. "We'll wrap it up without you," he'd say to counter any protest that she made. "We already had enough to nail him," he'd add, reminding her of what he had said in their first meeting, that her help was needed only to speed the process.

With a shudder, Maggie wondered if that wasn't where tonight was ultimately going to lead. If McCormick was taking it upon himself to pay Channing a visit that couldn't wait until morning, it could only mean that he had found something solid enough to issue a warrant.

"And I have your assistant, Maggie Price, to thank for tipping us off," she could hear Troy proclaim with a swell of pride as he snapped a pair of handcuffs on Channing's wrists.

She could picture Channing's face if that scenario came to pass, his blue eyes penetrating hers with the hatred of a man betrayed. A man who would never forgive her for the rest of his life.

"You're free to go now," Troy would tell her.

But she already knew that the price of such freedom had been bought by something that had come to mean much more.

Her lips began to move in a silent prayer. *Please let me be wrong. Don't let it be Troy who comes here.*

Knowing that she couldn't put off going downstairs any longer, or Brecht would appear at her bedroom door to drag her by the ankles, she took a deep breath and began her descent.

The doors to the study had been left open, and the sound of Channing's voice reached her even in the hall as he spoke to an unseen visitor.

"Legally," he was saying, "we can't be held accountable for it. From a moral standpoint, however—"

"We're not talking morals here, Mr. Channing," an unfamiliar voice interrupted. The flash of relief that Maggie felt that it wasn't Troy's was quickly canceled by the man's next words. "We're talking possible homicide."

"Not from the way you've described it," Channing said. "For someone who wasn't familiar with how poorly some of those passages were supported—"

"Are you sure you wouldn't like to have one of your attorneys here?"

"Unless I'm being formally charged with something, Lieutenant, I hardly think that's necessary."

Maggie had frozen outside the door, now conscious of just what kind of "incident" had brought the police out to Lynx Bay, and conscious as well that they felt Channing had a connection to it.

Maggie hesitated where she stood, clenching her hands until her nails dug into her palms, unsure of what to do next in spite of the fact that Channing had specifically asked her to join him.

"Like I said," the man continued, "we're still working on the ID."

"There wasn't anything on him?"

"Just one thing, but so far it doesn't tell us much."

"And what's that?"

"The victim had a broken watch in his hip pocket—the novelty kind you can get personalized?"

"Shouldn't that be a clue?" Channing asked, displaying humor even under fire.

There was a long pause.

"Does the name 'Clayton' mean anything to you, Mr. Channing?"

48

The gasp that fell from Maggie's lips was just loud enough to bring Channing into the hall.

"I caught my heel on the carpet," Maggie said hastily, but in his ever-vigilant eyes she saw apology. *I wish you hadn't heard that,* they seemed to say. *I wish you had come down sooner so I could have prepared you for this.*

Whether respectful of her lie or protective of his own interests, he played along with her casting a glance downward at the allegedly faulty carpet.

"I'll remind Brecht again to get that fixed," he said, his hand just touching her elbow as if in concern for her mishap. "Are you all right?"

"And who's this?" the visitor asked as Channing escorted her into the study.

"My assistant, Margaret Johnson," he said. "She's with me for the summer."

She extended her hand in greeting to the newcomer, hoping that her surprise at Channing's use of her alias didn't show. She'd have to ask him later why he didn't say Maggie Price.

"And this," he said to her, "is Lieutenant Finch."

Finch responded with a tight smile. He was a man of Brecht's height and stocky build but with a complexion and features that were decidedly Indian. His silky black hair was combed straight back from his bronzed forehead and temples, emphasizing strong cheekbones and a clean-shaven jaw. He frankly assessed her with his penetrating black eyes.

From his neck down, however, Maggie couldn't help but note that a man of such rugged attraction could have benefited from lessons on how to dress. He wore a polyester suit that looked like it had come out of the 1960s, and a floral tie wide enough to cover Iowa. Mahogany brown cowboy boots with scuffed and pointed toes poked out from the cuffs of dull gray pants that were neither stylish nor well-fitting. She'd have to remember to ask Troy if he knew whether his co-worker had a wife who picked out his clothes or whether he alone was accountable for the display of such bad taste in fashion.

"Do you have a minute to answer some questions?" Channing asked her.

"What's going on?" she asked, hoping her voice sounded natural, trying to hide her inner distress from the detective's probing stare.

"The lieutenant is here," Channing explained, "because there seems to have been an accident down in the tunnels early this evening."

"A fatality," Finch said, openly studying Maggie for reaction. "I have a few questions I'd like to—"

"Who was it?" she asked anxiously, her thoughts still focused on the unmistakable name she had heard outside the door—the first name of her father. "Was it someone on the crew?"

"Fortunately not," Channing replied.

" 'Fortunately,' Mr. Channing?" Finch echoed. There was an arrested expression of contempt on the Indian's face. "Is the loss of a human life that insignificant to you?"

"What I meant to say," Channing responded calmly, "is that Margaret and I consider the members of the crew to be friends as well as co-workers. While the death of anyone can be deemed a tragedy, Lieutenant, I was only pointing out that we're grateful it wasn't someone with whom we had a personal association."

"To paraphrase you, then, Mr. Channing, you're happy that it wasn't one of your own kind?"

Derek regarded him with an arched brow. "I don't believe my answer needed to be paraphrased," he said, "nor is it appropriate to imply the existence of any bigotry on my part."

Finch bristled at Channing's remark. "Negligence is the real issue here."

"Then let's stick to the real issue, shall we?"

Angry at being ignored, Maggie plunged back into the conversation. "Would one of you please tell me what's going on?"

Channing drew a deep breath before replying. "Apparently some kids were trespassing in the tunnels and one of them lost his footing. From what the police can tell, he tried to grab hold of some boards to break his fall and ended up triggering a cave-in."

"Or so it was made to look," Finch added.

A sudden wave of nausea suddenly overtook Maggie as she struggled with an awful premonition. "The boy who was hurt—"

"Killed," Finch corrected her.

"What is it, Margaret?"

"Was he an Indian?" she asked. "A teenager?"

She could sense Channing tighten, even though she was looking at Finch.

The cold snap of satisfaction that suddenly lit the policeman's eyes made her wish she had said nothing at all.

"What makes you ask that?" he challenged her.

She recalled Cleveland's aborted chase in the rain that afternoon and his defensive explanation that Channing himself had ordered the boy caught.

Could it be that her fears were premature, that she had jumped to the wrong conclusion without hearing the full story?

"Well?" Finch persisted. "Why did you ask if the victim was an Indian?"

"I'd just heard from some of the crew that it was an ongoing problem," she said.

" 'It?' "

"Kids getting into the tunnels." Maggie swallowed hard and lifted her chin, determined not to let him see how shaken she was. "They don't know how dangerous it can be if you don't know what you're doing."

"Apparently not. At least this one didn't."

It seemed like forever before he spoke again.

"Did you ever see any of them down there yourself, Miss Johnson?"

"See what?" she asked, pretending not to understand his question.

"Indians."

She wanted to look in Channing's direction, wanted him to say something that would remove the tortured dilemma between an answer that would implicate him in a new murder and a lie that would continue to mask his involvement in an old one.

In a voice that seemed to come from far away, Maggie heard herself reply, "No. I didn't see any."

Maggie stood at the French doors, watching the rain come down. In the reflection in the panes, she could see Channing return, even before he spoke. "How are you doing?" he asked.

"Has he left?"

"For the time being." Channing paused. "Should I ask you why you did that?"

"Did what?"

"I don't exactly live in a vacuum, Maggie. Whatever you thought you were accomplishing . . ." he hesitated, as if unsure of the right words. "It really wasn't necessary."

Maggie turned to face him. "Just tell me one thing."

Channing smiled. "I've never known you to stop at just one. Ask me whatever quantity of questions you want."

"Is it true that you wanted him caught?"

"Caught, yes. Dead, no."

"Why?"

"Why do you think?"

Her temper rose in response to his continual reversion to mystery. "He had a watch with my father's name on it," she reminded him. "Did you know about it?"

"Not until Finch mentioned it, no."

"I think that's more than coincidence."

"So do I," Channing agreed. "Particularly since I don't remember him ever wearing one. Not even the night of his accident."

The word *accident* stung her, reinforcing five years' worth of suspicion. Somehow, she found the voice to contest him.

"Murder," she said. "I've never believed it was anything else."

He was strolling toward her, his thumbs hooked in the front pockets of his jeans. Just short of her he stopped. "And do you still believe I had something to do with it?"

A thrill of frightened anticipation touched her spine.

"While you're thinking about an answer to that," Channing said gently, "there's still something I'm in the dark about."

"What's that?"

"Why did you lie for me tonight?"

Maggie's eyes met his, and in their depths lay the answer that both knew had been building for weeks.

49

It was the second time that she was going to set foot in his room, though Channing believed it to be the first.

Then again, maybe he knew everything. Knew everything and forgave her in spite of it.

Every fiber of her soul was perilously poised on the brink of the forbidden. So many mysteries, and yet, unquestionably, one fact loomed as clear: the quest to push him as far from her heart as possible had instead brought him closer to her than ever, leaving no room for anything or anyone else.

"If you'd rather go to your room . . ." he whispered in her hair just outside the door.

"Yours will be fine" she murmured, her voice barely above a whisper that the silken spell of passion wove around them, a spell that any second might be broken and lost forever.

"Are you sure?"

Maggie's hand covered his as he reached down to turn the knob and let them both inside.

That the invitation to his most private domain be conditional on how *she* felt was yet another dimension of the most complex man she had ever met. Only a single night ago, they had stood in another doorway and exchanged words far different from these, words that had sent him away. It was too late to retract the suspicions she had voiced about his involvement with Lynne-Mae, but, ironically, she now had a second chance in his arms just twenty-four hours later. Perhaps, in spite of all protests and obstacles, some things were simply cast by fate.

Tonight is ours, she told herself, determined to set aside all doubts, all suspicions, all association with anything else except for the man whose wet kisses were as urgent and exploratory as the hands that pulled her tight against the length of his body.

And though she might never know for certain, her pride contented itself with the belief that no other woman had crossed the threshold of Derek Channing's private quarters on the island at Lynx Bay.

There was no longer any turning back from the chemistry that both of them knew had existed from their first meeting. Whatever questions she might have asked him after Finch left—and there were many—had fallen back into silence when they had looked into each other's eyes. With one accord, their gazes had lifted and locked, sealing an unspoken covenant of desire.

Had Channing made the first move downstairs or had she? As he now closed the bedroom door behind them and she wrapped herself in the magnificent warmth of his arms, Maggie realized that the answer really made no difference. All that mattered at that moment in time was the fulfillment that only the intensity of lovemaking could provide.

Maggie's hands skated down the smooth planes of his back, delighting in how hard and bracing his body felt beneath the light fabric of his shirt. His legs were parted as they stood together just inside the door, and Maggie moved one of hers forward and raised it just enough to press against his crotch. He tightened his grasp on her waist.

"You little devil," he whispered.

"Takes one to know one," she teased back.

He slid one hand under her knee to assist her tantalizing massage. His tongue traced the soft, moist fullness of her lips, leaving them only briefly to nibble at her earlobe and huskily repeat the erotic invitation he had issued downstairs.

"And how long have you wanted to do *that?*" Maggie countered as she began to extricate his shirttail from his jeans and slide both palms up inside to caress the warm bare skin.

The sensation of his fingers working to unbutton her blouse was as heady as the hot whisper of his reply against the side of her neck.

"Only about seven hundred years," he said, expertly opening her blouse all the way to her waist and slipping his fingers inside the lace camisole to stroke her creamy breasts.

"You don't *look* that old," she said, intoxicated by his touch, his scent, his magnetism. "Or did you mean in another life?"

Channing bent his head down and pulled the lace aside with his teeth. "I don't know about *then*," he murmured, "but I know I'd spend the rest of *this* life looking for you if you hadn't come along." With the feverish fire that only first times ignite, his mouth seared a path across her breasts that left her weak, oblivious to all else.

Maggie groaned as his tongue hungrily moved from one nipple to the other, acknowledging the pleasure that was his to give and hers to enjoy without question or restraint. As her fingers raked through the black thickness of his hair, she felt him slowly descend to his knees and knew exactly what he was going to do next. The urgency to know, to experience every part of him made her dizzy with impatience.

"You'll notice I already took my watch off," he remarked, making them both laugh in reminiscence of the other time when they had found themselves in a similar situation.

"No lights either, I noticed," she said. "How well do you know Braille?"

His hands were moving in rhythmic circles over her bottom and then dipping below to trail the sensitive cleft between.

"Am I doing okay so far?" he asked with such seriousness that she laughed. "Was that a 'yes?'" he asked, planting a wet kiss on her bared midriff and then licking the evidence of it away.

"How would you have explained it to Brecht last night if he had walked in?" Maggie asked instead of replying, the touch of Derek's lips at her waist sending a warming shiver of anticipation through her whole body.

He unfastened her leather belt and slowly drew it through each of the loops to remove it, exhibiting a self-control that was even more of a turn-on than greedy ravishment.

"Oh, I think Brecht has the wits to have figured it

out himself," he remarked, laying the belt aside on the carpet and turning his attention to the zipper of her pants.

Much to her surprise, he hesitated.

"You can still change your mind if you want," he said, one hand poised over the zipper as the other gently stroked the curve of her derriere. Even in his fingertips, she could feel the throb of desire, the pulse of expectation.

"Why would I want to do that?" she asked.

"I just want you to be sure of what you're getting into."

"I *do* know what I'm getting into. I'm getting into bed with a man that I'm . . ."

Her last words died off, if indeed they were articulated at all.

"A man that you're what?" he asked.

Maggie was all too aware that the wrong words could destroy what was about to happen between them. And any words could be the wrong words, she warned herself, all too aware that by the morning light the situation could be radically changed.

Channing, however, was not about to let her get away with an unfinished thought.

"Maybe I should make it easy and say it first," he said. He had eased the zipper downward, and the knuckles of his hand slipped inside the opening to stroke the delicate triangle of peach-colored lace that matched her camisole.

"Say what?"

Only the pale outline of his face was visible, and yet the expression of profound tenderness on it just then seemed unmistakable.

"If we make love tonight, Maggie, I want you to

know that it won't be a one-night stand."

She could feel the tremor of his palm as he turned his hand inward and tentatively lowered it beneath the waistband, his fingers just grazing the silky delta of her womanhood.

"What would it be, then?" she asked, hardly able to breathe, to think, to imagine anything beyond the ecstasy that awaited her.

"How does 'forever' sound?"

50

She had been loved by other men in her life and loved them earnestly in return. Some she had even once imagined in a long-term role.

Not until Derek Channing, though, had she known the full definition of ravenous desire. Not until tonight had she experienced the overwhelming potential for passion between two people whose fierce zeal for independence had, ironically, brought them together.

Though they still played opposing sides in a real-life drama, the single-minded obsession with which they both sought to pleasure each other was as searing, as powerful as the white-hot heat that solders two metals.

After tonight, Maggie told herself, nothing would ever be quite the same. Nothing.

Any objections she might have harbored were all but forgotten as his mouth expertly moved over every inch of her body, his hands working magic as each caress warmed her skin, enticing her to stretch and twist, longing for more, longing for him.

That the energy of the anger toward him she had carried for five years would be unleashed in the present exhibition of such lustful and mutual craving was a scenario she would never have imagined. And now, the more he aroused her, the harder it was to imagine ever living without it.

Her conscience reminded her that as physically intimate as they might be on this electrifying night of discovery, still remained too much below the surface for her to say she knew him well. *Don't lose yourself to this*, her inner voice advised. But the earthy groans and purrs that fell from both their lips drowned out its heed for caution.

The smooth, concave hollow of her spine tingled at his descending touch.

"Oh, Maggie," he murmured, stroking her hip with a tenderness that compelled her to roll toward him, sending him back against the pillows.

"I'm yours," he cried, throwing his arms up in surrender.

She slid her palm across the dark mat of hair at his chest, delighting in his incredible physique that would put other men to shame.

"Surrendering already?" she teased. "You're being too easy."

"Actually, I'm getting pretty hard," he countered. "But don't take my word for it."

The remembrance of how lasciviously he had investigated her sweet, wet body before ever carrying her over to the bed generated a smile on Maggie's face that quickly erupted into laughter.

"I must have a comical technique," Channing said.

"I was just thinking about how long we stood at the door," she said.

"What about it?"

Her fingertips lingered on his taut stomach.

"It seemed like a long time," she murmured.

"We could call it 'extended doorplay.'"

Maggie began laughing again, in spite of the seriousness of their lying together naked for the first time,
their bodies about to propel their relationship into
another dimension. "How would you like a pillow
thrown at your head?"

"I think between the two of us," he replied, "we can
come up with something better. . . ."

Without need of further invitation, she reached
down to reciprocate with an exploration of his body.

"I think that this Braille thing has real potential," he
remarked after a moment, shuddering as her fingertips
shamelessly massaged him.

"You're in big trouble if you keep that up," Channing
whispered. "Literally, of course."

"I wouldn't have it any other way."

Unable to endure the anticipation any longer, Maggie drew herself up to kneeling and straddled his thighs.

Pleasantly surprised by her taking the initiative, he
drew her down over his body.

The gasp that broke forth from Maggie's lips as she
experienced him for the first time was matched by a
loud moan from Channing. Slow and measured at the
start, his deepening thrusts were the instinctive movements of a man who knew how to please a woman.

The muscles of her thighs and stomach flexed in
tempo with Channing's arched back and hips, now and
again his hands moving from her derriere to the front of
her body to squeeze the tender breasts that hovered
above him. Over and over, the sound of her own name
filled the room as he cried it.

As he aroused her passion his own grew stronger, all senses yielding to the unquestionable need for her that had been building inside from the first moment he met her.

"Slide your legs down a moment," he huskily instructed, gripping her tightly with both hands so that they would not break precious contact. Heat rippled under Maggie's skin as he agilely rolled them both over, pinning her to the bed as a willing prisoner of his own seduction.

Fire spread to her heart as he commenced their erotic rhythm all over again, breaking through whatever shell of self-protection still remained around the woman she used to be. Locked in an exquisite harmony not usually found on the first night of new lovers, it now seemed impossible for her to even remember that her hatred had once run deep, much less her jealousy.

"Yes . . ." she groaned, gasping for breath as Channing's pace began to build. Though she knew they were nowhere near the edge of the bed, her fingers dug into his skin to hold on, alternating among his broad back, narrow waist, and tightened buttocks.

Less than a minute later, their bodies both convulsed, uniting them with the hot testimony of their passion's consummation.

Tenderly he clung to her, their damp chests and midriffs pressed tightly together as they maintained the bond that still linked them physically.

"Sweet, sweet Maggie," he whispered, gently kissing the hollow at the base of her throat.

The feather-light brush of his lips on her skin dispelled thoughts of all else save the contentment of sleeping in his arms.

"Oh, by the way," he added softly.

"Hmm?"

"I think this changes our relationship."

51

She loved him.

It was her last conscious thought before she drifted into sleep and the very first one to which she awakened, still snug against his body, almost two hours later. Outside, the storm's fury had subsided into harmless rain. Inside Maggie's heart, however, any restoration of peace was not in the immediate forecast.

It had been easy—almost too easy—to make excuses for her vulnerability to his sensual attraction. United by the reality of an unexpected death in the tunnels, such common ground had been the impetus which had gotten them upstairs and into his bed. Mindful as they both were of the chemistry that simmered beneath the surface in their day-to-day contact on the project, it had taken this—the shock of a crime—to bring such passion to the surface.

Even without any training in psychology, though, she knew enough of human nature to recognize that tragedy was only a temporary adhesive, instantly bonding people who might otherwise have nothing to share. More often than not, once the trauma of the crisis passed, all that would remain of the spontaneous encounter was a bittersweet memory.

It could happen that way with Derek, she reminded herself, in spite of the words that he had moaned so passionately in her hair, in her ears, between her breasts. Come the first rays of morning light through his bedroom window, it was altogether possible that his whispered promises of love forever would already be history. They could well be convenient phrases that a man of his independence had never intended to honor in the first place.

There was no way that she could remain at Lynx Bay and continue to work for him if what had happened only a few hours before was just an indulgence of the flesh, a torrid release of pent-up emotions that had absolutely nothing to do with romance or commitment.

To see him every day, to catch a scent of his aftershave, to hear the smooth aristocratic drawl of his voice—such things, as simple as they were, would be unbearable if they returned to their former roles of boss and employee. If their romance didn't mean the same thing to him, she told herself, she would have no choice but to leave him as quickly as possible.

Beneath the leg she had draped over his, Channing suddenly stirred, the cool globe of his posterior sliding back against her flat stomach. Maggie shifted as well, hoping her own movement wouldn't awaken him. Not yet.

A shudder of apprehension rippled down Maggie's spine as the seed of a far more dangerous proposition planted itself in her head. What if he really *did* love her?

It would be impossible for her to even think of maintaining both a professional liaison with the Seattle police and an intimate relationship with the man she had been hired to spy on. Whether or not he ever touched her body again, it would be impossible for her to be objective. Sooner or later, she realized, her credibility would be called into question.

She was already withholding critical pieces of information from McCormick. While she could argue that revealing her feelings for Channing would worsen the blow of her rejection of Troy's own amorous advances, the truth was far more complicated.

With each piece of the puzzle that she contributed by her amateur sleuthing, Channing's day of judgment drew closer. Over and over, McCormick's words in Boston returned to haunt her. They almost had him, he had said. All they needed was Maggie's cooperation as a silent partner to bring the case to its rightful end. By the end of summer, Troy had promised, she would finally know what had really happened on the night her father died.

But what if they were wrong?

It wasn't the first time that she had considered it. Nor could she attribute her change of opinion to the newly discovered knowledge of Channing's unparalleled expertise as a lover. Too many variables had entered the picture since she first took on her assignment to expose him as a murderer. Too many variables that suggested that someone else—someone close to him—was the real villain.

Even if this night in his arms meant nothing to him by morning, the part of Maggie that desperately wanted to believe in his innocence now governed the decision she knew she had to make. One way or the other, she would have to make contact with Troy as soon as possible and beg off from any further involvement or espionage on behalf of his department.

"You're in love with him, aren't you?" he'd inquire on the heels of her resignation. No matter what excuse she offered, he'd see through to the truth and condemn her for it.

The harder job, of course, would be to fabricate an excuse to leave Channing and Lynx Bay. In her mind's eye she continued to see the vivid expression of betrayal that would be on his face if she were still on the premises the day of his arrest—if and when it came. A betrayal made even worse by the intimacy they had shared.

Without thinking, she tightened the arm that lay across his chest, an unconscious bid to pull him closer.

"Awake?" he murmured, his voice a low drawl that melted through to her very soul.

For an instant, Maggie considered pretending to be sound asleep, reluctant to break the magic of their time together.

"Hmm?" she mumbled in response.

He was turning toward her, momentarily disengaging their interlocking limbs as he adjusted to a new position.

"How are you doing?" he whispered, sliding his right forearm under her neck. His left hand, free from the covers, was stroking her cheek and pushing back stray tendrils of her hair.

"Doing fine," she replied, conscious that the soft flesh of her inner thigh was being prodded and teased. Against her better judgment, Maggie's fingers slid down to affirm his arousal.

"Find something you want?" he asked, hungrily

covering her lips with his own before she could fashion a response.

I want you, she would have said if he had let her. *I want this night to never be over.*

As their bodies once more found a rhythmic and satisfying union, a third unspoken wish outweighed all the rest. *I want you to be innocent!* she longed to scream.

"Sounds like the rain finally stopped," Channing remarked.

For the past hour or so they had alternated between sleeping and talking. Although she had no sense of what time it was, it disturbed Maggie that their sojourn in bed would be over much sooner than she would have liked.

"It's a good thing that the tunnels don't leak," she casually managed to say. "It'd sure be a muddy mess to go to work."

"Well, no one will have to worry about that for the rest of the week."

"Hmm?"

"Oh, Finch mentioned it when I saw him out," Channing explained. "The police are going to need a couple of days down there free of interference." His arms closed around her midriff as he kissed her on the nape of the neck. "I guess I'll just have to find something else for you to do. . . ."

His remark about the tunnels stirred a momentary flicker of panic in her. "We'll still need to go to the mainland, though, won't we?" she asked. "I mean, won't you be needed there if they have any questions?"

"I think the Seattle police can dial a phone as well as the next person."

Her subsequent silence was a mistake.

"Something the matter, honey?" he asked. "You tightened up just then."

"A lot of things on my mind." She hoped he wouldn't press it.

In the darkness that was slowly giving way to dawn, she saw him prop up on one elbow and rest his chin on the heel of his hand. "I bet I can guess what one of them is. Or should I say who?"

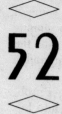

52

"*I had started* to tell you a story earlier tonight," he continued. "And I know how you really hate it when a story doesn't get finished."

In a moment, Maggie's anxiety level had roller coastered from high to low. Almost a hundred percent certain that he was leading up to "Troy McCormick," her senses flooded with relief when he said "Fiona" instead.

"Oh yes," she murmured as if she had completely forgotten about SkySet's daughter, thankful that the one secret she still kept from Channing was intact. "What about her?"

Channing resumed his narrative from where he had left off during their rainy walk up the beach path.

"You have to put it in the perspective that SkySet and Fiona weren't that close when she was growing up."

"Because she was in boarding school?"

"Because she was an ever-constant reminder to SkySet of the event that had brought her into the world.

Although she came to love Fiona over time, some of that emotional distance between them at the beginning couldn't help but influence their relationship. And the girl craved attention, even if she had to get into trouble to get it."

Inquisitive and incorrigible at every turn, her problems had been compounded as she moved into her teens and took on the dark, exotic looks of her maternal side.

"Twylar," Channing went on, "used to say that they should lock her in her room until she turned thirty and, even then, only let her out under supervision."

"I can see why you agreed, then, to let her come out here."

"Island life started to suit her after a couple of weeks. Not that I didn't have to get after her for being a nuisance, but I think the isolation from her peers cut down on some of her mischief."

"She must have driven Brecht nuts," Maggie said, reflecting on how her own resistance to authority had vexed the man since the first day she arrived.

"Actually, they got along better than you'd imagine. As I'm sure Twylar told you at lunch, Brecht already knew something about laying down ground rules for children."

Maggie felt color creep into her cheeks at his candid knowledge of their luncheon topics and was thankful that Channing couldn't see her. Had Twylar revealed it himself? she wondered, recalling the exporter's embarrassment at being caught on the phone in the lobby of the Pacific Crabhouse. Or had Lynne-Mae passed it on to Channing, having overheard Twylar's initial lunch invitation the night they had all come to dinner? She'd probably never know the answer, nor would it make any difference.

"So Brecht kept her in line?" she asked.

"As much as anyone could. He also grieved as much as her mother did the night that Fiona—" Channing stopped short. "I'm getting ahead of myself on the story."

It seemed to Maggie like an interminable time before he continued.

"The beginning of the end," he said at last, "was when David came back to the island."

"I didn't know you even had a brother," Maggie said. From all she had read and Troy had researched, Derek Channing had no siblings to share his last name or his family fortune.

"All of our lives would have been better off if I *hadn't* had a brother, believe me." The bitterness in his voice was unmistakable. "It was bad enough that he came back to claim something that wasn't his. That he played on Fiona's trust and innocence was worse than all his other crimes put together."

Practiced in the art of seduction and possessed of good looks to go with it, the younger Channing had literally swept the teenager off her feet and into the heady throes of first love.

"When SkySet found out Fiona was pregnant," Channing continued, "she came close to putting a butcher knife between his shoulder blades."

"What would you have done if she had?"

"Probably lie to protect her."

"In the name of justifiable homicide?"

"Unfortunately, it didn't come to that."

"Unfortunately?"

Channing heaved a sigh. "The only thing to David's credit was that he had the decency to marry her . . . not that he favored the idea. Had she and the baby lived—well, there's no sense in rehashing what can't be fixed."

"What happened to her?" Maggie asked when another long and peculiar silence broke the tempo of his story.

Channing pulled her close into his arms.

"Brecht and I came back late from the mainland one night and heard them fighting out on the ridge behind the house, the side where there's nothing but rocks that go down to the shore."

Maggie could picture the very spot he was talking about, a treacherous cascade of boulders with jagged points and faces too slick and narrow for any kind of footpath.

Channing was painting the scene for the tragedy that had unfolded that night, the devastating moment that neither his money nor his power had been able to prevent.

"She was screaming at him at the top of her lungs for lying to her and not being there when she needed him," he said. "David was just standing there and laughing at her the same way he laughed at everyone. It wasn't until sometime later we found out that he was seeing a girl back in Tacoma on the side."

Maggie felt the muscles of his shoulders and arms tighten.

"Brecht and I got out to the ridge as fast as we could. Fiona was hysterical at that point, and our first fear, of course, was about the risk that the whole situation posed to the baby." He shook his head. "She was just into her eighth month when all of this happened, and we couldn't chance her going into premature labor, not with the complications she'd been having since her pregnancy began. She was such a diminutive little thing to begin with. She probably wouldn't even have made it to eight months if it hadn't been for the care she got from her mother."

This prompted another question on Maggie's part, averse as she was to interrupting his story. "Where was SkySet at the time?"

"She had gone with us to the mainland that day for some shopping," he replied. "Things might have been different, of course, if she had come back with the two of us that night instead of remaining behind in Seattle to see a friend who was ill." Channing emitted a sigh. "Then again, it might have been even worse. . . ."

Brecht had started talking to Fiona to try and calm her down, Channing continued, but she was beyond the point of any reasoning. When David started down the rocks, Fiona's impulse was to run after him.

"She kept screaming that she loved him, and he kept laughing at her," Channing went on, his anger increasing. "I ran after her myself because I was afraid she'd slip and fall." He took a deep breath.

"I only had her in my arms for a few seconds. Only a few seconds and then she broke away from me to go after a son of a bitch who never even loved her."

Shudders wracked his body, compelling Maggie to hold him tighter. "She was dead before we could even get her to the mainland," he said, through his tears.

Though she never knew Fiona except as a name, Maggie felt her own tears come as well, tears for a young woman misled by false love, and tears for SkySet, whose daughter's birth and death were conjoined by acts of violence. The image of the woman, cloaked and silent, laying fresh flowers at Fiona's grave, heightened Maggie's guilt at ever imagining the housekeeper to be her enemy.

"What about David?" she asked after a long moment of silence broken only by Channing's muffled sobs.

"He played the grieving widower to the hilt. Of course, he blamed *me* for everything that had happened that night when, in fact, I had done all that I could to stop it." He reached up to smooth Maggie's hair with his free hand. "His last words to me at Fiona's grave were of hatred, that he'd pay me back one day for everything that he'd lost, everything that he thought I owed him." Channing paused. "The irony is that when he first came to Lynx Bay—and before he seduced Fiona—I'd almost convinced myself that we could really be the brothers to each other that we never had the chance to be in the past."

Maggie waited, sensing there was something else he was going to tell her.

"Unfortunately," he said, "the truth has a way of always catching up. I couldn't condone the career he'd chosen for himself to support his high style of living."

"What was that?" she asked.

"Forgery."

53

As she dressed a few hours later in the privacy of her own bedroom, Maggie could barely contain the burgeoning anxiety generated by Channing's story of Fiona and David.

An outlandish theory swirled in her imagination. It was too much of a coincidence *not* to be valid, she told herself, stunned at how the power of a single word dropped in conversation had suddenly opened a door she never considered.

Forgery.

The word echoed in her head like a mantra.

Too many loose ends, she now realized, were linked by a frightening common denominator from the past that not even Channing had brought himself to recognize.

Forgery.

Maggie laced up her shoes, silently congratulating herself that she'd had the willpower not to bounce off the walls in Channing's bedroom and exclaim that she'd just solved the mystery that hung over both their lives. What she had to do first was to get the information to someone who'd know how to take the right course of action. And there was only one person who could.

There'd be time enough to share it with Channing once the whole thing was over.

Renewed by what the last hours had wrought, it now seemed almost a lifetime ago that she had even entertained the idea of leaving Lynx Bay, of deserting the man she loved. Armed with new evidence that he himself had supplied, the idea of vindicating Channing after five years of misplaced suspicion was as exhilarating as the remembrance of loving him, of feeling him deep inside her body.

She just had to play her role a little bit longer, long enough to convince the Seattle police to listen to a theory that might finally unlock the truth.

It had to be his brother David behind the entire scheme to ruin him. Unbalanced by his own jealousy and grief, who else but his brother would have masterminded so hateful a plot of revenge?

"He swore at Fiona's funeral that he'd pay me back someday," Channing had said.

Her heart squeezed in anguish at the realization that her own father had been an unwitting part of that price.

Maggie's eyes fell on the manila envelope that she had taken out again that morning. Little, insignificant things that she had never noticed before now loomed as major discrepancies in the letter. Feeling as foolish as she did angry for her naïveté, the acknowledgment that his peers knew her father better than she did—well enough to see his high regard for Channing—was not an easy thing to accept.

"Your father would never have written such things about Derek," Lynne-Mae had insisted. And as she fingered the damning page of lies that Clayton Price had supposedly penned about his employer, Maggie knew that Lynne-Mae was right.

Had her father ever met David, she wondered, or at least been apprised of his threats? Fiona's death might still have been fresh enough for Channing to have shared the circumstances of it with his new foreman.

Maybe David had rigged a trap to halt, if not permanently block, a project dear to his brother's heart. Lynne-Mae's admission that it had nearly taken a joint act of God and Congress for the excavation to be approved suggested that a fatal mishap would not only close the tunnels down but slap Channing with a lawsuit. Maybe even a murder charge.

Maggie shuddered, disturbed by the unanswered question of whether her father had been a random victim of David's lethal spite or had, in fact, been the solitary key to expose him, a key that had to be destroyed.

Five years had obviously failed to exact the justice that David Channing so hungrily craved, though. With Clayton's death ruled as accidental and the work in the tunnels proceeding without incident, the passage of time had clearly only exacerbated his pain. Desperate to carry out his promise of revenge, he had miraculously managed to engage the aid of the one person with whom he shared a common bond of hatred toward Derek.

Maggie.

And in that moment of realization, there came an even darker understanding. She wasn't the only person who had figured out David's connection.

◦   ◦   ◦

"The 'tourist thing,' hmm?" Channing said in response to her plans for the day. "That's not such a bad idea."

"Everyone's been saying it's such a great city," Maggie continued, buoyed by his acceptance of her excuse to go to the mainland. "And goodness knows I haven't had any time before this to really see much."

Channing grinned over his coffee cup. "Sounds good. Why don't we make a whole day of it and wrap up with dinner at Ivar's?"

Maggie faltered. "What?"

"The last time I took a day off from work was too far back to even remember."

"Oh."

"Try to contain your excitement," he teased her. "You did want me to join you, didn't you?"

"I was just thinking that maybe . . ." Maggie's eyes met his, and she wondered if it was really true that two people could read each other more accurately once they had reached a certain level of intimacy.

"I wanted to do some shopping, too," she said, hoping to imply either hitting every boutique at Ranier Square or purchasing personal items of a feminine nature and embarrassing him.

"There must be an operative word in that answer just now that I'm missing," Channing remarked. "Are you saying you want to be by yourself?"

Maggie shrugged. "It's a free country if you want to tag along. I just like to move at my own pace, that's all."

"Well, since 'tagging along' isn't exactly my style, I guess you're on your own." As he set down his cup in its saucer, he frowned. "Sure it's nothing else?"

"Like what?"

"That's why I asked."

"Just some time by myself," she said, her voice purposefully softening. *Forgive me for lying to you about this,* she wanted to say, *but in the end you're going to see that I had a good reason to.* "A lot on my mind I need to think about," she added. "You know what I mean?"

He nodded thoughtfully. "Yes, I think maybe I do."

As she rose to leave the breakfast table a few minutes later, Channing surprised her by saying, "I want you to be careful while you're over there. This latest thing in the tunnels—well, I don't want anything to happen to you."

"I'll keep it in mind," she said, warmed by his concern for her safety and yet concurrently guilty with herself for having to lie about her real plans.

"Keep Brecht with you, too. I think it's a smart idea for him to stick with you today."

"But—"

"He really does need to get out more. Any objection?"

Maggie managed a weak smile of compliance. The day was not going to be as easy as she had hoped.

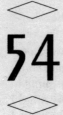

54

"*You know,*" Maggie remarked to her companion after an hour and a half of browsing, "there's a café up on the next block that has poppy-seed muffins to die for."

Brecht regarded her with a smirk. "We just passed an excellent bakery on Seneca. Perhaps you didn't notice it while you were buying everything in sight."

Maggie dismissed his suggestion with a wave of her hand. "Trust me on this," she said. "I've got a nose for these things. Look, I'll even buy you one and you can judge for yourself. Poppy-seed okay, or are you a blueberry kind of guy?"

"Danke schön, but I would prefer not to spoil my appetite with frivolities."

When it came to spoiling her day, though, the man was clearly an expert.

Since the moment they had come off the boat together, he had locked in step with her and remained within manacle length the entire time. Passersby, Maggie speculated, probably inferred from such ridiculous closeness that she was saddled with either a possessive mate or a well-dressed parole officer. Left to his own devices, of course, the man would no doubt opt to put her in a box with a good, strong lid on it instead of traipsing around the waterfront carrying her packages.

She reminded herself that it was Channing and not Brecht who had determined that she needed an escort for the mainland. Though he had surrendered the most private part of himself to her the previous night, the fact remained that Channing still held in reserve a critical level of suspicion.

Obviously she could not have contested his decision or the spurious rationale he had offered to justify it. It was simply an obstacle she would have to work around if anything significant were to be accomplished.

Time, unfortunately, was of the essence. Precious time that had already been lost wandering around Pioneer Square as her mind raced to come up with a workable plan that would not attract attention.

The café would at least be a start, she decided. She knew the place had a very practical and convenient telephone located back in the ladies' room. Not even Brecht, she thought, would be so zealous as to follow her there.

"You're not getting your order to take with you?" Brecht asked when Maggie slid into the nearest front table by the window of the café.

"I'm getting some coffee, too," she said as if it were the most obvious thing in the world. "Unless I grow another hand between now and when it gets here, I think it's easier to sit and have a breakfast snack in comfort, don't you?"

"As you wish, madam."

Brecht took the seat opposite her, his jacket falling open just enough for her to glimpse his ever-present weapon.

"I'm curious about something," she remarked when the waitress took leave of them.

"That seems to be a perpetual state with you," he replied.

Maggie indicated his jacket and the secret it hid. "Do you always wear that?" she asked. "I mean, is it like an American Express card that you never leave home without?"

"One never knows when a good defense will be necessary."

"It probably shakes them up in airport security, too. There's definitely no mistaking *that* little puppy for a hair dryer."

"No," Brecht agreed. "There isn't."

"Oh, excuse me?" Maggie caught their waitress before she could set down the mug of coffee. "Would you mind putting that in a styrofoam cup for me?"

She noticed Brecht's reaction to such a strange request.

"Some people say that styrofoam ruins the taste of the coffee," Maggie explained, wondering how long she could keep up such idiotic banter without him catching on to her hidden agenda. "Back in Boston, though, it's the only thing I ever drink out of. The weird things you get used to, huh?"

"Do you have plans to return soon?" Brecht asked.

"To where? Boston?"

"That is where you're from," he said, phrasing it as a statement instead of a question.

"I haven't thought much past the end of summer, to be honest."

If she were *really* being honest, Maggie thought, the answer would be that she'd finally found the one place she felt she belonged, the same place where her father had always wanted her to be. With Derek.

"Why do you ask?"

She already suspected that Brecht had made more than one pass by Channing's bedroom door the previous night and guessed what was happening on the other side.

Her question caught him in a sly glance at his wristwatch.

"If I'm keeping you from something else, don't feel like you have to hang around on *my* account."

"*Your* account, madam, is precisely why I am here," he reminded her.

"Just didn't want you to get bored."

"That," Brecht curtly replied, "has not occurred since the first day you arrived."

"I'll take that as a compliment. And would you mind not calling me 'madam'? I feel like I should be working the waterfront at the turn of the century."

Brecht merely nodded.

"You can tell I'm a real coffee drinker, can't you?" she remarked a minute later as she started doctoring it with packets of sugar and an inordinately large amount of cream. "I've never understood how some people can drink this stuff black."

"I believe it's a matter of taste."

"Spoken like a die-hard black coffee drinker," she said. "Are you sure I can't buy you a cup?"

As Brecht declined, Maggie reached over to the paper napkin dispenser. "There's just something about

East Coast coffee, though, that always seems better than what—" her wrist hit the top lip of the cup with just the right momentum to pitch the entire thing over and into her lap. The expletive that flew from her lips aroused not only the attention of the nearest customers but two waitresses as well.

"Where's your ladies' room?" Maggie cried as she tried to dab the front of herself with napkins and soak up the puddle on the table before it could spread any further.

"In the back," the waitress replied.

"Save my place," Maggie said over her shoulder to Brecht as she grabbed her purse. "I'll be back in just a second."

There wouldn't be time, of course, for a lengthy phone conversation with Troy, provided that she was even able to reach him. Too long an absence from the table would arouse Brecht's suspicions and interfere with her plan.

A hundred thoughts raced through her mind as she made her way toward the door. Thoughts that culminated in one thing she was now a hundred percent sure of: Derek Channing was innocent. All she had to do was convince Troy McCormick that it was *another* Channing who merited the attention of the Seattle Police Department.

As she turned the door handle, the irony struck her that Brecht might even applaud her undercover efforts on his boss' behalf if she were to let him in on what she knew.

Caution, however, dictated that she play all of her cards as close to the chest as possible for the next few hours.

Maggie opened the door and stepped inside, her optimism immediately plummeting at the sight of an obstacle that she had not anticipated.

55

There were three of them—a trio of leather-clad teenage girls virtually indistinguishable from one another except for the height of their lacquered, teased hairstyles and the shade of their fingernails.

Two looked up as Maggie came in. The third was too engrossed in her conversation on the phone to acknowledge even a nuclear holocaust.

"So I says to him, 'Get outa here,' like y'know he thinks I'm real stupid or somethin'? And he goes, 'Yeah, well, Darryl says so' and I says 'Darryl?' and Carolyn goes 'No way' and he goes 'Uh-huh' and we go 'What?' and he goes 'Well, y'know cuz like him 'n' Tony heard some dudes' and I go 'Tony?' and he goes 'Yeah, him 'n' Darryl says you guys were doin' it at the mall' and Carolyn goes 'No way' and he goes 'Yeah' and so y'know I says 'Why's that?' and he's actin' like y'know he don't know nothin' and so then I go—"

"Excuse me," Maggie interrupted, "but I really need to use the phone."

If looks could kill, she thought as three pairs of heavily overdone eyes met hers with lethal disdain.

"Huh?" said one of the girls in response to her request.

"It's an emergency," Maggie said. "I really need to make a telephone call."

"Like so it's not the only phone on the planet," the shortest of the girls said. The second one laughed.

"That may be true," Maggie replied, "but it's the closest one to where I'm standing."

"Say what?"

The third one remained permanently entrenched in her conversation as her two companions proceeded to debate the issue.

"So *hers* is important, too," they said in defense of their friend.

"It'll only take five minutes," Maggie assured them, annoyed that she even had to debase herself to such rude juveniles. Under any other circumstances, she would either have reported them to the management or found another phone elsewhere. With Brecht awaiting her return to the table at any moment, however, her options were limited.

Staring the girl down had no effect whatsoever, nor did her continued efforts to prevail upon the peers meet with any success. Maggie finally reached into her purse and withdrew her wallet, hoping that her smallest bill wouldn't be something exorbitant like a twenty.

"Five dollars for five minutes," she said, brandishing the bill under the nonstop talker's nose. "Deal?"

"Later, dude," the girl said into the receiver as she snatched the money from Maggie's hand and hung up the phone.

What had purchased a free line to call Troy's machine, however, hadn't bought privacy as well. Less than four feet away, the trio parked themselves as permanent fixtures lest she try to steal more than her allotted time. Consoled only by the fact that her words would have no tangible meaning to them, Maggie dialed the number.

"Hey, babe! What's up?" Troy said when he came on after his customary screening of the call.

"A lot more than you'd ever imagine."

"What's that supposed to mean?"

"It means I think you've had me spying on the wrong man."

"Sounds like we need to talk. Where are you?"

"We can't meet." Maggie quickly explained that Brecht had accompanied her from Lynx Bay and would afford her no chance for a face-to-face meeting. "Even the phone call's a stretch," she said.

"Twenty words or less then. What the hell's going on?"

"Just answer me one thing first."

"Anything. What is it?"

"Did you know that he had a younger brother?"

There was a long silence at the other end of the line.

"You *did* know, didn't you?" Maggie challenged him, as exhilarated about being right as she was disappointed that she had been lied to by a man she had trusted. "You knew from the first day you hired me."

Troy cleared his throat. "What if I take the Fifth Amendment?"

"You can take the entire assignment and shove it if you want," Maggie retorted. "What I want to know is why you didn't tell me that David was the one you were really after."

"Maggie—"

"I don't like being used, Troy."

"No more than I liked doing the using," he said, "but this one wasn't my decision."

"Whose was it then?"

"Old-fashioned thing called a boss, Maggie. It helps to keep the job if you do what they tell you, especially if Channing's in thick with the Commissioner. When this thing blows open—well, you get the picture."

There followed an awkward pause, neither one knowing quite what to say.

"How did you know about David?" he asked.

"Putting two and two together," she replied. "Listen, I don't have much time, and I've got this feeling something really awful's going to happen. I guess you heard about the Indian boy, the one Cleveland said Channing wanted caught?"

Troy clucked his tongue. "Looks like he got his wish. They send somebody out already?"

"Finch," Maggie replied, "and I think you're wrong about Derek."

"Yeah, well, knowing Finch, Channing's got a run for his money on this one. You didn't say anything about *us*, did you?"

"Of course not," Maggie replied. "But doesn't Finch already know?"

"Only as much as he has to."

Maggie let the cryptic comment pass. "You still didn't answer my question."

"Which one?"

"That you knew about David."

"Are you sure we can't meet somewhere? I hate this stuff on the phone when you sound so stressed."

"Yeah, tell me about it," Maggie said, eyeing the

three teenagers who were clearly growing restless.

"Look, I know I owe you some answers," Troy admitted.

"More than that, I think."

"Did Channing tell you about his brother or did you learn it yourself?"

"A little of both. And a lot more than I learned from you."

"So you know what happened to him, then?"

"Not from the night he left Lynx Bay, no. I can only guess that he's the one behind most of what's been going on, including the supposed letter from my father. Once you find *him,* I think it's all going to fall into place."

"Maggie—"

"I just want to know why you didn't tell me that to begin with."

To Maggie's delight, the three girls were actually leaving the room, muttering a string of purple phraseology.

Troy drew a deep breath. "The more you knew, the greater danger you'd be in."

"And you thought I couldn't handle it?"

"No," Troy said. "I didn't know that I could trust you."

"You could have trusted me with the truth."

"That," Troy said, "would depend on your perception of what the truth is."

"Only that you set me up to spy on someone who's innocent in order to help catch someone who clearly isn't. *That* is the truth. And I think you've known it all along, whether or not you'll admit it."

There was a long pause. "Yes," he said at last. "I've known it for the past five years."

"Then why—"

"Knowing and proving," he said, "are two entirely different animals."

Maggie wasn't sure whether to feel euphoric or depressed. Troy's promise to investigate her idea of a connection between Cleveland and Derek's black-sheep brother was overshadowed by the fact that he had purposely withheld critical information from her.

"Blood is thicker than water," Troy reminded her. "You still can't trust that Channing's not hiding him out somewhere on the island to keep us from finding him."

But Maggie was confident that if there were anyone hiding on the island, she would have noticed by now. "It's Cleveland who's got the hidden agenda," she said, reiterating what had led her to such a conclusion.

"Try to call me back in a little bit," Troy said. "I may have something we can go on. Oh, and one other thing—"

"What?"

"Be careful."

Maggie stopped in her tracks as she reentered the café after hanging up, disconcerted to see that the three girls she had displaced were seated with a fourth companion directly behind Brecht, their strident voices carrying just enough to reach her in the doorway.

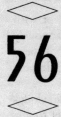

56

"*So y'know like* she's cussin' us out y'know like her hair's on fire or somethin' and says it's like this majorly big emergency—"

"Yeah," her friend across the table piped up. "And so she's gettin' in Lisa's face like she's real pissed—"

"Then she goes like she's gonna get a gun—"

"And we're like totally sweatin' it, y'know?"

"So she's like crazy and she goes and like throws this money at Lisa instead and goes 'You better shut up when I say to, bitch' like she's queen o' the hive—"

"And then she goes y'know and like grabs the phone right outa Lisa's hand!"

"Get outa here," their listener said in disbelief.

"And like she's goin' like she's got this emergency—"

"Emergency, my ass," the first girl grunted. "She gets on it y'know and she's like totally pissed at her ol' man and she's goin' on like how she woulda went and busted his—"

Their embellished version of the encounter with Maggie jolted to a halt as the three simultaneously looked over and recognized their target of disdain. "That her?" the fourth asked in a voice well above a polite whisper.

Maggie slid back into her seat without acknowledging that she had heard any of their conversation, nevertheless imagining her run of luck that morning to be just about the worst in the universe.

"Bitch," one of the girls muttered just loud enough in Maggie's direction as the group immediately vacated their table and made a beeline for the ladies' room.

Brecht's ever-watchful eyes met Maggie's.

"Perhaps," he said wryly, "you might take one of the Carnegie courses on how to be less objectionable to total strangers."

"I'm sure I have no idea what you're talking about," Maggie replied.

"I see your cleaning efforts weren't effective," Brecht remarked, indicating the coffee stains on Maggie's clothes.

"I guess I'll just have to go shopping for something new, then."

"Might I suggest something in a brown print for future such incidents."

"Maybe in another forty years." She found it hard to envision herself in a matronly paisley just for the sake of concealing spills. Patterns like that might be fine on little old ladies, but—

A sudden stab of inspiration sent Maggie's spirits into an upward climb, and she smiled in spite of her present circumstances.

"Oh, speaking of doing some shopping," she said, "there's something I've been meaning to get to all week. You don't mind a side trip to Queen Anne's Hill later today, do you?"

Troy's lack of specificity about when she should try to call him back left Maggie with no choice but to hazard a best guess, her intuition opting to stall for as long as she reasonably could. Certainly if the fruits of his investigative labor hadn't yielded what he needed over the stretch of five years, it wasn't likely he'd wrap it up in a half hour.

Even with the information Maggie herself had provided about Cleveland's potential liaison with Channing's brother, McCormick's reference to political sensitivity was a sure sign that he wouldn't trade caution for speed.

"Why do you think I haven't done something *before* now?" he had asked her. "There's no ninety percent right on this one, Maggie. To make it stick, it's got to be one hundred."

Maggie felt her anger return as she replayed Troy's other words in her head.

"When it's all done with," he had promised her, "I'll explain the whole thing over dinner."

As long as she was expected to cooperate with the police department in seeing the case through to conclusion, she'd do her job. Once it was resolved, though, no explanation in the world would bring back the father she loved. Nor would any candlelight dinner change her opinion of the man who had purposely endangered her life.

57

Cora Marquart squinted and blinked in the doorway like a nocturnal animal suddenly exposed to bright light.

"Maggie Johnson," Maggie repeated after Cora's initial dismissal of her as a door-to-door salesperson.

"No, dear," Cora apologized. "I'm afraid you have the wrong house. We're the Marquarts, not the Johnsons."

"*I'm* a Johnson," Maggie said, surprised that she had made so minor an impression as to have been completely erased from Cora's memory.

Cora shook her head and fingered the lopsided cameo pinned to the neck of her floral dress. "Well, I don't know what to tell you, dear. You might try the next street over. I think some Johnsons used to live next to the Baileys." Cora scowled. "Or was it Johanson? No, no, they were the young black couple, and she used to model for Bon Marché. Very tall. Very pretty. I wanted to be a model once myself," she said, "but they only want you if you're tall and you don't mind wearing your unmentionables in front of everyone." Cora vigorously shook her head. "I'm just old-fashioned."

"Maybe I should start over," Maggie said. "I'm—"

"Did you know the Johanson girl?" Cora asked. "Isn't it funny how all the pretty girls at school all know each other? And Johanson and Johnson are so close, you could practically be twins."

"I suppose," Maggie nodded. "Just like you and your sister, Nora."

Cora's mouth fell open in astonishment. "How did you know I had a sister named Nora?" she asked.

"I had cocoa with both of you," Maggie explained, hoping to jog the woman's memory back to life. "We sat and talked about Old Seattle."

"Well, Nora would be the one to know about anything *old*," Cora proclaimed. "Did you know that she was born five minutes before I was?"

"Yes, I remember you mentioning that."

"And she's never let me forget it, either. 'I'm the oldest so I should go first'—that's what she always says." Cora shook her head. "She just never gives a body peace about that."

"Is she home today?" Maggie asked.

"Who?"

"Nora."

Cora pursed her lips. "I'm not sure, dear. It's such a big house, you know. We sometimes go for days without seeing each other. Not that that's a bad thing. Just because we're twins doesn't mean we have to be joined at the hip 'til we die." Cora sighed. "Of course, it would be worse if we were Siamese, wouldn't it? Do you ever wonder what they do if one of them dies first?"

"I've never really thought about it," Maggie said.

"It would probably be Nora. She always has to be first at everything, you know." As if noticing them for the first time, Cora pointed at the bouquet of flowers in Maggie's hand. "Very pretty," she remarked.

"They're for you and your sister," Maggie replied. "I wanted to thank you for the lovely talk we had."

"You shouldn't have," Cora said. "Nora hates it when people cut her flowers without permission."

"No, no," Maggie explained, "I bought these at the—"

Cora suddenly grabbed her forearm and whispered confidentially. "Did you know there's a man standing by that car who's been watching you the whole time?"

"Oh, he's with me. Listen, do you and your sister have a few minutes to chat? There are a few things I need to fill in on my notes from the last time and I was hoping—"

"Well, I'd have to ask Nora but I'm sure she'd say it was okay."

"*What* would I say is okay?" Nora echoed, coming into the foyer at that moment.

"Could you wait here just a moment, dear?" Cora asked, partially closing the door so she could talk in privacy to her sister.

"Who are you talking to?" Maggie heard Nora inquire.

"I don't know," Cora said. "I've never seen her before in my life."

Nora opened the door again.

"She forgets things when she doesn't take her medication," she said with a sigh. "Who did you say you were again, dear?"

"Maggie Johnson. I'm doing that research project on Pioneer Square?"

"She's related to that nice black girl who used to do

the modeling," Cora added. "The tall, pretty one?"

"Oh don't be such a goose. They don't even have the same last name."

Cora reached up and patted the side of Maggie's face. "You have the very same cheekbones," she observed. "That's how I knew right away."

Nora's glance toward the driveway sharpened. "Did you know that there's a strange man watching you?" she asked Maggie, unabashedly pointing a bony finger in Brecht's direction.

"He's with me," Maggie said, wondering how much longer she'd have to linger at the front door before they invited her in.

"Nice suit he's got on," Nora remarked. "Expensive-looking."

Cora's eyes widened in excitement. "Is *he* a model, too?"

"Just a friend," Maggie answered, resisting the impulse to laugh.

"Any friend of yours is certainly a friend of ours," Cora announced. "Would he like to join us for some cocoa?"

"Oh, I don't think so," Maggie said quickly. "He's on a very specialized diet. A medical diet."

"What's wrong with him?" Nora asked.

"It's this permanent growth he's got right about here," she said, indicating on her own body the place next to the side of his ribs where she knew his gun rested. "He's had it for years, and nothing can get rid of it."

Cora bit her lip. "Oh dear," she murmured. "The poor man."

"What about tea?" Nora offered. "Can he take a cup of tea if he can't take cocoa?"

"Do you have any fresh gooseberry?" Maggie asked. "It's the only thing his doctor lets him have."

The two sisters exchanged an anxious glance and simultaneously shook their heads.

"That's okay," Maggie assured them. "I think he can wait until we get home."

"What pretty flowers," Cora said, effortlessly shifting subjects. "Did you grow them yourself?"

"No, actually I—"

"They look familiar," Nora cut in with a dramatic arch of her pencil-thin brow. "In fact, they look *very* familiar."

"I *told* her not to cut them, but she just wouldn't listen to me."

Before Maggie could protest her innocence, Nora was taking the bouquet from her hands.

"Well, the damage has already been done," she said. "We may as well go put them in some water."

"Come along, dear," Cora urged Maggie as Nora started into the hall without them. "We'll sit down and have ourselves a cup of cocoa while she's fussing."

"She must be very proud of her garden," Maggie said, allowing herself to be propelled into the parlor by Cora as Nora disappeared into the kitchen.

"It's all the poor dear really has, so I suppose it's good that she likes it so much. I've often told her that she must be part mole for all the time she spends rooting around in the dirt."

"So you never hired another gardener to help out?"

Cora laughed. "Oh we've never had one to begin with, dear. No, no, that's been Nora's job since she was a girl, and Mama's before that. Women's work, Papa always said. Did I tell you Papa once worked for the railroad?"

"Oh my goodness!" Maggie suddenly exclaimed.

"Well, lots of people did, you know," Cora went on, misinterpreting Maggie's reaction as a response to what she had just said.

"I'm sorry," Maggie said, "but you just now reminded me of something I completely forgot to do for my boss."

"I did?"

"And it's a lucky thing you did, too. Do you have a phone I could use? It'll only take a minute."

"Oh, certainly. Let me show you where it is, dear."

"Show her where *what* is?" Nora asked, emerging from the kitchen with the flowers in a crystal vase.

"I reminded her of something. What was it again, dear?"

"Just need to use your phone a second," Maggie repeated, pausing for a moment to admire the woman's handiwork with the floral arrangement. "Those are really nice," she complimented Nora.

"Thank you," Nora said. "I grow them myself."

"How do you know they're not listening in?" Troy asked when Maggie told him where she was calling from.

"They're perfectly harmless," she said. "Did you find out anything?"

Troy hesitated. "Do you have any idea how hard it is for me to admit that I'm not always right?"

"Admitting to anybody or just to me?"

"I ran a couple of your thoughts past my former partner," he said. "He happens to think they might hold water."

"And?"

"And he proposed something that—well, I'm not sure you're up for."

"What's that?"

"Would you be willing to talk to him?"

"You've lost me," Maggie said. "What's the big deal about talking to your partner?"

"The operative word is 'former.' He got his ass kicked off the case, courtesy of your buddy Channing."

Maggie bristled at Troy's allusion but said nothing.

"It's like I told you about Commission politics," Troy reminded her. "It could just have easily been *me* getting bumped down the ladder for lack of discretion."

"I thought things like that took more than one vote."

"Depends on who's voting. I assume you already knew that Channing's in thick with Pete Barstow?"

"I wouldn't quite say 'thick,' but go on about your partner."

"Let's just say he's got some information that puts things in a new light. If you hadn't told me what you said about Cleveland—"

"When does he want to meet?" she asked, anxious that she had already spent too much time on the Marquarts' phone.

"I thought when you rang it was him calling me back," Troy said. "If you're sure you want to do it, can we shoot for late tomorrow?"

Maggie bit her lip. "If I can. It'll take some real maneuvering."

"Let me call you right back. How long are you going to be there?"

Maggie read the number off the face of the phone. "I can't really overstay my welcome," she said. "I told Brecht I was stopping in just to say hi."

"Stall as long as you can, babe," Troy said. "You know I can't call you at the island."

"Oh, hello," Cora pleasantly greeted her as Maggie returned to the parlor. For an instant, she was almost expecting to be asked again who she was and what she was doing in their house.

"Do you need any help with the cocoa?" Maggie offered, surprised not to find a tray already laid out.

"Cora spoke out of turn, I'm afraid," Nora said. "We have to be at Dr. Gwynn's this afternoon for our check-ups. We mustn't be late or he charges extra."

"Oh, yes," Cora said. "We go see Dr. Gwynn every six months."

Nora tilted her head in her sister's direction. "You'd think she could remember something we only do twice a year."

"Do you go to Dr. Gwynn, too?" Cora asked Maggie.

"No, but I'll keep him in mind if you think he's good."

"Oh he's as good as any. A little full of himself some-times, and he could use a better barber—"

"Stylist," Cora corrected her. "They call them stylists now, Nora."

"Whatever." Nora was on her feet, a sign of her impatience for the visit to end. "Well, it was nice of you to stop by. Please give our regards to your mother."

"Oh, yes," Cora said. "We never see her anymore."

Maggie tried fervently to come with a credible delay, but both sisters were swept up in the momen-tum of saying good-byes and going on about their business. As they opened the front door and very nearly pushed her out, Maggie couldn't help but notice that Brecht had not moved from where she had left him.

"I do hope your friend will be all right," Cora whispered. "I had a cousin with a growth once on her right knee. No one ever asked her to dance."

"It was a goiter, Cora," Nora said, "and it was under her chin."

"That's what I said," Cora insisted. "You never pay attention."

Maggie heard them continuing the argument through an open window after the door had been closed behind her.

That, and the sound of a telephone ringing.

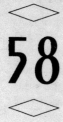

58

Had she been by herself, Maggie would have lingered on their front step, certain that the incoming call was the Seattle detective and that the Marquarts would come out to see if she was still there. Or she might even have knocked on the door and fabricated an excuse about leaving her car keys and needing to come back inside and retrieve them.

That call was for her, she just knew it. In full sight of Brecht, however, it would have been awkward if they *did* come out and tell her she had a phone call, for he would surely wonder how someone just happened to know where to track her down.

She broke from her state of immobility and proceeded down the drive toward the car. Troy would simply have to find some other way to contact her about the meeting with his former partner.

"They enjoyed the flowers you brought?" Brecht asked, opening the door for her.

"They mentioned it several times, as a matter of fact. Thanks again for helping me pick them out."

Brecht nodded.

"Well, we probably should get back to Lynx Bay," Maggie suggested after he slid into the driver's side, anxious to be on her way. "Did you know it was this late?"

"It is frequently much later than one thinks," he replied philosophically, inserting the key in the ignition.

As he shifted the car into gear, however, the worst of Maggie's expectations came to pass: the Marquarts' front door opened and the two of them tumbled out.

"There appears to be a problem," Brecht said, applying his foot to the brake.

Not as big a problem as there's going to be, Maggie thought, noting that the twin at the forefront was enthusiastically waving a piece of paper over her head.

"Yoo-hoo!" Cora shouted at them.

"Yoo-hoo!" Nora echoed.

"Let me see what they want," Maggie said, almost bolting from the passenger side and slamming the door behind her before they got any closer. She hoped that Brecht would stay put and not roll down the windows to listen.

"We were so afraid you'd gone," Cora said breathlessly.

"The phone rang just after you left," Nora added. "We were afraid that you'd already gone."

"He said it was very important," Cora said.

"*Very* important," Nora echoed.

"Well, I really appreciate it," Maggie said, reaching for the paper. Cora, however, was noticeably reluctant to part with it so soon.

"I'd better read it to you," she said. "My handwriting just isn't what it was back when I was a girl."

"And it wasn't very good then, either," Nora cut in. "*I* always got the penmanship honors at school, you know. And when I did, Papa took me for an ice cream. Sometimes two flavors on the very same cone."

"I'm sure I can decipher it," Maggie said, impatient to take the note before Cora started reading it out loud.

"Ice cream is so expensive now," Nora said. "It's not like it was back when we were growing up. Highwaymen—that's what some of those grocers are."

"Oh, dear," Cora said in dismay. "These glasses need a good cleaning, don't they? It's a wonder sometimes that I can see my own feet."

"Most of the time she can't even *find* them," Nora said. "Her glasses, that is. Her feet are always at the end of her ankles." She laughed at her own wit. "Did you think I meant her feet when I said that?"

Maggie heard the car door open behind her and knew that Brecht was stepping out.

"It's a good thing I was wearing them when I was writing down the message," Cora babbled on, "or it wouldn't make sense at all."

Nora reached out and vigorously jiggled Maggie's forearm. "Should your friend be driving a car with his condition? I'd think that would be awfully dangerous to other people on the road."

"Why don't you go ask him how he's doing?" Maggie suggested. Weak distraction that it offered, the garrulous Nora was better than nothing under the circumstances. "He'd probably like that."

Nora frowned. "He's not contagious, is he? At my age, I can't afford to catch something contagious."

"Of course not. In fact, talking to people is very good for his health."

"Does this look like an M or an N?" Cora asked, thrusting the note under Maggie's nose.

"Well, as long as he's not contagious," Nora said, "I suppose there's no harm in it." Smoothing her dress and patting the sides of her hair, Nora proceeded down the drive to address the strange man in the three-piece suit.

"I really should have had Nora take down the message," Cora said, "except I was the first one who picked up the phone. I usually do, you know."

"I hear you have a goiter," Maggie heard Nora loudly announce to Brecht. "I had a cousin once with a goiter and no one ever asked her to dance." Had she not been preoccupied with the dramatic urgency of the moment, Maggie would have laughed aloud.

"I definitely got the time right," Cora said. "He said five-thirty tomorrow. You can even ask Nora. I'm always accurate on things like time."

"I'm sure I can figure out the rest."

"I even repeated it to him after he said it just to make sure I heard it right," Cora went on, clearing her throat so she could speak up a little louder. "I said to him 'Was that five-thirty tomorrow?' and he said, 'Yes, five-thirty-tomorrow.' Nora was right there."

"At least you can't see it," Maggie heard Nora tell Brecht. "My cousin's goiter was hanging right out there in front of God and everyone." Nora clucked her tongue. "We used to call her Turkey Tilly."

"It's this name part I can't figure out," Cora scowled. "I think he said 'Under Munroe's,' but that wouldn't make any sense, would it?"

"Have you considered surgery?" Nora asked Brecht.

"Munroe's makes perfect sense," Maggie said. "And I really appreciate you taking the message for me."

"But how could you meet him *under* something?" Cora inquired. "Maybe he meant across or next to. And yet I'm sure he said 'under.'"

"My cousin died young," Nora said. "Not to mean that you're going to die young. It's just a statement of fact."

Maggie glanced at her watch. "I hate to run, but I really need to get my friend to his doctor's appointment."

Cora brightened. "Which doctor does he go to? Dr. Gwynn? Nora and I have gone to Dr. Gwynn for years."

"No, someone else. And he charges extra if we're late."

"So does Dr. Gwynn," Cora said in amazement. "Do you think they *all* do that to their patients? It doesn't seem like a very nice thing to do, does it? What if you miss your bus? What if your watch stops after breakfast?"

Nora broke off her one-sided conversation when she noticed Maggie approaching her.

"You're not leaving already, are you?" she asked. "You just got here."

"Don't want to overstay our welcome," Maggie said, her hand on the car door handle.

"I hope Cora got that message right from your friend." Nora sighed. "Every day she slips a little bit more, you know."

Maggie gave an okay sign with her thumb and forefinger. "No problem."

"She said I got the Munroe part right," Cora told her sister. "I said he said to meet him under Munroe and she said it was right, although I told her I just don't see how."

"How can you meet someone *under* something, Cora? I swear you're getting dottier every day."

"Am not."

"Are too."

"Am not."

"Your friends," Brecht remarked as he eased the car down the driveway, "are very colorful."

"I think crazy is more the word," Maggie replied. "They don't make sense from one breath to the next, do they?" She refrained from the impulse to suggest that they had confused her with someone else and delivered an erroneous message. Maybe he'd dismiss the entire incident as isolated lunacy and not give it another thought.

Brecht glanced over at her with an amused look.

"Oh, I don't know," he said. "I found the experience of listening to them to be most interesting."

59

It was unnerving enough that Brecht suspected something. That he suspected something and yet didn't say a word about it was driving Maggie to distraction. It was not unlike those times, she recalled, when she had fancied herself eluding him and yet still sensed that he was right around the next corner, cognizant of her every move. It was enough to drive a person crazier than Cora and Nora.

What little conversation they had on their return trip to Lynx Bay so obviously avoided any reference to the Marquart sisters that she was certain he'd seek out Channing the very second they docked and tell him everything he knew.

"She made at least two telephone calls, sir," Maggie could imagine Brecht saying. "A rendezvous is scheduled for five-thirty tomorrow beneath Munroe's. I felt you should know."

Would he click his heels together before leaving the

room, Maggie wondered, his mission of espionage effi-
ciently seen through to conclusion? Somehow, she had
a feeling he was going to enjoy informing on her.

To the surprise of both of them, however, Channing
was not on the island.

"This would appear to be for you," Brecht said,
handing Maggie a sealed envelope that bore her name.

"Have you steamed and reglued it already?" Maggie
asked facetiously, "or do I actually get the first peek at
this?"

"One needn't resort to the practices of amateurs," he
replied, withdrawing a similar envelope from inside his
jacket. "He left me word of his whereabouts as well."

*Having a business meeting in Anacortes tonight and
staying over*, Channing had written, along with instructions for her to fax some documents on his desk first
thing in the morning. *Dinner tomorrow on the beach at
six if it doesn't rain? I love you.*

Maggie returned the letter to the envelope and
slipped it into her pocket.

Well, that decides it, she told herself. Impatient as
she was to hear what McCormick's ex-partner had to
say, the meeting would have to be postponed. Even on
the off chance that Brecht hadn't heard a thing Cora
said, there was no way Maggie could be two places at
once, not with an invitation as direct as Channing's.
The memory of his kiss flooded her senses with longing,
reminding her of how much she wanted to be a part of
his life, to reconcile the past and move forward. If he
wanted her, she couldn't refuse.

Idiot, her conscience chided her. The trouble that
Troy had gone to in arranging the meeting at all *would*
reconcile the past, and here she was contemplating
delaying it for another night of passion. Was she that

afraid of the truth about Channing? As she pulled out the note to read it again, she realized that what she was more afraid of was his inevitable discovery of the truth about *her*.

"SkySet isn't feeling well," Brecht told her later. "Do you wish to eat alone tonight or join me for lamb stew?"

"Lamb stew?" Maggie repeated. "She really shouldn't have been doing any cooking if she didn't feel all right."

"SkySet," Brecht replied, "is not the only one on the island who knows how to wield a ladle."

His response was clearly not the one Maggie had expected. "A ladle or a Luger?" she teased.

"I've been known to utilize the latter," he said, "if my skill with the former is criticized without cause."

"*This* I've got to see."

"Will an hour from now be a satisfactory time?"

"Works for me. Need any help?"

Brecht considered her question for a moment before answering. The thawing in his tone a moment ago was apparently only a temporary aberration. "I'm sure you have *other* things you need to attend to," he said.

He knows, Maggie thought to herself. *He knows that I'm going to try to make a phone call sometime this evening, and he's going to torment me with it until I crack.*

"Not really, but I'm sure I'll think of something."

"Yes, madam. I'm sure you will."

"Give a holler if you set the kitchen on fire."

"You'll be the first to know," Brecht assured her, leaving Maggie to her own devices. Leaving her, as well, to the challenge of contacting Troy.

The trouble was, of course, that Maggie had absolutely no idea how to orchestrate a message to the mainland without Brecht or, for that matter, SkySet knowing about it. Throughout the time she had spent at Lynx Bay, she had never determined whether outgoing calls were monitored.

With Brecht already suspicious about her parting conversation with the Marquart sisters, she couldn't risk dialing Troy's number to tell him that the meeting was off. Nor could she simply fail to show up beneath Munroe's Drugstore tomorrow at five-thirty and let him draw his own conclusions. Knowing Troy, he would jump to the worst and try to come after her.

There had to be something that she just hadn't thought of.

With an hour to go until dinner, Maggie decided to turn her attention to whatever Channing had left behind on his desk for her to handle. Though she had until tomorrow morning to send the faxes she could perform the arduous task of looking up phone numbers and filling out transmittal sheets. At least it would take her mind off of her dilemma.

As she entered Channing's study, her thoughts returned—as they always did—to the first day she had met him. How he had kept her waiting and how she had felt overwhelmed by the presence of so many stern Channing men looking down on her from every wall. His portrait would be up there with the rest of them someday, she thought, wondering when he'd find the time or patience to sit still long enough for a painting.

For an instant Maggie remembered something, a stray, puzzling thought that had occurred to her while she was at the Marquarts'. She closed her eyes to try to recapture what it was but met with no success. Some-

thing short and simple that Cora had said. Or was it
Nora?

Irritated by her lapse of memory, Maggie crossed to
the desk and the short stack of paperwork that Derek
had left for her.

Like other things he had asked her to send out, the
documents were related to various Channing holdings
throughout the world. Commerce, real estate, philan-
thropic commissions—Channing appeared to be
involved in every type of venture in existence.

*No wonder he never had time to run off with anyone
before he met me,* she thought.

Then she remembered what it was that she had
thought of at the Marquarts'.

They knew *exactly* who they were talking about in
the scandal, she affirmed a moment later as she ran her
hand over the brass nameplate at the bottom of the last
portrait. The nameplate of Derek's father. Elliott
Homer Channing.

60

While *Troy might* be able to justify his manipulation of the truth to protect her, his blatant discrediting of two innocent old ladies was reprehensible. "We've never had a gardener," Cora had distinctly remarked to her just that afternoon. And yet Troy had not only made up a fictitious gardener's flight from the Marquarts' employment but the name "Homer" to go along with it.

What *else* has he lied about under the aegis of political sensitivity? she wondered.

Brecht's voice cut into her thoughts. "Something wrong with the lamb?"

"What?"

"You were frowning as if you'd tasted something unpleasant."

Maggie hadn't realized that her annoyance with McCormick was registering on her face.

"Oh, no, it's great," she replied. "As a matter of fact,

if the bodyguard biz doesn't pan out, I'm sure there's a chef's hat out there with your name on it."

Brecht responded in German.

"Sorry," Maggie said, "but that one just went over my head."

"I know," Brecht replied and helped himself to another ladle of his savory creation.

Maggie awoke well before dawn after a restless night of bad dreams and anticipatory jitters. No earthshaking ideas on how to contact Troy had come to her, escalating her awareness that a little over twelve hours remained before their meeting was supposed to take place.

As she lay in bed and replayed their last phone conversation, one phrase of it continued to bother her. Why had Troy expressed some reluctance about her talking to his partner, she wondered, suggesting that she might not be up for such an encounter. That it was the first time he had even mentioned *having* a partner puzzled her as well, much less that his partner had been more intimately tied to the original case than McCormick himself.

Obviously, she decided, there were peculiar workings of law enforcement beyond the comprehension of ordinary civilians.

One thing *was* certain, though. And that was how much she loved Derek. Once this was all over, there'd be no more room for doubts or lingering ghosts.

"Up already?" Brecht remarked, nearly startling Maggie as she entered the kitchen to make herself some coffee.

"Just want to get all those faxes out of the way," she replied, knowing that he'd be watching her like a hawk all day.

"Do you have plans to go to the mainland later?" he inquired.

Maggie tensed. "Why do you ask?"

"Just asking," Brecht replied. "If you do, of course, Mr. Channing would like me to accompany you."

"You'll be the first to know," Maggie answered with a blitheness she didn't feel.

"Damn," she muttered a few minutes later as she closed the study doors. Today was going to be even worse than yesterday, with Brecht stubbornly insistent on squelching her freedom. Maggie's glance wandered toward the phone, but she dared not use it.

Maybe he's just psyching me out, she thought. *Maybe he wants me to think he's going to eavesdrop and he's really not doing anything at all.*

Maggie dismissed the idea quickly. Brecht was too good at his job to rely on the uncertainty of mind games. He probably even had a telescope trained at that very second on the shoreline, she imagined, just in case she decided to get creative and throw a note out in a glass bottle. "I believe you dropped this from the window, madam," she could hear him say. "Perhaps you might explain it?"

Mentally taxed by questions for which she had no answers, Maggie focused on the task at hand and picked up the first batch of material to be faxed. As she fed the first of the sheets into the machine, she suddenly noticed something she had missed the previous night. Detective Finch's business card, just like the one he had handed to Maggie, lay on top of Channing's address book.

"Call if you think of anything helpful to the investigation," he had said to both of them when he left Lynx Bay. At the time, Maggie had pocketed hers without even looking at it.

A smile unexpectedly found its way to her face as she now read the small print in the lower left corner.

"Perfect," she murmured, wondering how she could have missed so obvious a solution to her problem of contacting Troy McCormick and leaving Brecht none the wiser.

It was a perfect solution in more ways than one, Maggie realized as she watched the single sheet slide through the fax machine. Even if Brecht were to waltz in, he'd think nothing about what she was doing as the evidence literally slipped out of Lynx Bay right under his own nose.

Like the telephone bill, Channing's fax statements were issued on a monthly basis. Only three days ago, Maggie had seen the latest one come in and noticed that it just listed the numbers dialed, not the names of the specific parties. Given the volume of faxes sent, it seemed like a workable plan to sandwich a message to Troy at the police department in with the other jobs Channing had left on his desk. All she had to do was destroy her outgoing cover sheet and she was home free. By the time the next monthly fax statement arrived—if he even checked it that closely—this whole mess would be resolved. At least she hoped so.

As the digital display confirmed that her message had reached its destination, Maggie quickly folded and pocketed the sheet she just sent. "Can't make our appointment today as planned," she had neatly printed on Channing's customized cover-paper. "Will give you a call when I can. Maggie."

Then Maggie programmed the next of Channing's jobs, a fifteen-page brief to a law firm in San Francisco.

"Finished already?" Brecht inquired as she returned to the kitchen for a refill of her coffee.

"Got a long one going," she replied. "I swear sometimes that machine is so slow, you could walk the message to its destination."

The telephone rang. Brecht, being the closer, set down the book he was reading to answer it. "Just a moment," he said to the caller. "It's for you," he informed Maggie, handing her the receiver. "The Seattle Police Department."

Maggie feigned puzzlement while her head screamed every expletive it could think of. "Yes?" she said into the mouthpiece, knowing even before she heard a voice that it had to be related to the fax she had just sent.

"This is Captain Harding," a man said. "I'm calling about a fax we received for Lieutenant McCormick?"

"Uh-huh?" Maggie said, wishing that she had either obliterated the phone number on the cover sheet or used a blank piece of paper instead.

"What was the nature of the appointment you had?" the captain asked.

Maggie cast a glance at Brecht. Even though he had resumed reading, Maggie knew that he was listening to every word.

"Oh, nothing important," she replied. "Just something I'd talked about following up when time permitted."

"I beg your pardon?" the captain said. "I'm a little confused here, ma'am. Were you working on a case with him?"

"That's right," Maggie replied, delighted to have been asked something she didn't have to phrase as a voluntary statement.

"Which one was it?" the captain asked.

"Maybe you could just have him give us a call later." Maggie circumvented his question, hoping that Brecht would assume she was taking a message for Channing.

"I'm afraid that won't be possible, ma'am," Captain Harding replied. "Lieutenant McCormick was killed in an accident."

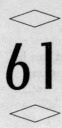

61

Channing's tall shadow fell across the sand. "Brecht told me you'd be out here," he said.

Maggie looked up from where she had been sitting for the past two hours, her back against the seawall. "Did he also tell you why?"

The screech of gulls as they looped through the sky on paths of near-collision almost sounded like laughter, mocking the folly of the humans below.

Channing extended his hand to pull her to her feet and into the protective and forgiving circle of his arms. "Why do you think I came back early?"

Had someone told her at the start of summer that she'd one day break down and confide anything to Brecht, she would have laughed. When the telephone slipped from her hand in the kitchen that morning, however, his presence had strengthened rather than frightened her.

"My God," she had said over and over, struck numb

by Captain Harding's shocking revelation. "I can't believe it."

"You must not take the guilt for it," Brecht told her after listening to the entire story that spilled forth, a story that she could no longer keep to herself. "There are some things over which we have no control."

"All the same—"

"In the end, Fräulein, it would not have made a difference."

In retrospect, she didn't even remember the moment Brecht had taken her hand and patiently held it while she talked, only that she had looked down and suddenly noticed it. Noticed as well for the first time that his eyes weren't those of a cold enemy but of a warm friend communicating concern. That his intention from the beginning had been to protect her in the same selfless way he protected Channing made her realize what an inaccurate judge of character she had been.

"You knew that I was involved with him from the start, didn't you?" she asked. Oddly enough, Maggie almost felt cleansed to admit it out loud, to finally tear down the barriers she had erected from her first day on the island.

"I suspected," Brecht replied and said no more.

"I'm sorry," she now blurted out to Derek, burying her head against his chest. "I'm sorry I ever lied to you or that it ever went this far."

"Maybe if it hadn't," he whispered softly into her hair, "we would never have gotten together. At least we have *that* to thank him for, don't we?"

Maggie tilted back her head to look at him. "What happens now?" she asked, knowing that their problems were far from over, and the mystery of her father's death far from laid to rest.

Gently, he caressed her tear-stained cheek. "Well, I'd say we've got a telephone call to make and a meeting to keep at five-thirty."

"Even after—" Maggie faltered, conscious of the unexpected twist that Captain Harding's news had introduced to all of their lives.

Channing anticipated what she was going to ask.

"There are *some* things we still have to our advantage," he pointed out. "As far as the other party's concerned, well—there's been no change to the rendezvous." A muscle flicked angrily at his jaw. "Brecht told me that you still want to go."

"I'm expected," Maggie reminded him. "Don't you think my father would want me to see it through?"

"He'd want to see you safe. And I think he'd expect me to ensure that in his absence."

"He'd also want me to know the truth."

Channing forced a smile through his stern countenance. "You have an answer for everything, don't you?"

"Just about."

"Well, the only answer *I* want is to what I'm going to ask you when all of this is over."

Maggie shook her head. "I can't even think about that now," she said, still stunned by the magnitude of what had transpired and what still remained. "Much as I love you, Derek, I just—"

Channing laid his index finger against her lip. "When the circumstances are right," he said. "Besides, I don't think I'm likely to forget it between now and then."

Assailed by the dull ache of foreboding, not even Channing's warm embrace could dispel the reality that her own stubbornness and blind faith had played them both into the enemy's hands. "There's something I need to ask *you*," Maggie said. "Something before we go back to the mainland."

"Name it."

"The meeting at five-thirty," she murmured. "You know that he's going to be there, don't you? That he's been the one behind the entire thing?"

Even if he had said nothing in response, the look on Channing's face affirmed the truth.

"It was only a matter of time," he replied gravely. "Only a matter of time before it came down to this."

Maggie checked her watch against the granite pedestal clock in front of Munroe's Drugstore. Five minutes and counting.

Channing would already be down in the catacombs and waiting for them both to arrive. "What I still can't figure out, though," he had said before they parted, "is why he'd pick a place with only one access." Given the lengths that their common adversary had gone to so far, it didn't make sense that he'd choose a meeting site with a single exit door.

Munroe's, flanked by a gift shop on one side and a narrow alley on the other, sat atop one of the smaller, half-block hollows in the underground network. Accessible by a metal basement door at the back of the building, its existence served no useful purpose for the project, nor were its brick support walls or low-slung splintered ceilings any enticement for serious exploration.

"If he's got a key like the rest of us to get into it in the first place," Maggie said, "doesn't that suggest that he's pretty familiar with the layout? What if there is another route that nobody knows?"

Channing maintained that the risk of creating another route, much less successfully concealing one, was too high. "Either he's stupid or he's cocky. "Whatever the case, all you have to do is act as if nothing is wrong and get him down there for us."

With misgivings increasing by the minute, Maggie crossed the street toward Munroe's.

She hadn't expected to find a note with her name on it wedged into the clasp below the door handle. Tentatively she withdrew it, not recognizing the handwriting within and yet knowing exactly who it was from.

Not safe for us to meet here as planned, it read. *Will wait for you behind Café Dolce on Yesler until six with the truth about your father. Please be there.*

The scowl that started to crease Maggie's brow at the prospect of a new meeting place nearly eight blocks away quickly faded with her discovery of a brief second note penciled in lightly below the original. *We've got you covered.—Derek.*

In spite of her anxiety, Maggie caught herself smiling, almost amused that a man as sly as Channing's brother had failed to anticipate that anyone besides herself would read the instructions first and take appropriate action.

As she started to return the keys to her purse, however, a sound behind her from the shadows of the alleyway made her freeze.

"Hello, Maggie," the voice said. "You're exactly on time."

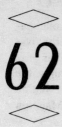

62

Too late, Maggie realized that she had just walked into a trap. Prepared and well-rehearsed as she had been to confront the man who had killed her father and deliver him to justice, she had never anticipated the raw vulnerability she felt now in knowing that Channing and the police were waiting for her at a phony location eight blocks away. A location she would never reach.

Maggie turned to meet the gray eyes that she had unwittingly trusted all summer. The same gray eyes that she had recognized in his mother's portrait in the attic and yet—until a few hours ago—had not made the final connection.

Play it through and act natural, her conscience told her, knowing that her only chance of survival—as well as stalling—was to let him continue to believe that she still thought of him as Lieutenant Troy McCormick.

"So what's with the change of plans?" she asked in feigned confusion, indicating the note she had removed from the door handle.

"What's with the postscript?" he countered, one corner of his mouth twisted upward into a smile that was neither friendly nor amused.

Before Maggie could fathom a convincing reply, the hand at his side now came into view, revealing that he had planned their rendezvous with a specific intention in mind: that only he would walk away from it.

Maggie recoiled from the sight of the gun yet refused to let it override her determination to keep him off balance. "What's going on?" she challenged him. "Are you trying to scare me out of my wits or something with that?"

Channing's brother, however, was just as resolved to maintain his appointed agenda.

"Unlock the door," he instructed. "I think we could do with some privacy, don't you?"

Maggie hesitated as if puzzled, when in fact her thoughts were on whether she dared risk trying to run the long and narrow distance out to the street or scream in the hope that someone might hear her. Once he got her out of sight and down in the tunnel, she knew she was almost as good as dead.

"I don't understand," she protested. "I thought we were supposed to get together with your ex-partner."

"Dear, sweet, gullible Maggie." He sighed as if wearied by a recalcitrant child. "You still haven't figured any of it out yet, have you?"

Maggie swallowed hard and lifted her chin, drawing on the only tangible ace that might convince him they were on the same side. "I know that Derek killed my father," she said. "And with whatever your partner has to add to that, I think we've finally got him exactly where you want him."

David Channing smiled. "No, Maggie. The only person I've got exactly where I want right now is you, short-lived as such pleasantness will be. Certainly you've heard the expression 'an eye for an eye'?"

Maggie's lips parted to stall him with another purposefully inane question, but in two strides he had closed the fragile distance between them.

"Unlock the door," he repeated. "I'd really rather not be here when your Sir Galahad returns."

He didn't speak again until they had descended into the lower level, its depths now dimly illuminated by a kerosene lamp which he hung on a hook.

"I guess the first order of business," he said, "is to get the introductions right." David shook his head. "It's funny, isn't it, what people will believe when they want to?"

"What do you mean?"

"I mean that, back in Boston, you didn't hesitate for a second to accept that I was with the Seattle Police Department and that I needed your help on a case. Remember?"

In the lamp's weak, yellow glow his features took on an evil quality, making Maggie wonder how she could ever have read kindness, much less an intimation of romance, in the same face that was now triumphing so openly at her expense.

"You do remember, don't you?"

Maggie refused to dignify his question with a response.

With a shrug, he moved on with his story. "First off, my name's not really Troy McCormick."

A part of Maggie still wanted to feign astonishment, to buy herself precious time with whatever means she could. But she knew that the outcome could well be the same no matter what she said.

"It would be an odd coincidence if it were," she said.

David raised an eyebrow. "What was that?"

"The real Lieutenant McCormick was killed in a skiing accident at Snoqualamie Pass last winter," she replied. "Did you have a hand in that, too?"

David whistled. "You *are* smart, although I'm afraid I can't take the credit for my alter ego's clumsiness on his day off." David's brow furrowed. "What gave me away?"

"Maybe just a lot of things finally coming together."

"Unfortunate for both of us that way," he said, studying her. "We made a good team for a while, didn't we?"

When Maggie offered no answer, David chuckled. "Since you know who I'm *not*," he continued, "I suppose you also know who I *am*."

She nodded. "Yes, I know that, too."

David scowled. "Then I guess this is going to be a shorter conversation than I'd planned on." His gray eyes met hers. "Because if you know *that* much, you know I can't let you live to tell anyone."

"How do you know that I haven't already?"

"You mean Big Brother Derek?" he said. "Oh, I had a feeling by that little starry-eyed look you've been melting into lately that he'd added you to his stable of fans like everyone else."

"What's *that* supposed to mean?"

"Exactly what you *think* it does, Maggie. Exactly the kind of crap that yours truly has put up with since the day I was born."

As the anger in his voice built, Maggie now heard as well with frightening clarity the assessments made by Derek, the Marquart sisters, and, most recently, Brecht—that David Channing had succumbed to his liabilities rather than rising above them. The unwanted son, the child of another man, the bitter competitor whose looks and intellect could never garner the adoration that came so easily to his older brother.

"He pushed my wife to her death," he said. "Did he bother to tell you that?"

Maggie's breath burned in her throat. "It was an accident," she said. "Fiona fell while she was trying to go after you."

David flashed her a look of disdain. "Accident?" he echoed. "It's about as much an accident as what happened to good ol' Clayton, isn't it?"

It was all Maggie could do to keep from flying toward him, his sardonic expression filling her with more rage than she had thought herself capable. "What *did* happen?" she demanded.

"You're wasting my time with your questions, dear," he said, sliding his left index finger along the smooth metal barrel. "Besides, does it really make that much difference if I'm going to kill you anyway?"

"I came this far. You said yourself I'd know the truth at the end."

David smirked. "I *did* say that, didn't I? Well, I suppose I shouldn't go back on my word to a lady." David paused a moment before continuing. "The truth is, Maggie, it wasn't your father I was even after."

"Derek, then?"

David shook his head. "Cleveland."

"But why were you—"

"End of the questions," he cut her off, pulling back the hammer of the gun as he pointed it toward her chest. "I'm really sorry, babe."

A single shot and a guttural scream of pain split the dank stillness of the catacomb.

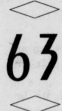

63

It happened so fast that, even seconds later, Maggie could only conjure a confusing, frenetic blur of recollection.

One moment, David's gun had been trained at her heart. In the very next, the sudden impact of a bullet from across the darkness had not only knocked the weapon out of his right hand but left him gasping in horror at the sight of gushing blood that splattered down his wrist from where his thumb and the heel of his hand had been.

Too paralyzed to move, Maggie watched in shock as David frantically pulled out his front shirttail to try to swathe the ragged wound, his eyes maniacally darting toward the floor in a desperate search for his fallen gun.

Somewhere to Maggie's right, a familiar German accent addressed him.

"If I were you," Brecht said as he stepped forward, "I would not bother looking for it."

◦   ◦   ◦

Maggie shivered in spite of the warmth of Channing's jacket draped over her shoulders as they sat together at police headquarters. Brecht, behind closed doors for well over the past hour, had still not emerged.

"How much longer do you think they'll talk to him?" she asked Derek.

"Shouldn't be too much more," he replied. "Just standard paperwork."

Her mind still spinning in bewilderment, Maggie found neither cohesion nor sense in the whirlwind of events that had just transpired, particularly Brecht's decision to spare David's life.

"He could've killed him," she said, stunned by the accuracy with which Brecht had literally disabled their opponent's attack.

Channing nodded. "If he had wanted to, yes."

Maggie's green eyes met his, her lashes still moist with tears from the aftermath of so frightening an experience. "I'd just think that for all the things your brother had done to other people . . ." Maggie let the words trail off, her remembrance of what had nearly happened down in the tunnel superimposed on a montage of faces—her father, Fiona, the Indian boy.

"It wouldn't have been Brecht's place to exact payment for David's crimes," Channing replied after a long moment of reflection.

"What if *you* had been the one to stay behind instead?" she asked. That both men possessed the foresight to suspect a potential trap had ultimately proven to be Maggie's salvation. Brecht, Derek had explained in the car, had insisted on being the one to remain beneath Munroe's in the event that their hunch was correct. German intuition, Derek labeled it.

"If *I'd* been the one?" Derek sat there, gazing into some private space that, for the moment, Maggie was not a part of. "I doubt I would have done anything different."

"Because David is a part of you?"

"Because he always *has* been," Channing quietly answered, absently stroking Maggie's hand. "His was the choice to turn against it."

Though Maggie understood that the details of David's treachery wouldn't fully be known for weeks— maybe even months—to come, she had learned enough just in that day from her own assimilation of memories to combine them with Derek's and Brecht's own words. From that emerged a jagged picture of revenge so inconsistent with the good-guy image "Troy" had projected that it was no wonder she had never connected the brother and the detective as one and the same.

"He said it was Cleveland he tried to kill," Maggie told Derek. "It wasn't even my father he was after."

"A case of being in the wrong place at the wrong time," Derek murmured, sharing Maggie's pain for the waste of so worthy a life as the man they had both cared for. "My guess," he said, "is that he tried to get Ken to screw up the project, get it closed down. Maybe afterward he reconsidered and decided to shut him up instead."

"And Cleveland never said anything to you?"

"The bottom line, honey, is that Ken benefited by your father's death. The best he could do was keep his mouth shut and hope that he never got blackmailed."

"You don't think he had a hand in it himself?"

Channing didn't even hesitate to reply. "If he helped David at all, it was by shooting off his mouth after a few beers. That's probably how David even heard about *you*."

"Five years is a long time to plan something, though," Maggie pointed out. "If he knew about me back then—"

"Five years is also a long enough time for Cleveland to forget about him. When Twylar called me up to tell me that he'd seen him—"

"Twylar?" Maggie recalled their lunch at the Pacific Crabhouse and the startled look on Twylar Zarzy's face.

"David must've been checking up on you," Channing explained. "By the time that Twylar got himself out to the front of the restaurant, he was already gone."

"What about the Indian boy?" Maggie asked, realizing that she herself had provided David with the full description of what the youth had been wearing, as well as the last place he had disappeared. Now sickened by the knowledge that her information had directed David right to him, Maggie couldn't help but feel a heavy ache of guilt.

"I'm not sure we'll ever know," Derek said. "I do know there was a boy who would've been about the right age back then that your father took a liking to. One of the crew mentioned to me that he'd started coming around again about the time I hired you. If he'd been down in the tunnels the night of the accident and saw something, or specifically saw *David,* maybe he was trying to get close enough to warn you to be careful of him."

Maggie looked down to discover that her fingers had clenched in anger. "He didn't have to die."

"If he *was* a witness," Channing quietly explained, "David couldn't afford to let him live."

"What about the watch? The one with my father's name on it?"

"Just a shot," Channing shrugged, "but maybe David wanted us to think that the Indian kid had something to do with your father's death, maybe even that he stole the watch off his wrist and kept it. The only problem being, of course, that your father never wore one. David wouldn't have known that."

Maggie shuddered, finding it incomprehensible that one man could possess so much hatred toward a brother.

"What's going to happen to him, do you think?" she asked.

Neither one of them had seen David since his arrest, nor inquired about where he had been taken. More than once Maggie had caught herself wishing that a second bullet from Brecht's gun had ended their nightmare once and for all, a wish that she could never bring herself to express out loud to the man she loved so deeply. Given the inequities of the judicial system and David's own capacity to twist the truth, it was not beyond the realm of reason that he would not serve a full sentence for his crimes, that he would one day be free again to threaten their existence and their love.

"I really don't know," Derek replied, slipping his arm around her shoulder and drawing her close. "I only know that, whatever happens, we'll find a way to deal with it together."

Across the room, the door to Captain Harding's office opened and Brecht stepped out, having completed his statement to the police. "What do you say we all go home and get a good night's sleep?" Channing proposed as Brecht joined them.

"Back to work in the morning?" Maggie asked, linking her arm in his. "We've still got a treasure to find, you know."

"Speak for yourself, Ms. Price," Channing replied with a wink, "but I've already found what I've looked for all my life."

Epilogue

One Year Later

"Well, Mrs. Channing," Derek proclaimed, leaning over her hospital bed to admire the newborn life cradled in her arms, "I'd say the dynasty has finally been broken."

Maggie laughed. "After six generations," she replied, "I'd say it was high time for it." In her husband's eyes, Maggie saw the reflection of wonderment and delight at his seven-pound baby daughter, the first Channing girl to be born since the 1800s. "Have you told Brecht yet what we're going to call her?" she asked.

Derek shook his head. "I thought I'd leave the honor to you, my love."

"What's taking him so long, anyway? Didn't you two ride up together?"

"I think he got sidetracked at the stuffed animals in the gift shop," Derek said, not taking his adoring gaze off the baby.

"It's hard to picture him doing that," Maggie remarked. "Do you think he'll pull his gun on 'em if they don't come along peacefully?"

"Smart aleck."

A tap on the door made them both respond at once. With the upper half of his body partially obscured by a three-foot plush gray elephant, Brecht entered Maggie's hospital room.

"Oh, good," Derek commented on his friend's selection. "I see you bought something politically correct."

"Good grief," she said, bending her head to whisper something to the baby.

"What do you mean 'don't listen to them'?" Channing teased. "That little girl's entitled to an empire."

"Right now," Maggie countered, "I think she's more entitled to a good nap."

Brecht said something softly in his native tongue, awestruck by the tiny person swathed in a pink blanket.

"You know, it still ticks me off when you do that," Maggie said.

"I know," Brecht replied.

"I'll just hazard a guess here," Channing said, "but he either said that you're holding the world's most beautiful baby or that he's misplaced his aunt's red pen in the broccoli."

Brecht continued to stare at the child. "Have you named her?" he asked.

Maggie and Derek exchanged a meaningful glance.

"We've decided to call her Greta," Maggie said.

"A good Germanic name, don't you think?" Channing added, awaiting his bodyguard's reaction.

Brecht's lips began to part, and for the very first time since she had ever met him, Maggie saw a broad smile of happiness and satisfaction spread across his face.

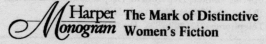